Stumbling Through
A Wartime Childhood

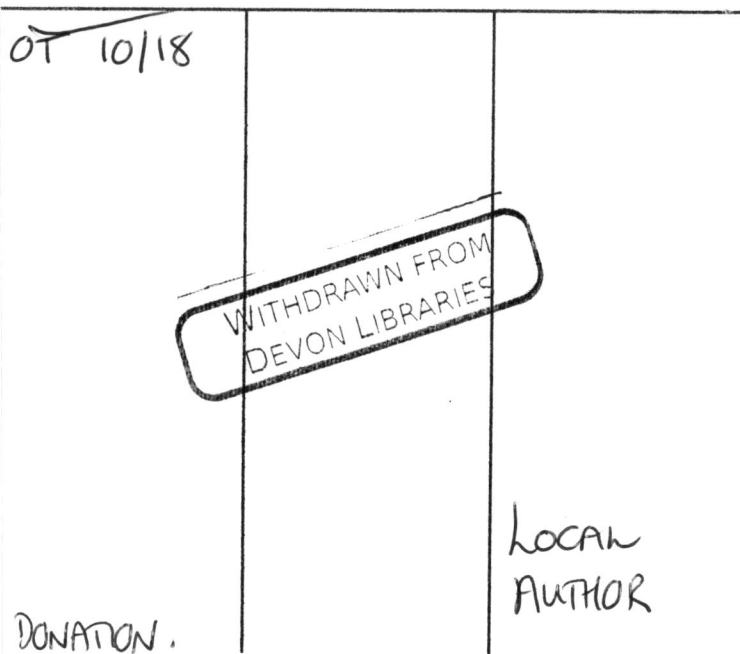

Stumbling Through
A Wartime Childhood

Philip Algar

Published by www.lulu.com

STUMBLING THROUGH
A WARTIME CHILDHOOD

ISBN 978-1-291-71605-4

Book formatted by www.bookformatting.co.uk.

Contents

Books by Philip Algar

Humorous novels

With Immediate Effect
It's Just Not Village Cricket
It's Just Not Village Politics

Other fiction

Stumbling Through A Wartime Childhood

Biography

Goodbye Old Chap

Business books

Careers In Oil & Gas
Industrial Emergencies And The Media
Managing Industrial Emergencies
Your Problem, Our Story

About the Author

Philip Algar, B.Sc. (Econ), F.I.J, has written nine books. Initially an economist in the oil industry, he was subsequently a freelance editor, writer, lecturer and occasional broadcaster for many years and worked in 30 countries. He contributed regularly to UK and overseas publications on energy, economics and crisis management and also wrote a regular and humorous column for a national newspaper and for a business magazine. Now he concentrates on writing books, two of which were published by the Financial Times. He has written three satirical novels: one pokes fun at office life and business and the others take a satirical look at a village as it tries to defeat the efforts of local and central government, backed by commercial interests, to change the character of the village for ever.

In The Beginning

Casual remarks can start wars, alienate friends, change individual lives for better or worse or simply float away, unheeded, on the disinterested winds of time. A chance comment in a gloomy and dingy pub in Newcastle, in 1926, was to change the lives of two adults permanently. Peter Adams, an ambitious 27 year-old officer in the Merchant Navy, handsome, dark and short, was having a drink with his life-long friend Joe Yates. Peter, clothed in an old sports jacket and grey trousers, was better dressed than his friend, who was wearing his bus conductor's uniform, and the other men in the pub who, mostly, looked haggard, shabby and troubled. Some, bearing war wounds that would never heal, hobbled to the bar. Everyone in the pub faced seemingly permanent problems of jobs and money. Those who were drinking Newcastle pale ale, at sixpence a pint, aware that they could not afford too many drinks, were taking time to imbibe whilst enjoying the relative freedom that the surroundings offered. Perhaps for an hour, they could escape from the harsh economic reality that dominated their lives although conversation was not easy as the Corporation trams clattered passed en route to the Wingrove depot.

The Kensington, which belied its rather superior name, had seen better days. A crumbling balcony on the first floor threatened anyone standing underneath it and the outside walls, previously white, were now black as decades of dirt left their indelible mark. The window sills, covered with cheap ornaments, were enveloped by grime. Smoke from the roll-up cigarettes from the shabbily-clad customers was drifting upwards to the yellowing ceiling which was illuminated occasionally by a shaft of sunlight from the late evening sun which penetrated the dirty windows. A few inadequate light bulbs, bravely struggling to combat the gloom, made little impression. The black wooden tables and chairs, decades old, were uniformly uncomfortable and unimpressive and the floor was covered by a faded and worn-out carpet. That said, this spartan setting at least offered a temporary alternative to the patrons' crowded, inadequate and frequently unsanitary homes and the domestic rows caused by financial hardship. The pub and its few patrons conveyed a defiant gesture towards a hapless, brutish and worrying life.

Peter had used his leave to complete his studies. Success would allow him to command vessels in foreign waters and a higher salary. His leave pay would only be granted when he re-joined one of the company's vessels, in the Far East, which meant that he would have no income for five months. He understood the financial problems suffered by his fellow-drinkers.

Joe and Peter had been friends since childhood, so could discuss confidential matters free of embarrassment. Years before, they had exchanged innocent stories about girls when they had realised that they existed. Today, however, as elsewhere in the country, the talk, initiated by Joe, was about the recent industrial troubles.

'What will the miners do now as General Strike's been called off after just nine days? It's difficult to realise that it happened in this county, but there was no public transport, the newspapers weren't published, the iron and steel industries were shut down, docks were idle and armoured cars patrolled the streets of London. Now, to make matters worse, I've just heard that Spencer's steelworks is to close so another 2,000 men are without work. God, how I hate bloody government and the bosses. They treat us like slaves.

'The poor devils were only striking to avoid having a pay cut forced on them by those swines who own the mines. It wasn't as if they wanted more money. You see, before year's out, they'll be forced back to work but what really gets me is that so many bloody volunteers from the so-called upper classes supported the government by driving buses and lorries and working telephone exchanges. To them it was all great fun and I despise the so-called students who helped. Did any of them think about those of us who face unemployment and worry about where the next meal is coming from? No, of course not. This country's riddled by class and I can't see it changing unless there's a full scale revolution, as they had in Russia. It'll come and I just hope that it's in my lifetime.'

Peter nodded in agreement. He was not surprised by the appalling way in which the working class was treated. He was part of it and he knew how hard it had been for his father, working in a local factory for long hours and little pay. He had died, worn out, at the age of 45. It was as if the country was divided into two unequal parts and that he and Joe, who shared a northern and working class solidarity, were in the wrong one. Joe decided to move to what he hoped would be a more agreeable topic.

'Anyway, lad, when will you hear if you've passed your exam?'

'I've passed.'

'That's bloody great, lad, you deserve it. Why didn't you tell me earlier when I was going on about the General Strike? Let me buy you a pint.'

'Thanks but it's my shout. I'll have a half off you later.'

Peter, who had been earning about £4 a week, knew that his friend would have been earning about half that so was being tactful, not least as Joe had a young son to support. He returned with two pints.

'I suppose you'll be earning pots of money and joining the upper class?'

Peter smiled. 'After my experiences as an apprentice in the war, at £10 a year, I think I'll always worry about money, it's in my blood, but I'll never forget my roots. Anyway, I'll have to wait for a promotion and that could be years. I had a letter yesterday, telling me about my next appointment. I've got to go to London soon and then on to Singapore and I'll be in the Far East for the next three years.'

Joe, who sometimes was not keen on a weekend shift, although he had to accept for financial reasons, was astonished.

'You mean you'll be away for three years? Don't you mind

being away for so long? I would. There's so much I'd miss, even in this country where we seem to be on the verge of a revolution every month. I'd miss my family, especially my lad, and I'd miss going to football.' Peter smiled and, in a way, envied Joe for his life-long support for Newcastle United who were doing very well. They had won the FA cup in 1924 and were very successful in the First Division championship.

'Yes, I'll be away for three years. I don't really have a choice, there aren't too many jobs around these days, at sea as well as on shore, and my salary, when I eventually get it, isn't too bad but they won't pay me until I sign on again in Singapore. I've prised a small advance out of the company but I've got to be careful. Frankly, there's not much to keep me here. I like football but it isn't as important to me as it is to you. Cricket is more important for me especially as Yorkshire, the county where I was born, won the championship last year. I wish I'd been in London to see the match with Middlesex. There were 71,000 people present over the three days and Percy Holmes scored 315 not out. Do you know, they played 32 matches, winning 21 and drawing the rest. That's quite a record.'

A discreet cough encouraged Peter to forget cricket and he continued.

'I've always envied you as you're part of such a close family and relations with my own family aren't good. In fact, I haven't spoken to my brother, Frank, a greedy swine, for some time and, as you know, my mother and I don't get on and I blame her for giving me such a harsh, unkind childhood. Did I ever tell you that when I became an apprentice not one member of the family came to see my first ship? Not one. That hurt. Life at sea, when I could have been killed at any time in the war, was very hard: we worked 77 hours a week, the food was terrible and there was no tuition. I really resented those years and now I'm determined to have a better life, even if it means being away for so long. At least I'll see a different part of the world. I haven't got a girl friend, so I'm happy to go. Maybe I'll find one in Singapore?'

'What about that attractive Mary?'

'She was not a girl friend, just a friend who happened to be a girl.'

Joe's leathery and pale face, occasionally illuminated by a penetrating and winsome smile, looked much older than his 28 years. He had been involved in hand-to-hand fighting at the end of the war and continual worry about jobs and money had left an indelible mark. His short hair was already in retreat and he walked with a slight stoop, as if anxious not to be seen. Like millions of ordinary, decent and innocent people, he knew poverty. He hoped that, one day, he might be trained as a bus driver but he was realistic and expected to remain a conductor. He would have liked to do something else, but jobs were rare and, like millions of workers, he had no other experience. He considered himself lucky to be employed and, although the pay was not generous, he could provide some kind of living for his young son and wife, Freda, who helped to keep the family finances from disaster by having a part-time job cleaning the homes of the more affluent.

'When you go to London, does the company pay for an overnight stay?'

Peter sighed. 'No, they won't pay. They'd say it was my fault for living in the north. I'll have to pay but I'll find somewhere cheap.'

Joe looked sympathetic. After thinking for a few moments, he made a suggestion.

'I've got a friend who lives in London. Ann Lambert. She's a very kind woman. Her husband was killed in the early days of the war and she hasn't re-married. Her adult son has married and she lives alone with her daughter, Susan, who, I suppose must be about 16 now. Would you like me to write to Ann asking if she could give you a bed for the night?'

'Thanks, Joe, I'd be very grateful.'

Peter then accepted a half pint from his friend. Half an hour later, the two embraced briefly, aware that many days would pass before they met again, and made their emotional farewells. Each wondered what the next three years would bring.

A few days later, Peter heard that Ann Lambert would be

pleased to see him and helpfully told him how to reach her home. Peter wrote a short note saying that he was most grateful and confirmed when he would be in London. Several days later, he arrived at Kings Cross. Legend claimed that this was the scene of a battle between the British and Boudicea and that she had been buried beneath one of the platforms but Peter's thoughts were concentrated on what his life in the Far East might be over the next three years, not over the next 24 hours.

He knew he was right to sign a three-year contract but he would miss some aspects of life in England, especially the Yorkshire county cricket club. He smiled to himself that such a trivial aspect could even float into his mind. A more immediate challenge now confronted him. This was his first visit to London and he felt intimidated by the bustling, busy crowds in the noisy station. Everyone was rushing and, unlike him, they all seemed to know where they were going. Many girls, presumably office workers, were laughing together and some couples, arm in arm, made Peter, who realised that he would be 29 when he was back in England, wonder if he would ever find a wife. He was in one of the largest cities in the world yet felt lonely. So far, life had not treated him well. His parents had shown him no affection and, when he went to sea, in the war, he had survived three serious incidents each of which could have cost him his life. Now, trying to improve his lot, he was going abroad. Would his life change for the better?

It was difficult to see clearly across the station because some of the smoke from the engines had not yet forced its way through the small aperture in the roof into the capital's atmosphere. There was also an unmistakeable smell of the smoke. He had experienced it before, when travelling locally, but it was nothing like the comprehensive stink that now attacked his nostrils and permeated his clothes. He had some difficulty finding the right underground line. Pushing his two cases on to the tube train was not easy but it was even more difficult on the bus that Ann had told him to catch from the station that was the nearest to her home. The space for luggage on the bus was designed to accommodate office workers' briefcases or shopping, not luggage for someone about to spend three years on the other side of the world.

After a short walk from the bus stop, Peter re-checked the address whilst standing outside a well-preserved semi-detached modern house in the suburbs. The wide road, on which little traffic was flowing, was lined with trees and a few cars were parked outside some of the larger houses. There were no children playing in the street and the small front gardens were neat, suggesting regular maintenance. His parents' tiny terraced back-to-back home in Newcastle could hardly have been more different. Like the pub, it was coated with black grime and seemed to sag forwards, as if challenging gravity. It was too small for the family and the only toilet was in the small back yard which backed on to a narrow lane which became a depository for any rubbish, including that thrown out by the butcher next door, who had converted his ground floor into a shop. There was no front garden, of course: a narrow pavement meant that someone could lean out of the window and touch a passer by. The street's cobble stones echoed to the frequent sound of horses reluctantly pulling carts. No, pride in the home, suggested by his initial glance at the London house, was second in Newcastle to surviving. Peter was astounded at the impression of luxury, the like of which he had only seen in newspapers, and he was going to spend the night in this palace. What would Ann be like? He had never asked Joe how he knew her and this intrigued him as did the thought that she might not know he was working class.

He knocked on the solid front door which was opened promptly by a young girl who, initially seemed surprised, not least as, for some seconds that seemed like minutes, Peter failed to identify himself. Standing by his two large cases might have suggested that he was an optimistic salesman anticipating keen demand for his products. However, salesmen speak and Peter was struck dumb. Uniquely, he was overwhelmed on meeting a girl. When he recovered the power of speech, he stammered that he was Peter Adams and that his friend Joe in Newcastle had been in touch about his staying overnight.

The attractive girl rallied and, showing more maturity than was usually associated with those of her age, said 'I'm very pleased to see you. Please come in. I'm Susan'. Peter rallied belatedly and shook hands. She tried and failed to move one of the cases but Peter assured her that he could manage and heaved them clear of the front door so that Susan could shut it. At this point a plump Ann appeared. She was probably in her forties and well dressed but her fashionably short and prematurely greying hair made her look rather austere although her smile suggested otherwise. Introductions were made and Peter immediately thanked her for her hospitality.

'It's a pleasure to meet you. Joe told me all about you and I'm happy to help.' Peter wondered what, precisely, he had passed on. For example, did she know that he had little money and was on his way to the Far East for three years? Was that important?

'Susan, show Mr Adams to his room and where the bathroom is' 'I'm sure you want to wash after your long journey.' He returned and she resumed. 'I never like travelling on a train. They're always so dirty and the smell of the smoke makes me feel sick.' It would have been easy to infer that Ann was a snob but that would have been wrong. She was kind and considerate and made an effort to put Peter at his ease, as she detected that he was not particularly experienced in socialising. Peter, proud of what he called his working-class roots, felt unsure how to conduct himself with someone whom he imagined was middle class.

Ann wanted to know about her friend Joe.

'He seems ok but like so many of us, he's got his problems. The General Strike really angered him. He was upset not just by the strike but by what he called the toffs and the students who enjoyed driving the buses and trams and trying to undermine what he and millions of others regarded as the reasonable demands of the miners. When he heard that the strikers had overturned a tram, he was really pleased but he was angry that the government put armoured cars on the streets of London. That seemed unnecessary and provocative.'

Peter suddenly wondered if Ann shared these views. After all, he told himself, she lived in this very posh house. Had he been too candid? There was no need to worry. Whatever class she was, she was considerate and she soon demolished any concerns that Peter felt.

'Yes, I agree with Joe. The hard-working miners only wanted to avoid having a pay cut. When I read that some 300,000 volunteers rallied to the government cause, I did wonder if we were heading for a civil war and those students and toffs as Joe called them, made me really angry too. Then you see what the politicians get up to and you wonder why there isn't civil war. How much longer must we tolerate these men who seem to think that they have a god-given right to dominate our lives, whilst enriching their own?' Peter was reassured and had noticed that during Ann's brief speech, Susan had been nodding in agreement. He was with friends.

'You must be tired after your journey. Can I get you a cup of tea?'

'Yes, please.'

Ann left the room, leaving Peter alone with the girl who had reduced him to total silence. Guessing that he was about ten years older than this most attractive girl, Peter knew he ought to take the initiative and the ensuing conversation concentrated on Susan's job in a bank. Apparently she was also an active member of the company's swimming club and, as far as money allowed, liked to be fashionably dressed. One glance from Peter confirmed this. Did he know that an American had been the first woman to swim the English Channel? Fortunately he did and this enabled him to maintain the conversation without having to struggle to find a new topic.

Susan dutifully asked about life at sea and Peter told her what it was like to be an apprentice during the war. He soon realised that he was making it sound unpleasant so he switched to tales of overseas countries he had seen and, which to her, were places that she might know from lessons at school. He said that, in Africa, for example, he had seen some natives who had painted watches on their wrists as they could not afford the real thing and in some parts of the world, the water was so clear that you could see the fish swimming just above the ocean floor. He added that the fish were striped, as if they were wearing rugby jerseys and Susan, who knew nothing about rugby, smiled.

Ann, who had arrived with tea and biscuits, asked about Singapore. Peter had been there and he spent some time talking about the outward voyage. 'As soon as we moored at Port Said, the Egyptians swarmed on board. There were fortune tellers, magicians, stamp dealers, barbers, carpet merchants, dealers selling scarabs, amber beads and small boxes made from olive wood from Jerusalem.' Prudently, he omitted reference to the persuasive males who sought to sell pornographic pictures.

'The gullible were offered pieces of wood from the cross on which Jesus was crucified. Young boys wanted us to throw money into the harbour from one side of the ship and then they would swim under the ship, on to the other side to recover the money. I wasn't convinced. I think that they were different boys even 'though, to my eyes, all the boys looked the same.'

Susan wanted to know if Peter had been through the Suez Canal.

'Frankly, it looks like a large ditch. It wasn't very inspiring. It's very dull and all you can see is sand on each side, broken only occasionally by a signalling or control station and, just now and again, an attractive building that stretches down to the canal. In some places, the banks are so high that ships approaching around a slight bend showed only their masts and funnels which make it look like as if they were floating in the desert.'

The daughter recalled having been told something at school about Hong Kong. Had Peter been there?

'Yes, we docked in Hong Kong, for a month, whilst repairs were carried out on our very old ship. Most things in the shops, especially clothes, were so cheap. We were invaded by tailors, shoe makers and what were called sew sew women who wanted to repair our uniforms. The tailors, if they couldn't repair a suit, offered to turn it inside out and make a new one that way. The main shopping street was very busy and it was fascinating just looking at the few expensive shops that were selling ivory, jade, pictures, vases and silks. I enjoyed watching what was going on in the harbour where the tiny sampans, which are little vessels, drift around like water beetles. Apparently, families are born, live and die on them, making a living ferrying people from ship to shore. The junks seemed slow and clumsy, and they often had an eye painted on each bow. There was constant noise and bustle as the boats and ships scuttled around but somehow collisions were avoided. One part of the harbour was dominated by ships sailing between Hong Kong, Canton and Macao and it seemed as if a ship was leaving or arriving every few minutes. It was as busy as Kings Cross station. Unfortunately, there were many robberies on vessels in dock so we had to mount a 12 hour watch to ensure that nothing was stolen.'

The women were clearly impressed but Peter was most anxious to put this all into perspective.

'I've been very lucky but it's not all fun. We work hard and when I started my career at sea, the conditions were appalling. We worked 77 hours a week and my pay during the four years of my apprenticeship during the war was damn all.' Peter decided against mentioning that, in the war, his vessels had been mined, torpedoed and involved in a collision and that he had had to jump for his life. He was keen not to be seen as a hero, especially as he was well aware of the final sacrifice made by millions in the war that was supposed to be the war to end all wars.

'What I've seen in some countries, is decent humans having to live and work in appalling conditions yet, somehow, they seem happy with their lot in life. It's made me realise just how lucky I've been.'

Peter, realising that he was close to dominating the conversation, apologised for talking too much and asked Ann about her own life.

'Joe told me that you used to be on the stage in London, in Drury Lane, I believe.'

'Yes, we had a tailor's shop but in my earlier days, I was on the stage.'

Susan, sitting beguilingly cross-legged on an armchair, uncoiled herself and told her mother not to be modest.

'Mother not only appeared frequently in the West End, either acting or singing, but was on the stage with Sarah Bernhard.' Peter, impressed, said that Ann must have been very good to appear in the same shows as the very famous actress. Prompted by a meaningful stare from her daughter, Ann recounted some stories, including the occasion when she missed her cue to leave the stage, being dominated by Bernhard, so improvised and sat down, listening to the next few moments' monologue, before it was possible to leave.

'I felt so embarrassed. I wrote an apology to her, explaining that I was captivated by the performance of such a fine artist. She replied that she was grateful to have such a compliment from one artist to another. Did you know that she had broken a leg on the stage and, after that, had to rely occasionally, on holding on to her fellow performers? I remember that one show we were in, my arm was quite sore after supporting her through the whole of one scene.'

After a few more minutes conversation about the theatre, Ann led Peter to the well-furnished dining room. 'I'm sure that you must be hungry and I hope that you like shepherd's pie.' Although he did not know about such a pie or the food enjoyed by shepherds, Peter daringly said that it was one of his favourite meals. Later, having enjoyed the meal, and helping with the washing up, it was difficult not to stare at Susan. She was slim, had shining brown hair, down to her shoulders, and blue eyes that demanded attention. Her face was attractive rather than beautiful. She was only sixteen but she seemed mature without being precocious and had contributed sensibly to the conversation during dinner. Peter, still hypnotised, wondered if.. No, it was silly. He was some ten years older and was just about to sail to the Far East, where he had to remain for three years. How ironic that one reason that he had decided to go abroad was that he did not have a girl friend. Now, if he had been able to stay in the country, just possibly, no, it was absurd and he banished any further such thoughts.

The following morning, after a fine fried breakfast, the three left the house together and caught the bus. When it reached the local underground station, Ann remained on board, wished Peter good luck and said that she hoped to see him again one day. He re-iterated his thanks and joined Susan briefly as the two headed for different platforms. When the time came for parting, Peter, who had thought about this in advance, was unsure whether he should just thank Susan or whether he should shake hands. He opted for the latter. Somehow, it seemed rude not to. He watched her go to a different platform and soon she was but one person in the crowd and, as she vanished down an escalator, Peter was disappointed that she did not glance back at the young man who knew he wanted to marry her but feared he would never see her again. Three years in the Far East suddenly seemed an eternity.

When Peter reached Port Said, he posted a letter to his hosts in London, thanking them for their hospitality and including some details about the voyage and Port Said itself, as well as his address in Singapore. Would there be a letter from the daughter there? He tried hard not to think of her as Susan as that implied a degree of familiarity to which he felt he was not entitled. There was no letter awaiting him and, having tried to persuade himself that he should not have expected one, he was, nevertheless, surprised at how depressed the absence of a letter made him. The gods rewarded him for his patience and, some days later, he received two letters. The first was from Freda, Joe's wife, and he wondered, immediately, why she was writing to him. If anyone was to write, surely, it should have been Joe? Nervously, he ripped open the envelope. It was bad news, very bad news. His best friend was dead. His bus had swerved, to avoid hitting a dog and Joe, helping someone who, foolishly, had jumped on the bus as it was in motion, was thrown off. The passenger was all right but Joe was hit by a passing car and died three days later in hospital. Why did this sort of thing happen to the good people? Peter's belief in God, not for the first time, was challenged. How would poor Freda manage financially? Later that day, Peter wrote to her and arranged for her to receive some money.

The second letter had an equally powerful, but happier impact on Peter. It was from Susan and it was so long that Peter realised immediately that it had to be more than an acknowledgment of his earlier letter thanking the pair for their hospitality. Eagerly, now freed from the restrictions imposed by time spent studying, he began what was to become a series of long letters in which he described the places he visited and the unusual sights that he thought might be of interest to her.

Early in 1929, Peter's vessel was to return to the United Kingdom and he was excited at the prospect of finding out if he had a future with the young Susan. They had been active correspondents and as the ship crawled to the UK, he felt that he was justified in being hopeful. She had not only responded to his letters but had sent him photographs of her and her friends on holiday in Broadstairs, Seaton and Bournemouth. Soon he would know the worst or the best. Why did his vessel move so slowly? His impatience, excitement and concern grew the closer he was to England and his mood varied. Surely, long letters and photographs suggested that he had some hope? However, there was an age gap of about ten years and her letters might just mean that she was polite and was told by Ann that it was only good manners to write back. Was she just a pen pal? Although he had many acquaintances on the ship, he did not know any well enough to ask if they thought, on his evidence, he had a chance of advancing his relationship with 19 year-old Susan.

His immediate future was in the balance. This time, he was to be paid at the beginning of his leave and he had saved some money whilst overseas: he was determined to enjoy his stay in the UK but he knew that he could be disappointed. After one week in Newcastle, spoiled by his dominating mother who seemed angry that he was not spending all his leave with the family which would have allowed her to abuse him daily, he caught the train to Kings Cross. As the train wheezed into the station, Peter had convinced himself that it was foolish to assume that his life, hitherto unremittingly unhappy, was about to change. The train had been slow at times and Peter felt frustrated whilst at other times it was going so fast that he was unsure whether he wanted to know yet what the future held for him. For as long as he did not know, there was hope. Rejection was final. He had told Susan when he would be at the station and the moment when he would know his fate was now imminent. As he left the train, paradoxically both optimistic and pessimistic, he did not have long to wait. A beautiful young woman came bounding towards him and without any self-consciousness, flung her arms around the man who became the happiest male in London. He would not need a hotel room in the capital.

Later in his leave, Peter bought a second-hand Morris in Newcastle and, after nearly an hour's tuition, drove it to London. The happy couple spent many hours together and whilst waiting for Susan to emerge from the bank, each afternoon, Peter wandered around London, enjoying the museums, art galleries and, occasionally, a matinee at one of London's many theatres. He might have been the happiest he had ever been, but the Wall Street crash, later in the year, resulted in many thousands of Americans losing all their savings. Then the London market slumped and the depression set in. In the UK, more than three million would lose their jobs and the economic conditions proved fertile for the development of communism and fascism which were to cause the deaths of millions of people.

The relationship was developing fast and Peter was accepted by Ann's family. He had often wondered what it was like to be part of a friendly family. Now he knew. The pair enjoyed a holiday together in Bournemouth and, back in London, Susan said 'We've had a great holiday together but you suddenly seem glum. What's the trouble?'

'I've just had a letter about my next appointment. I've got to join the ship on 19th November, at Tilbury docks. As I've spent so much time out in the Far East, I asked for a position on a tanker trading on the run to the UK and at least they've agreed that. I'll be acting chief officer and that means that I shall get £23 a month. Of course, I've always known that I'll have to go back but now that the date's come, it makes me realise what I'm going to miss.'

Parting was painful and when Peter was transferred to a vessel trading in the Far East, although his monthly pay rose to £37, he was denied the opportunity of possibly putting his relationship with Susan on a more permanent basis. The two continued to exchange long letters and Susan met Peter whenever he came into a UK port. By 1931, five years after the timid knock on the door of a suburban house, the pair were engaged. Peter wanted to marry the following year but, in the January, he told Susan that he feared that his salary might not be enough.

Not for the first time, Susan assured him. 'We've both got jobs and it may be difficult at times, but I'm sure that we'll cope. Many people manage on much less.' Peter agreed and marvelled at the maturity of his young fiancée. In early 1932, his vessel docked at Plymouth. He caught a train to Paddington, where he met his fiancée and Ann and one of her friends. The quartet were to look at houses as Peter wanted to buy one whilst he was in the country for just a few days. Within a few hours, a terraced house, built in 1906, near Alexandra Palace in North London had been selected.

'Well, what do you think of it?'

Susan, clearly impressed , asked tentatively 'how much is it?'

'It's £1,200 which, I know, is a hell of a lot but I've saved some money and the mortgage would be spread over at least 30 years. I've worked it out. Ignoring interest rates, that's about £3 a month. It's got four bedrooms, a lounge, dining room and it's connected to mains electricity. Only a quarter of houses have power like that.' His fiancée wondered if they could afford it.

The foursome thought it through for a few minutes over an inexpensive cup of tea in the Palace grounds. Peter and Susan had decided. 'Well, if we both think we can cope financially, let's do it.'

Peter returned to Plymouth the following evening, tired and excited and looking forward to his marriage, which had been postponed until July to coincide with his next leave. Before the great day, he sent Susan a cheque for £100 to spend on setting up their new home. She acquired furniture for the lounge and bedrooms, kitchen utensils, carpets and lino and other essential items, for £95. As the wedding approached, Peter felt ill. It was not a concern over commitment to Susan: he had never been so sure of anything. It was the familiar problem of money. Additionally, he had been upset physically by some particularly difficult weather as the ship struggled to stay upright in some very unfriendly seas and the general mood had not been helped as one member of the crew had attacked the captain.

Sunday, 9th July 1932, Peter's wedding day, was sunny and everything went well. As Peter later wrote to Joe's widow, saying how much he owed her husband for the introduction, 'Susan looked beautiful and I couldn't take my eyes off her during the entire ceremony in our local church. We had our wedding breakfast in our own home and had 30 guests in the lounge. It was all that I wished for. We went to Torquay for our honeymoon but I was very tired when we reached the hotel at 10.00 in the evening. It had been the best day of my life and I didn't want it to end. The weather was beautiful and we wandered around Torquay which has fine gardens, beaches and countryside. We saw *Private Lives* at the Pavilion and spent some time on Oddicombe Beach and visited *HMS Stuart* in the bay and Kent's Cavern which is millions of years old. Apparently, Napoleon compared this region to Italy when he was awaiting deportation and exile to St. Helena. Surely, this part of the world must be as beautiful as any on the continent. None of this could have happened but for Joe. I'll always owe him more than I can ever say. I shall always miss him. He was a true friend.'

Later that year, Peter was on leave again.

'Isn't it good that we can relax in our own comfortable home, just the two of us, listening to the Cenotaph service on the wireless?'

'Yes, but it'll be better when we can afford a proper table to put the wireless on.' Susan smiled as she said this and put her arm around him. 'It's our own little piece of the world where we can retreat to leaving the cares of the world outside the front door.'

When Peter received a letter confirming his next appointment, a table for the wireless and much else seemed to vanish further into the distance. 'Look at this', he said, angrily brandishing the document. 'I've served as chief officer for four years and my next job is as a second officer. Why? Worse still, it means that my monthly pay has fallen to £16, my lowest for nine years, and all this so soon after being married. This is dreadful and I don't know what I can do about it.' Susan, seeing that he was really worried, struggled and failed, to say something that was, at once, sensible and helpful.

'Do they say why you will be the second officer, especially as you're qualified as a master?'

'No, but I do know that the shipping world is in difficulties.'

Ironically, he joined his ship which would be near Newcastle for four days so, after some deliberation, he invited his parents to visit him. Neither came but Susan joined him for a few days. Their first parting away from home, as man and wife, was painful. It was on a cold, cheerless, dank and dark morning on Hebburn-on-Tyne. The narrow cobblestone streets around the docks were grey and the occasional flickering street lamp illuminated the deserted and bleak buildings. The steady drizzle echoed Peter's emotions as they walked to the nearby station. His heart was heavy and sad. They kissed briefly and furtively, in a shop doorway littered with yesterday's newspapers, like a young boy and girl flouting parental orders, rather than a married couple and, as Peter turned away, his spirits plunged to a new low. Susan was his world. How, after being alone for so many years, could he now cope without her?

The months rolled past and the global political and economic climate looked increasingly serious but they were cheered by the fact that their first child was expected in late 1936. Some people questioned the wisdom of bringing a child into what seemed to be a potentially very dangerous world but Peter and Susan were overjoyed. The family life that Peter had been denied was now just months away and he intended to enjoy every available minute, watching his child grow up.

Was This A Christmas Pudding?

The Royal family suffered an annus horribilis in 1936 although it did not realise that because nobody had studied Latin. London in December 1936 was dry and mild and there were 59 hours of sunshine but, fortunately, a Frenchman had invented sunscreen earlier in the year. Just before Christmas, the sun shone metaphorically and literally on a nursing home in North London and on the 26 year-old blue-eyed and brown-haired and hitherto slender Susan Adams. Peter had visited his wife earlier in the month, but had to return to sea before the big day. His vessel was routed to Curacao and then on to San Francisco but, perhaps fortunately, he did not know was that he would then remain in the Far East and that it would be January 1939 before he would see his new son.

Doubtless, Susan was wondering how her life was to change, unless she was pre-occupied with comments in the newspapers that the Tasmanian Tiger had become extinct. Tim later admitted that he could not recall his own thoughts at the time, on the Tasmanian Tiger problem or anything else, as he joined 8.6 million fellow Londoners. There is no plaque to commemorate his birth. Presumably, keen to disassociate themselves from someone who was to be so mediocre for so long, the owners of the nursing home, some years later, turned the building into a community centre where those 21st century local residents, who had surrendered their guns or lost their cats, or who had lost their guns or surrendered their cats, could receive appropriate counselling. Tim's lack of public recognition was sustained throughout his life. He was never asked for his autograph by grubby children and even clean ones shunned him.

Born three years before the outbreak of the Second World War, Tim denied that his arrival influenced anything, least of all war. For many years, he had no phone or typewriter, such were the straitened financial circumstances of the Adams family, but this was not then construed as a violation of basic human rights. Few people realised that he had turned up. The infant did not know that King Farouk had ascended to the Egyptian throne but the king was similarly ignorant about Tim's arrival. The new baby knew nothing about the Spanish Civil War which had started in the year of his birth, the outbreak of hostilities between China and Japan or the German army marching back into the demilitarised Rhineland.

He did not know that Austrian-born Adolf Hitler, whose father was the illegitimate child of Maria Schicklgruber, who worked for a Jewish family, had spent some of his early life on the streets of Vienna, selling postcards of his artwork. This knowledge of local traffic probably inspired him to launch the Volkswagen car in 1936 and to direct his army into Austria in March 1938. The car was designed by Ferdinand Porsche who was identified later with sports cars. These became very popular when young financiers, gambling with other people's money, replaced manufacturing in the UK economy some decades later. Tim did not know that Somozo had been elected president of Nicaragua just 15 days before his birth but there was no shame in this. Somozo was hardly a household name, even in his own household.

If Tim had been aware of all this and the fact that the Nazi party secured 99 per cent of the votes in an election, he may have opted to stay where he was, but, as Mrs Thatcher said, decades later, there was no alternative. Tim would have sympathised with the unemployed of Jarrow, 300 of whom marched to the capital in October, despite frequent bad weather, to protest against poverty and unemployment and who were ignored by Prime Minister Stanley Baldwin. He retired the following May and died in 1947, aged 80. Baldwin, who disapproved of Edward V111's light-coloured suits, was the only prime minister to serve under three monarchs in the same year. Similarly, Tim was one of the few chaps to be born in a year when the country had been ruled by three kings, two of whom were known as George. This royal rumpus made George a very popular name for new UK males.

BBC Radio journalists were pre-occupied with the aftermath of the great fire which destroyed Crystal Palace in London on 30th November and their television colleagues failed to mention Tim's birth but the service had only commenced a month before his arrival and their news-gathering system was not fully prepared, even for an event that had been known about nine months earlier.

King George V had died on 20th January and was succeeded by Edward V111, who was never crowned. Edward wanted to share his life with Mrs Wallis Simpson, whom he had first met in 1934. This irked many politicians who were doubtless irritated also by her odd first name. Was it normal, even for an American woman to be called Wallis? As one letter to a newspaper observed, it was a 'dashed odd name and casts doubt on the whole rummy business'. It was a time when first names were very confusing as shown by Albert when he became George at the end of the year.

Edward abdicated on 10th December. (The following year, he and his wife, now demoted to being the Duke and Duchess of Windsor, visited Hitler which prompted even more anger in the UK government than the Duke's choice of suit.) In December 1936, Prince Albert, who was to become George V1, agreed to take the job, which was jolly decent of him as he was not all that keen but jobs for members of the royal family were rare. Some 1.8 million people, nearly 14 per cent of the workforce, were unemployed.

Gatwick airport became operational in 1936 and the £15 million Golden Gate Bridge was opened in November. This was good planning as Tim used both several decades later. Billy Butlin opened his first holiday camp in the UK, at Skegness, but this was a waste of time as Tim never went there but that's the kind of risk you have to take to be successful in business. The Olympic Games were held in Germany in August and the coloured American, Jesse Owens, who had broken five world records in one day in 1935, upset Hitler by winning four gold medals. Unlike other successful American athletes, Owens was not invited to meet Hitler, as he had challenged the theory that Aryans were the master race. In August of 1937, Hitler opened the Buchenwald concentration camp.

Vesuvius erupted and Queen Mary made her maiden voyage to New York. That's the ship, not the queen, who at 68, was a little old for such energetic swimming. The German airship Hindenburg crossed the Atlantic in 46 hours, excluding check-in time. In May of the following year, it exploded over New Jersey, killing 33 of the 97 passengers and injuring many more. In Italy, Mussolini nationalised the country's banks, creating a precedent that was partly followed by the Labour government in the UK some decades later. In November, Germany and Italy recognised Franco's Spain which should not have been too difficult: it had been in reasonable atlases, available from good bookshops, for some years.

In late 1936, Tim was ignorant of what was happening in Germany, being unable to read any of Winston Churchill's speeches. Realising that he was not literate at this stage, nobody offered to read them to him, which was curious given his subsequent interest in history, politics and economics. He might have heard some of WC's speeches on the wireless but Tim had a propensity to snoozing so might have missed them. Having, doubtless, worried how to solve the Euro crisis in the early part of the next century, he spent many hours asleep in his large pram, the design and size of which was probably the basis for the Mini car in the Sixties. The sheer enormity of the pram probably prevented him, in a horizontal position, from seeing the clouds of war developing on the horizon.

As far as Tim could recall later, there were no conversations in his presence about Poland or Germany, but adults were careful in what they said in front of the children so perhaps he was fooled or comatose. Now it's the parents who cannot understand their children and their strange texting language. It was fashionable then to spell out certain words but Tim did not remember anyone spelling out a potentially grim message 'W. A. R is coming.' If they had, he might have guessed that it meant that wonderful Aunt Rosemary was planning a visit, although why that should have been in code, nobody knows. She was a good woman but had nothing whatever to do with the espionage services but she might have been very professional and kept her secret to the grave. Rosemary rarely visited Susan during the war but that was not necessarily suspicious as she had moved to Devon and Rosemary was in London, allegedly looking after her family.

Other comments might have been in code, such as 'do you think that the G will beat the F?' (Germans and French for those who don't understand this style of patter.) That might have been speculation on whether the Gunners, (Arsenal) might overcome Finchley although Tim might have guessed that this could not have been about a football match as these two teams were light years apart in skill in 1939 which has remained the case, notwithstanding the latter merging later with the Wingate club and Arsenal selling their best players to other clubs.

This was the world into which Tim was born. Despite trawling through some of the most complete history books written before, during and after his birth, including some by genuine experts as well as by irritating gardening pundits who assume that, as celebrities, they can do anything, Tim never found a record of his arrival, apart from a birth certificate and some photographs of a small bundle wrapped up in blankets. But for the lack of a sprig of holly, it might have been a picture of a blanketed Christmas pudding. There is no incontrovertible proof that he was born but, for purposes of this story, it must be assumed that he was.

Tim, who arrived without even a cheap pocket watch, learned that he arrived on the evening of Wednesday 23rd December, just in time to miss the six o'clock news on the Home Service on the wireless. In those days, the headlines were not repeated at the end of the news and his birth was even ignored on the later bulletins but this did not upset him as he was asleep. Immediately after the event, which had changed her life, Susan was emerging from a dream. As she told a nurse, 'I thought that I heard carols and assumed that I'd gone to heaven'.

'Well, I can assure you, dear, that you're still on earth but when you see this truly gorgeous, handsome and obviously intelligent young boy, you might think that you've entered your own private heaven. You're very lucky to have such a fine young child, who may well become internationally famous.' Just possibly, the response might have been less effusive.

One day later, the new mother, if she had had access to a television set, which she and virtually everyone else lacked, could have watched the newsreel at 9.15 pm and then Old Time Music Hall. She could have sampled Dairy Box and Quality Street confectionary, created earlier in the year, whilst reading a book from Penguins, which set up in 1935. Susan enjoyed reading newspapers and noted that one was obsessed by a 24 year old who was on trial for stealing £4-10-0. More positively, a new airmail service to Africa was planned. Susan was pleased for her son as, even if he never needed to send a letter by air to Africa, it was thoughtful of the officials to organise the service on the off chance.

Anthea Barnes, a neighbour and mother of two young boys, was visiting Susan just after the birth. After the two exchanged predictable comments and Anthea had gushed enthusiastically on seeing Tim, Susan asked her friend whether she had seen a story in the papers about the Post Office claim that its 20,000 bicycles covered 120,000 miles a year.'

'No, but I'm hoping that you can tell me all about it.'

Demonstrating her mathematical skills honed in the bank, Susan said 'that's six miles per machine per year or, about 30 yards a day, assuming a six day week'. Anthea looked impressed but then noticed that the newspaper left on the bed was decorated by rows of figures.

'Wouldn't it have been more efficient for the postal delivery staff to walk? A few yards must have been devoured by taking the machines to the open road so it must be assumed that many cycles were rarely used. One day in the future, you mark my words, the Post Office will be in severe financial trouble, then the government will put money into it and sell it to their friends in the City.'

Anthea was about to speak but Susan had not finished. Picking up her paper, she read out some more figures. 'Alternatively, could each machine cover 120,000 miles a year, which would imply over 300 miles every day? Assuming a ten-hour day and ignoring time spent in delivering the mail, that suggests an average speed of over 30 miles per hour.' What Susan did not know was the power of drugs in later years but, doubtless, all this cycling was paving the way for British success in the 2012 Olympics.

Anthea, thinking that all this was rather silly, although Susan was enjoying herself, tried a different conversational tack.

'Have you been able to contact Peter to tell him he's got a son?'

'I've tried to reach him but so far, poor chap, he doesn't know. Anyway, how's your family?'

'Well, as you know, James isn't due for leave from the army until some time next year he's a corporal now, and the two boys are a handful. Occasionally, they play up because their father's away but, on the whole, they're good.'

In February 1937, Peter received a photograph of his new son when he was on a vessel when it docked in Kobe in Japan. Lest there be any doubt, it was Peter Adams who was overseas. His son remained in London, spurning all forms of travel unless he was wrapped up warmly in a pram, and who confined his external activities to visiting the shops or Alexandra Palace grounds. Peter, looking at a photograph of his son, noted that 'at first I laughed because he looked such a funny little chap. Not at all good-looking'. When, later, people said that his son was like him, Peter conceded that Tim was rather handsome.

The infant's early months were dominated not by discussing the loathsome Hitler and his evil ambitions but by consumption of food products, packaged in a fine red circular tin by Cow and Gate, and regular naps. He had not heard of Winston Churchill, who had first stood for Parliament in the same year that Peter was born. A UK poll in 2008, the results of which reflected the standard of British education after some 60 years of 'progress', revealed that 23 per cent of the respondents thought that Churchill never existed whilst 58 per cent maintained that Sherlock Holmes was real. That's surprising, given the television coverage devoted to Churchill but, admittedly, there was a recent series on Mr Holmes and, doubtless, seeing him take drugs, many people, identifying with this current habit, thought that he was real. Churchill was, surely, just the name of an insurance company.

Some people said that Tim resembled a bald version of Churchill. However, over the years the similarities between the two faded. For example, the only painting Tim did was on his home and he never built a wall. Of the two of them, Churchill is the only one to have a statue in Parliament Square, or anywhere else, and Tim never smoked a cigar. They never met but Tim saw Churchill, nearly 30 years later, in early 1965, but, as he was dead, lying in state at Westminster, there was no opportunity for a chat.

Neville Chamberlain became prime minister in May 1937, despite his awful shirts and collars. Tim did not hear his speech, in 1939, which confirmed that in the absence of a reply from Germany, the United Kingdom was at war. Occasionally, we still have trouble with emails. Did Chamberlain ask for a read receipt, when he contacted the German leader? Perhaps that was a day when he was deluged with spam and the response from Hitler was overlooked? Letters, too, can be lost in the post and, hopefully, the Post Office personnel were not on strike or had cut the number of daily deliveries to reduce the incidence of their staff being bitten by dogs. Perhaps the reply was caught up in junk mail and was accidentally thrown away or maybe the delivery men were servicing their bicycles?

Earlier, the press photographs of this odd and strangely-collared character waving a piece of paper around, in September 1938, and claiming that we could expect peace in our time, had induced fear in the more far-sighted. Within five days, with the agreement of Britain, France and Italy, Hitler led his troops into the Sudetenland. Hitler may have outwitted the UK prime minister but it was clear that the British moustache really was a moustache whilst that which adorned the German's face looked more like a dirty mark which had defied routine washing. He must have had problems if the fanatical, foolish fuehrer favoured fistfuls of fresh fusilli.

NC always referred to Mr Hitler but Tim later contended that the murderous thug was not entitled to any courtesy title. The man was a bloodthirsty lout and that was doubtless Tim's considered but unspoken opinion as he contemplated his third birthday. Neville

Chamberlain was to resign on 10th May 1940, the day that Germany launched attacks on Holland, Belgium and Luxemburg, and was succeeded by Winston Churchill.

Britain and France had declared war on Germany on 3rd September 1939 : within hours, the first air raid siren had been heard but it was a false alarm. Before long, the German air force was dropping propaganda leaflets on the UK. These were eagerly sought by housewives who used them as toilet paper, which reflected both a desire to save money by spurning a more professional product and a comment on the contents of the leaflet. The USSR invaded Poland on 17th September and Finland at the end of November. On 19th September, the aircraft carrier HMS Courageous was sunk by a U Boat. (During the entire war, U boats sank more than 2,700 merchant ships, two battleships, six aircraft carriers and nearly 100 other British vessels.) On the same day, the Royal Air Force dropped leaflets over Germany and by the end of the month, the British Expeditionary Force had sailed to France. Anticipating war, the UK government had required all men of 21 years or more to register for conscription in May.

One of the UK administration's early decisions was to require blackout material to drape all windows. Street lighting ceased and all vehicles, allowed a maximum speed of 20 miles per hour, were restricted to the amount of light that they could use. Consequently, in the first few months of the war, there were more fatalities caused by road accidents than by enemy action. The first bomb to drop on the UK fell on the Shetlands in November 1940. In June of that year, Italy had declared war on the United Kingdom and this resulted in many Italians being attacked in their home towns in England.

The Move To The West Country

Peter was on leave in summer 1939. His happiness at being with his wife, and seeing his son for the first time, had been undermined by the incessant talk of war. He had decided that, before he faced a very uncertain future, he must do whatever he could to reduce the danger to his family. His main fear was that London was an obvious target.

'I hope to God I'm wrong, but I think that war's inevitable and that we must brace ourselves for the worst. I was never fooled by that Chamberlain idiot, who ought never to have become prime minister, waving a piece of paper around and stupidly claiming that it was peace in our time. He must think that we're all as daft as him. There's no doubt on Hitler's intentions and they've been clear for some years and what did we do during those years? Nothing. The height of our planning, if we had any at all, was to dream up how to evacuate many thousands of children from dangerous areas and to plan the manufacture of gas masks. Oh, yes, we also were good at appeasement which must have encouraged Hitler. We've promised to support Poland if they're attacked but we all know that's an empty gesture. There's nothing we can do for them. We felt that Hitler would suddenly go away and we even ignored Churchill, whose political skills and knowledge of history suggested that conflict was inevitable. Now, we're about to reap the whirlwind and who can be sure of the outcome? If America doesn't join in soon after the war starts, we should be very concerned. I don't think they're bothered about Germany and Europe. They're more worried about the Japs. Last time, you may know, they only entered the Great War when it was nearly over.'

Susan did know because it was a point that she had heard Peter make before. Indeed, she had heard most of Peter's speeches before.

'I just can't see how war can be avoided. It will be truly bloody and civilians will be in the front line. In the Great War, the war to end all wars, ha ha, more than 2,000 civilians in the UK lost their lives due to military action. Your mother lived through that as you did as a very young girl, and I've no wish for you both to have to suffer that again. We lost twice as many civilians as the Germans. Now advanced bombing techniques means that many thousands of people could lose their lives. Obviously, London will be the obvious target for those murderous huns. I don't want you, Ann and Tim exposed to the dangers. You've got to move out of London.

'You know what appalling loss of innocent life occurred when the Italian swine bombed Abyssinia and they and the hideously obscene Germans attacked civilians from the air during the Spanish civil war. Two years ago, the town of Guernica was destroyed by the German air force. The Japs killed 5,000 civilians from the air when they bombed Canton last year. Then, of course, the Germans have been building up their air force whilst we do nothing, pretending that peace will prevail. We really need Winston to take over from the pathetic Chamberlain. The man doesn't understand what's going on and he's leading us into a disaster from which we may not recover in our lifetime. Something must be done. We can't influence whether we go to war or not, but I can ensure that my family isn't in London.'

Susan looked at him quizzically but experience told her not to interrupt.

'Apparently, official thinking is that, as soon as the war begins, tens of thousands of Londoners could be killed in a matter of weeks. They're even planning to produce vast numbers of cardboard coffins.'

Susan shivered and nodded. His comments had frightened her. She was not surprised to hear her husband's opinions but the reference to coffins somehow changed the almost abstract discussion of war between nations to the deaths of thousands of innocent civilians like her. He had spoken like this before but his views now seemed more clearly defined, and, worst of all, totally plausible. Like millions, she feared that war was inevitable and that the UK had been negligent in making fundamental preparations and in building military capacity. Even the newsreels showing the UK's military preparations suggested that the country was preparing for a re-run of the First World War and featured the digging of trenches and filling sandbags. Sandbags could be used to absorb bomb blast, but what was being done to build up the military? As she had complained to Anthea, it was as if we had learned nothing whilst the Germans had advanced their thinking significantly. Both women rejected the argument that Chamberlain's approach was to buy time and, like many others, felt that he should not be in office at such a crucial time.

Susan responded to her husband's speech.

'I agree. I'm as worried as you but what can we do? We can't afford two houses. This one is expensive enough and I don't think we've time to sell it and to buy another one somewhere in the country. You're due to go back to sea soon and we don't have much time to work out what we could do.' Then, as if suddenly aware of what might happen, she leaned towards Peter, smiled and hugged him. 'I don't want you to go but I know you've no choice. We need the Merchant Navy and the Merchant Navy needs you. Anyway, who's going to buy a house in North London when a war seems imminent? I don't know what we can do. I'm really worried.'

A grave-looking Peter, who realised that he had upset his wife, not least by mentioning coffins, revealed that he had a possible solution. 'Whatever happens, you, Tim and Ann must go to somewhere which should be safer. I've been making some enquiries but I didn't want to worry you with the details until I had some firm ideas and knew that they might work. I've found a very small cottage in St. Mawes, near Falmouth, in Cornwall which we can rent for six months. It's too small for the three of you to live in for very long so I've agreed provisionally with the agents that you can then move to a rented house at Preston, near Torquay, that will be on their books later, for the rest of the war. How would you feel about that?'

'What about this house? We can't sell it so we'd have to rent it out and I can't imagine that anyone would want to live here with a war possibly weeks away.'

Peter permitted himself a wry smile. As usual, his perceptive wife had immediately identified a possible problem. 'Just for once, you're wrong. I've found someone who is keen to rent this house and, what's more, he wants to keep it for the duration.'

Susan was impressed but mildly irritated that Peter had done all this without even consulting her but she said nothing as, to use a familiar family phrase, it was all for the best. She realised that Peter wanted to organise the move before he returned to sea and she was in no mood to argue. What was important was that they would leave London and that this would relieve Peter of worrying about the family. Soon he would be gone and, being realistic, no one could know when the two would meet again or, God forbid, ever. This unwelcome thought induced an immediate sense of heavy melancholy and, with some difficulty, she hauled her thoughts back to the proposed move.

Together, united in gloom, they decided that, when war was declared, it would be sensible to move to the west country. Seven years before, they had enjoyed their honeymoon in Torquay. It had been the happiest few days of Susan's life and now it was to be her home during a war the outcome of which was impossible to predict. She would use her earlier memories to offset the worry of not knowing where Peter was and, indeed, and she shuddered at this, whether he was alive. Being on an oil tanker during a major war must be one of the loneliest and potentially most dangerous occupations. She stretched out her hand and took his and squeezed it before kissing him gently on the lips.

How long would the Adams be away from the capital? Unlike the optimism at the beginning of the First World War, there were no euphoric claims that it would all be over in a few months. The signs were that, unless the UK was forced to capitulate early in the conflict, it would be a long war. Susan had her doubts about France being able to withstand a severe onslaught from the Germans who had spent years and huge sums in modernising their forces, and feared that, without a prompt American intervention, which seemed most unlikely, the outlook was really bleak. How would the family fare during the war? What sort of city would London be after the war, especially if Peter was right? The United Kingdom had been slow to re-arm and horrific as the possibility was, both Peter and Susan even speculated on whether the UK could win the war, especially without any major ally. Susan was desperately worried that Peter, the captain of a small and virtually unarmed oil tanker, would be very vulnerable but she tried not to contemplate a life without the only man she had ever loved. Even thinking of what might happen induced tears and as they planned their move, Peter noticed that she was struggling to avoid crying. He put his arm around his wife's shoulders and silence, more eloquent than words, prevailed.

Peter moved Susan, Tim and Ann from their North London home to Cornwall. That is not to suggest that he hired a white van, or indeed a van of any colour, and drove the family to their new and temporary home. Captain Peter Adams was overseeing his small ocean-going tanker as it was prepared for war with elderly guns that might have been useful only at the Battle of Trafalgar. More precise wording is required. It was not his vessel: it belonged to GOC Petroleum and they entrusted him with it, the crew of 32 and its precious cargo. If it had been his, he would have spent more on modern weaponry and less time in the dangerous Atlantic where heavily-armed German navy vessels were to roam at will, often disguised as innocent merchant ships.

St. Mawes was part of a harbour which claimed to be the third largest in the world. The local castle, built between 1539 and 1545 by Henry V111, was part of a strong chain of defensive fortresses designed to protect the southern coast of England. It was ironic that the region was now regarded as relatively safe in yet another example of man's inhumanity to man. St. Mawes was a small village where the local residents were mainly occupied in fishing. The narrow, cobblestone lanes and elderly white-washed cottages would have been recognised by locals long since resident in the cemetery by the side of the generously-proportioned church. The

Londoners, known as 'incomers', were welcomed warmly. There were very few children in the village and Tim was popular and was often offered sweets when he was riding around the castle grounds on a very small tricycle.

Susan, Tim and Ann had spent a few very crowded days in their rented cottage in Gibraltar Terrace and were joined for just two days by Peter. They all dreaded the moment when they had to part, perhaps for years, perhaps for ever, and, when the time came for Peter to go, Ann, failing to fight back the tears, said, 'I don't really know what to say. Words are so inadequate but I pray you'll be all right and that God will look after you. I promise you, I'll do my best to help Susan and Tim. God bless you.' Peter, whose views were that, if God was so omnipotent, war would have been averted, was less confident on the possibility of divine intervention, but he swallowed hard, took his mother-in-law's hand, squeezed it, then kissed her on the cheeks. 'Thank you, I know you'll look after Susan and the boy. Please don't worry, I know I've a tough job but so have millions of us and I'm sure that, one day, there'll be peace and we'll all be reunited.'

Susan and Peter were struggling to avoid crying, for Tim's sake, and it was only after some discussion that it was decided that he should accompany his parents on the short walk to the harbour. The three walked down the hill to the ferry to take Peter from St. Mawes to Falmouth, en route to war and an unknown destiny. Local residents pulled back their curtains, waved and shouted out 'good luck'. The more elderly, who had seen action in the First World War, muttered a prayer as Peter, in his uniform, passed their neat little cottages which seemed a world away from conflict. Even those who did not know the couple gave a thumbs up signal. They all knew what could happen and felt sorry for Susan and the well-behaved young boy. The couple walked in silence and Tim followed in their wake, kicking the occasional stone as if to relieve himself of the sadness which seemed to be enveloping his family. There were no words that could convey the emotions accurately. When they reached the harbour, Peter, only just holding back the tears, picked Tim up.

'It's time for me to say goodbye old chap. I've got to go back to my ship now but I'll see you again soon. Please be a good boy and help Mama and Nana all you can.' So saying, he lowered his son to the ground gently, kissed him on both cheeks and patted him on the head. He knew that there was a real possibility that he might never see him again. He had had a difficult First World War. Would he survive the new conflict? The spectacle of her husband and son hugging, for possibly the last time, proved too much for Susan and the tears were flowing as Peter clasped her passionately muttering into her ear 'you know I've always loved you and always will. Please, whatever happens, never, never, forget that.' His words were drowned by the siren on the ferry indicating that its departure was imminent. Peter kissed his wife again and whispered 'I'll be back, my love. Never give up hope, never, whatever happens'.

He strode towards the ferry and as he turned round, for the last time, and waved, Tim shouted 'goodbye daddy!' and watched as his father went out of sight. Peter sobbed quietly to himself before regaining control. Would he ever see his family again? Why were we at war? When Susan and Tim returned to the cottage, Ann made tea but mother and daughter did not speak. They both knew that the next few years would be catastrophic for millions of people around the world and there was nothing they could do but wait and hope.

Six months in the tiny white and picturesque Cornish cottage passed quickly. It overlooked the sea and Susan, when not walking to and from the small shops, which necessitated a walk along a steep and very narrow lane, spent some time in the garden. She was grateful to have her own mother with her and she also made a few new friends, one of whom had also moved from London. Ann, now more portly and greyer, had the knack of calming her daughter when she was overtaken by worry and fear and was to prove to be her best friend.

Occasionally, Susan spent some hours, tending a few plants before sitting in the garden, which overlooked the sea hundreds of feet below. She knew that they would be moving to Torquay before the flowers blossomed but somehow it was a small gesture of confidence in the future. Although it was now early winter, the weather was mild and the temperature comforting. She sat, staring at the calm and seemingly innocent water, marvelling that it looked so serene and that elsewhere, humans were being slaughtered. Was Cornwall part of the same world? Peter was probably in the Atlantic and faced daily dangers. She shuddered at the thought that at any time, he could be captured or blown up. Somehow, gazing at the sea brought her closer to her husband. Because of wartime security, she had no idea where he was and not knowing was beginning to gnaw away at her belief. Occasionally, the company gave her some indication but it was always out of date so its value was limited.

Tim, too young to understand that the world was going mad, enjoyed living so close to the sea. This change of scene gave him some new things to do in his spare time, which was all day, every day. He developed a facility for digging large holes on the beach and the fact that the tide soon undid his labouring seemed not to bother him. He also enjoyed pedalling fast on the paths surrounding the local castle. Susan vowed to sustain his ignorance for as long as she could but, when she made this promise to herself, she had little idea of just how difficult that could be. What she did not know herself at that time, was that within weeks of the beginning of the war, Peter's vessel had been involved in an incident. In December 1939, his tanker was some 15 miles south of Hastings, steaming eastwards, towards Beachy Head. The weather was overcast, with low clouds and moderate visibility. Peter had ordered a gun drill for 16.30 and went to the bridge at about 16.00. The second officer was already present and was anxious to impart some news. Breathlessly, he stammered 'I've seen an aircraft with black markings on its wings and sides. I think it's a Heinkel 111 bomber. It's certainly not one of ours'.

Almost immediately, a snarling German aircraft swooped from the clouds. As it came ever closer, Peter swung the vessel as hard as it would go to starboard and when the bomber was about 50 feet overhead, the gun crew fired a single shell and, although it missed, it may have surprised the enemy pilot whose bomb was well wide of its target. As the bomber approached a second time, Peter swung the ship violently again and the second bomb missed by an even wider margin. 'By Christ, the swine means business.' As the second officer offered this opinion, the German pilot raked the deck with machine gun fire. A third bomb missed the tanker but some damage had been sustained to the vessel and one machine gun bullet, which had pierced the deck, was embedded in the second officer's desk. For saving the vessel, a grateful company gave the crew an extra month's wages which meant £53 for Peter who later described the attack as a 'mild affair'.

After six quiet months, the family moved to the rented house in Preston, near Torquay, some 180 miles from London, and just 32 miles from the naval docks at Plymouth and close to the historic city of Exeter. In the spring of 1941, the Luftwaffe launched the first of seven major attacks on Plymouth. Almost 1,000 bombers dropped more than 200,000 incendiary devices. On 21st and 22nd of March the city centre was destroyed. There were 602 alerts and bombs were dropped on Plymouth on 59 occasions during the war. Civilian deaths in the city throughout the entire war were assessed at 1,174 and a further 1,092 were injured sufficiently seriously to be detained in hospital.

In 1942, between the end of April and early June, the enemy, using the Baedeker tourist guide for Germans, killed 1,637 civilians and destroyed some 50,000 homes in Exeter, Canterbury and Norwich. All were subjected to later attacks during the conflict. The German efforts were in retaliation for the allied attacks on the Hanseatic League city of Lubeck when 312 civilians were killed and some 15,000 homes were damaged or lost. The RAF released some 4,000 tonnes of bombs, including about 25,000 incendiary devices. During the main retaliatory attack on Exeter, in May 1942, 75 tons of high explosive and 10,000 incendiary bombs were dropped, killing 161 civilians and injuring another 476. Exeter was only 25 miles from the Adams home. In the early part of 1944, the invasion forces gathered in South Devon and elsewhere in the region and it was astonishing that the area, which included Exmouth and Dartmouth, escaped, relatively lightly, during the entire war. One unconfirmed rumour claimed that a German pilot saw D Day preparations in South Devon and reported accordingly on his return to his home country. He was ignored and, allegedly, executed.

The new home, Camellia House, built in the 1920s and painted black and white, was in a quiet and short residential road which, in the virtual absence of traffic, was, at different times, a tennis court for the local girls or a football pitch for the boys. It led to nowhere in particular which was true of most roads in those days. There was nowhere to go, apart from the shops, about a mile away, school, the beach, the church or the surrounding countryside which was dominated by steep hills. The local people all knew each other, united by the deprivations of war and the joys of gossip. Life was uncomplicated: the objectives were to find enough food, to stay warm and healthy, to comfort each other and to avoid being killed.

The type of soil deterred the growth of camellias and favoured hydrangeas and the property was semi-detached so was only half a house. However, Hydrangea Half-House lacks impact although the home was a charming residence, deceptively large and doubtless well worth an early inspection by a discerning buyer. There was a modest garden, front and back, two reception rooms, three bedrooms, a bathroom and a separate toilet. The outside lavatory was also home to hundreds of old copies of the *Daily Sketch* and numerous spiders, who had moved in for the duration and, presumably, a good read. This newspaper was used as toilet paper, which was then the usual final service provided by out-of-date papers, or for persuading a coal fire to ignite against its will, but the sheer size of the hoard would have sufficed to meet all but the most dramatic levels of demand. A stirrup pump, a bucket of water and a hod full of sand were parked close to the newspapers.

Tim had a question.

'Why do we have so many papers in the outside lavatory because, if they caught fire, the house would soon burn to the ground?' Susan, who thought that advantages of using the paper for toilet purposes outweighed the risk of fire, decided against telling the whole truth. This tactic was always employed if there was even a slight risk of upsetting her young son. Shielding him from the grim reality of war was her prime objective, apart, of course, from finding sufficient food for the family, whose numbers had been increased with the arrival of a new brother for Tim. Harry had been born in early 1940. 'Don't you worry, dear, our house isn't going to catch fire.' She asserted this as confidently as she could and hoped that her words sounded more hopeful than she really felt. She omitted the last part of her useful response which, in the circumstances, would not have helped, 'in any case, dear, there's a war on'.

An old-fashioned type of clothes horse dominated the kitchen. It consisted of long wooden strips, held together at each end by a black bracket and washing was folded over the strips and then the entire contraption was hauled upwards to remain suspended just below the ceiling whilst the contents dried. Because the heating in the house was inadequate, the device always seemed to be raised with clothes and towels draped over it. Consequently, there was always a smell of dampness and some condensation on the windows but, even if the occupants smelt a little, they were clean and Tim's yellowing and often mended round-neck Viyella vests were free of splinters. The floor covering, a brown and mature lino, curled up at some corners of the room, seemingly sneering, confident that it knew that it could not be replaced as there was a war on.

The available space in the kitchen was severely restricted when a Morrison shelter, named after Herbert Morrison, the Minister for Home Security, was installed, next to the pantry, in 1941. The shelter, six feet six inches long, 4 feet wide and 2 feet 9 inches high, consisted of four strong pillars which supported a flat and very heavy and strong top intended to prevent those inside from being squashed if the house fell down. The back and sides had hooks which allowed grids to be fastened to prevent flying objects from attacking the inmates. Families whose income exceeded £350 a year had to pay £7 for each shelter but they were otherwise free. Half a million had been erected by 1941. Tim, pleased that the family had such protection, wondered how, if the house had fallen down, the family could escape but wisely decided against seeking an answer lest the response was discouraging. Susan did her best to make the shelter comfortable and some cushions and blankets softened the impact of the draughty linoleum floor and elderly rugs, which had been bought second hand after a pre-war career on the back seats of someone else's car, helped to keep cold at bay. Several books were kept in the shelter and Ann often read to the two young boys in an effort to lull them to sleep.

The small scullery floor was made of red tiles that were permanently cold but which were polished regularly to no apparent effect or purpose. It was virtually compulsory to clean everything in the house at least once a week even if there was neither justification nor discernable improvement afterwards. It was what households did and, remarkably, it was deemed important to do some chores that were hardly necessary when there were no washing machines, fridges, or household appliances to ease the load. Inevitably, there was little time for socialising except to exchange gossip, rumour and, just occasionally, genuine news. The elderly wooden cupboards in the kitchen and scullery were painted a depressingly dark brown and had blistered which allowed Tim to pop the bubbles when he felt so inclined, which was often, until he realised that excessive activity would reduce the potential for future fun. The kitchen also had a pantry which, because of its small but open aperture was always so cold that no self-respecting piece of valuable food would have dared to go bad. It knew that there was a war on.

The front room was called the best room although, because there were only two, it should have been called the better room but Tim, at this stage in his young life, did not realise this so was silent. It was seldom used except at Christmas when a festive but small, cheerful and pink-faced pre-war Father Christmas took up residence on the trolley near the door, alongside a modest Christmas tree that always shed its needles long before 12th night, which seemed to be when the festivities, such as they were, and the season of goodwill, were replaced again by the reality of war.

The small dining room, which looked out on to the back garden, via a modest and open-fronted roofless conservatory, was also used for lounging but there wasn't much of that because everyone was permanently busy. Cleaning, shopping, cooking and taking Tim to school took a large part of Susan's time as did worrying about

Peter. A large black wireless, which provided limited and approved information about the war and entertainment to divert attention away from the conflict, dominated one corner: it took some time to warm up and made impressive but rude sounds as it lumbered into what passed as life.

A lightening conductor was attached to the main back window, on the left of the room, hidden behind a curtain. Whenever a storm threatened, Tim's grandmother made her usual speech. 'A storm is brewing, you mark my words. Tim, come away from the window, you don't want to be struck by lightening, do you? People don't want to be hit by lightening.' Ann enjoyed inviting listeners to mark her words but this comment about the people was used occasionally when she was uncertain about her own opinion and sought the tacit agreement of others. In this instance, Tim agreed that people didn't want to be struck by lightening but he was not sure what it entailed and how serious it was. His ignorance induced fear. Without waiting for a response, and denied the opportunity of asking what, precisely, would happen if he were hit by lightening, Tim was ushered away from the window. Later, he discovered that occasionally, apparently, people who sheltered from storms under trees were hit and their faces became permanently distorted.

'Mama, why is it that so many people around here have sheltered under trees when it's raining?'

'That's a very odd question. What do you mean? Why shouldn't they shelter under trees?'

'Well, nana told me that if you shelter under trees in a storm and you get hit by lightening, it can change your face. So many people around here have funny faces, I though that they must all have been hit by lightening.'

Susan did her best to reassure her son that people were struck by lightening only rarely and what he thought were funny faces were not funny but old. She added, perhaps tactlessly, 'many of us get funny faces when we're old'. Tim wanted to know when his mother might acquire a funny face and, for good measure, he asked if his father already had a funny face. Susan did her best to reassure her son that his parents did not have funny faces and would not for many years, if at all. 'Not everyone gets a funny face as they get older.' Tim pressed on, fruitlessly, asking when he would be old. Apparently, it was many years away. On being told that the thunder was caused by the clouds having a fight, he suggested that someone should tell them to stop. Occasionally, Ann even envied Tim who was hardly aware of what was happening around the world such was their success in shielding him from the brutal truth.

A large and dark sideboard was parked against the dining room wall and its surface was dominated by a 'tree' the leaves of which were small yellow, dirt-attracting plastic-like beads of unknown origin. This ornament came from Singapore as did two very black 1930's elephants which stood, impassive, on either side of the tree. A glass dish became home to a few home-grown apples. The fireplace was opposite the sideboard and poor quality coal or wood often used to spit through the inadequate guard, landing on the rug or on the well-worn carpet, creating a very nasty small of singeing.

Tim occupied the small bedroom in the front of the house. To his left, he could see a large lamp-post, a pig-food bin and a post box and idly wondered if anyone accidentally posted some waste food and gave a letter to the pigs. To his right, he could gaze up the road towards the Oldway estate which was being used by the Royal Air Force. In the First World War, part of the mansion had been converted into a hospital and now the building was used for training. The furniture, in Tim's bedroom, not in Oldway, which he had never visited so could not discuss, was frugal but sufficient. A large black box, always covered with a dark yellow cloth, was positioned under the main window and he used to sit there staring out during school holidays, at the empty road and watching pedestrians on their way to wasting a few more hours of their lives queuing at the shops for minimal but much-needed supplies of food. He also pondered what life was like in what he had heard Susan refer to as peacetime but could not come to any real conclusions. He would not have to spend part of the night sleeping in the shelter in the kitchen but there must be more to peace than that. The other bedrooms were occupied by Susan, who then shared her room with his new brother, Harry, and Ann, whose room was at the back of the house.

Upkeep of the small front and back gardens was undertaken by a man who had greeted senility prematurely. Mr Ellicombe, grey, portly and with ears that seemed too big for his head, or possibly, his head was too small for his ears, was probably only in his late fifties but was sufficiently energetic to push the hand lawnmower over the grass once a week during the season. It was not heavy but it was doubtless more cumbersome than the one that was advertised before the war as being 'easy enough for the lady of the house to control'. His rustic features were hidden behind a giant moustache that made Hitler's look pathetic although Tim never saw them together so an objective comparison was difficult. He, Ellicombe, tied his trousers at shin level with string so that the last few inches looked as if they were of the same material as the rest of his bags but separate. Perhaps Hitler favoured the same trick when working in his own garden?

The front garden was bounded by a brick wall and a black gate which allowed entrance to a modest path. To the left, there was a narrow lawn leading to the enormous hydrangeas which formed an alcove. To the right, a square lawn tried to survive and four red stone and steep steps led to the front door which was protected by a triangular but tiny roof which kept off perpendicular rain whilst keys were being sought. The small but very productive back garden yielded apples, pears, blackberries, blackcurrants, gooseberries, tomatoes, potatoes and some vegetables. The output was impressive: the spur was hunger but some space was given to daffodils, irises, flags, tulips, roses and peonies. Tim was particularly proud of his lupins and the area outside the small scullery window was dominated by a proud display of aubrietia which seemed to remain in bloom from about February to November. Tim spent many hours playing in the garden.

Local gossip maintained that the man who lived opposite was involved in the black market. He was widely disliked as he had a German-sounding name and, allegedly, played no part in the war effort. The neighbours on one side were an elderly couple, the Bradburys, who appeared to Tim to be in their eighties, but who were probably no more than sixty. They were friendly and did what they could to help Susan and Ann. An elderly widow, Mrs Strachan, lived on the other side: like Ann, she had lost her husband in the First World War and had not re-married. The kindly Mrs Strachan liked to observe the New Year ritual of first footing. She may well have enjoyed others but this is a topic on which there was no information. The lady might have taken real delight from hurling a haggis over the fence whilst standing on one leg and playing the national anthem, although no such Scottish delicacy was ever found in the garden which, surely, undermines this idea.

'Tim, I've just had a chat with Mrs Strachan. She wanted to know whether you would help her celebrate the New Year. I said that you would.' Tim knew that this meant that he had to push open her front door as it was important that her first visitor of the new year was a dark-haired male. Tim then had to shout out a New Year greeting before hurling a lump of coal down the hall and into the kitchen door, having caused much mess en route as the example of primary fuel bounced over the carpet, occasionally kissing the wall as lustily as a young man on seeing his girl friend for the first time for months but with rather more damage.

'Yes, of course, I'll do it but what's it about? It causes a mess on her carpet or wall and why does whoever does it have to have dark hair?'

'I really don't know, dear, but she appreciates what you do and, let's remember she never complains when you go round to collect a ball you've kicked over the fence or on that occasion when your shoe accompanied the ball on its way into Strachan country. Anyway, she's lonely and a good neighbour and she's Scottish. We must make allowance for their strange customs.'

Wartime

In the early years of the war, Tim and his friends knew little about the conflict and his knowledge, even later, would not have secured him a pass at GCE O level History until the dumbing-down process was established and the exercise of human rights meant that all who sat examinations must pass. He knew that, occasionally, he had to leave his bed to spend some time in the shelter but he had no experience or knowledge of peace so assumed that war was natural but he could not understand why adults, who did not know each other, seemed determined to cause death and injury.

One night, in August 1941, the four year old Tim could not sleep. He had woken up suddenly, provoked by a sound that, at first, he could not identify but it was not an air raid siren which was what usually aroused him. He climbed out of his bed and bravely walked towards the door and carefully pulled it open lest its squeaks indicated that he had escaped. He might avoid detection if he seemed to be smaller so he crept, on all fours, and sat on the top stair. The noise was coming from the kitchen and he realised with increasing horror, if not understanding, that his mother was crying. Ann was trying to comfort her but he heard his mother speak between her sobs.

'It's nearly six months, now and I still don't know if Peter's alive or dead. Six long, awful, painful months when he's been officially declared as missing. Six months. I don't know how I could live without him. He's my life. He's all I've ever wanted. I'm going through hell.'

Tim winced. All he knew was that his father was on a ship and that it was difficult to find out where he was. He had often asked 'how's daddy?' but the responses, although not specific, were always reassuring. Had he just heard that his father might be dead? Was that really possible? Was he dreaming? He shivered with fear, sorrow and sympathy for his mother at a level which belied his young years. He tried very hard to remember what his father looked like as if that were a sign of respect, but failed and felt guilty. For the first time, he realised that adults could cry really loudly. Hearing his mother made him want to cry but he had to stay silent to find out more about his daddy.

'Why must I suffer like this? What have I done to deserve this? I think about it every minute of every day and I even dream about it. Sometimes we're together, walking in a London park, and it's peacetime and then I wake up and immediately know that it was just a dream. Some days I convince myself he's alive and then I realise just how dangerous it must be in the Atlantic and think that he must be dead. We know that our ships are being sunk and brave men killed at sea and I ask myself why Peter should be spared. Why can't someone, somewhere, tell me? Doesn't anyone know? Do they know and they're not telling me? This is a permanent nightmare. Not knowing is destroying me and trying to be cheerful, especially in front of Tim, is becoming so hard. Poor little boy, he doesn't know the agonies I'm going through and he must never know. If the worst has happened, how do I tell him? At least Harry's too young to know. Why can't anyone tell me if he's alive or dead?' Susan broke down again and her sobbing convulsed her whole body.

Ann tried to comfort her daughter but her words, nobody's words, could be of any real consolation and she knew this. She did point out that it must be very difficult for anyone to know what was happening in the Atlantic which, according to the last information from his company, was where he was. Ann bit her lip. Mentioning the Atlantic again was unwise as it was common knowledge that many German naval vessels were operating in the area and the Allies were losing thousands of tons of shipping and, worse still, hundreds of men. Hastily, she tried to blot out the comment about the Atlantic but the damage was done.

Susan resumed. 'Just think, he's on a tanker, carrying oil, in the Atlantic, where U boats are patrolling looking for victims. He could have been blown up or drowned. Please, God, if you exist and I don't think you do, make him safe on his ship or in a prisoner of war camp. Why, why, can't someone tell me? Somebody, somewhere, must know. I can't go on like this. What can I do? How can I find out?'

Ann tried again. 'He's a brave and sensible man. I'm sure that, he would do everything possible to save his crew, his vessel and, of course his own life if it came to it. It's not like peacetime. Communications are difficult and I'm sure that's the reason that we haven't heard. I feel that he's all right and that before long, you'll hear.' She was tempted to add, 'mark my words' but decided that was unwise. She also refrained from telling Susan how, in the First World War, her own husband had visited her in a dream, saying that he had come to say goodbye. Later, Ann discovered that was precisely the time when he had been killed. Somehow, she realised that the lack of such a dream would not allay her daughter's worry.

'I have some days when I convince myself that he's alive, possibly in a prisoner of war camp, then I have other days when I'm sure that those German swine have killed him and he's on the bottom of the sea, still on his ship.' Susan sobbed again. 'Please God, let me know soon and let me escape from this horrific uncertainty. Why are you putting me through all this? What have I done to deserve this? I really wonder if God ever listens to us as we hear of more and more horrors. If He is omnipotent, why does He allow all this senseless slaughter? Does He exist? We used to sing "all things bright and beautiful, the Lord God made them all". What about all the bad things?'

Ann pondered a response but soon realised that she could not offer anything apart from putting an arm around her daughter.

Tim, hearing this, padded back to his bedroom, lest his own crying revealed that he had been listening. He shut his door, dived under the bedclothes and began sobbing uncontrollably. He would do everything he could to help his mother. He felt guilty as he could not even remember what his father looked like but he resolved not to ask any questions about him. He would tell no one, not even his friends, who often boasted about their fathers who were actively involved overseas. He would share his mother's worry in the hope that, somehow, that would help and would wait for news and he would always, always, be good. All this suddenly made sense. Tim had noted that people often asked his mother, 'any news?' He had not really understood this question but now all was clear.

A few weeks later, an ebullient Susan, was crying again but this time she was wearing a beaming smile which illuminated her tear-stained face.

'Tim, I've just had some marvellous news. Daddy's alive and well. He's in a German prisoner of war camp so at least he won't be at sea for the rest of the war at risk of being blown up at any minute.' Then, her faith restored, she said 'thank God'. Ann, sitting in the corner of the room, was already weeping with relief and Susan, no longer able to restrain herself began to cry more violently and smile at the same time, shaking gently. All this emotion provoked Tim and he, too, was soon crying, not this time with fear and sorrow, but with genuine happiness. Showing a maturity beyond his years, he put an understanding arm around his mother and wept quietly with her.

Tim's knowledge of the war expanded modestly as did his scrap book. The press used maps in which the allied advances or retreats were indicated by stark black and white massive arrows which indicated progress or withdrawal. They often covered even entire nations, suggesting that the map of the world was not red, as often claimed, but black. Seemingly, entire countries were on the move and, in some instances, this was almost true. All this was puzzling to a young chap who had gradually accepted that something grim was happening and that his father was languishing in a German Prisoner of War camp.

Tim had the occasional postcard from his father in the camp, expressing the hope that he was well, being good, and looking after his mother and that he loved him and hoped to be home soon. What more could the poor man say? Tim's responses sought to assure him on these issues but when in expansive mood, he also told him that he loved him, as Susan had required, and was doing well at school. This latter claim was good for PR, paternal relations. The former was difficult in that Tim could not recall having met the chap but he must have been all right as his mother seemed very fond of him. Susan received the occasional letter from Peter but he was always careful not to offend the censor but, as far as she could deduce, he was healthy and coping with his predicament well.

The Torbay area was not totally free of the physical impact of war. Although raids were relatively rare, they did cause some damage. Houses with roofs missing and some walls knocked down, as if they were toy homes, wrecked by a bad-tempered child, was a poignant scene, even for a little boy. Seeing ruined or burned furniture and some of the family's private possessions, scattered indiscriminately around the wreckage, for all to see and for the wind to scatter, was very sad and, somehow, the knowledge that this had happened whilst Tim was awake, in the shelter, made it even more real. Fellow human beings had recently lived in this wreck. Had they survived? What had they done that was so bad that the Germans wanted to kill them? Sometimes Tim and his friends were accused of bad behaviour. How could adults condemn them for childish pranks as grown-ups murdered other fellow human beings? It did not make sense and nobody even tried to explain it. Perhaps there was no explanation. As he'd heard his mother say, if God made all things bright and beautiful, who was responsible for all the damage and deaths and, if God was all-powerful, why did He not stop it?

In October 1942, Susan and Tim were on their way to the shops when Susan stopped to have a chat with a friend. After some brief mutual preliminary enquiries about the friends' health had been exchanged Susan asked 'Have you heard from Douglas lately? Is he all right?' The friend, looking blank and wan, and obviously trying to control herself, paused as if trying to find not just the right words but the skill to control her tears, said 'he's dead: he was killed at El Alamein in Egypt'.

'I'm so sorry. That's terrible. We'll all miss him. If there is anything I can do to help, at any time, please let me know. He was a brave and fine man and you can be proud that he did all he could for us all. I'm really sorry.' The real horror and immediacy of war dawned afresh on Tim. Damaged houses were one thing and he knew that his father was a prisoner but someone that his mother knew had been killed was on a different scale. Douglas would never see his mother again and Tim clung on to his. What kind of world was this? What had Douglas done to deserve being killed? Tim just could not understand this war.

One afternoon, as Tim was just about to go downstairs, the doleful dirge of the siren wailed out its warning. Enemy aircraft were approaching. The noise of the siren, now compounded by the rasping engines of the hostile aircraft, en route to trying to kill people, depressed the young boy whose imagination was beginning to make him unhappy. The following day he was talking to his friends.

'I heard the siren when I was upstairs and was on my way to our shelter in the kitchen. I'd reached the landing on the stairs and looked out of the window. A bomb was about to hit Oldway, close to our house.'

His friends, George, Edward and James, all of whom, judging by their names, came from staunchly royalist homes, were listening intently. They had never seen a bomb landing so Tim had an advantage and a captive and rapt audience.

'Just after I saw the bomb, the blast blew me down the stairs and my feet didn't touch the carpet. I landed in a heap at the bottom of the stairs and the first thing that I knew was my mother shouting out, 'Tim, come down, now, you must have heard the siren. You know that, whenever you hear the siren, you must go into the shelter immediately. Now, be a good boy and do as you're told.'

'It seemed unfair as I'd just fallen down the stairs in a world record time, but when I groaned a little, she soon found me and asked if I was all right.' His friends seemed impressed and asked if he really had been injured as he had floated over and missed about ten stairs.

'No, I was ok.' He thought that this admission might lessen their admiration so he added, 'but, of course, I was jolly shaken and bruised'.

Tim was a very worried little boy and was hounded by concerns which might have been very rational to him but silly to others. One day, after another air raid, he asked Susan if he could wear some clothes in the bath.

'Why do you ask me that, dear?'

'Well, you know how the other day I was blown down the stairs?'

Susan nodded. Given his appetite for telling, and even embellishing, the story, she was unlikely to forget it. In the latest version, he had not only come down the stairs rather more speedily than intended but his landing had taken him as far as the front door, and, as he admitted to other enquiries, 'I was very lucky not to have crashed into the door'. He hinted darkly, that this could have been very serious for both the door and him.

'What will happen if there is a raid when I am in the bath? Would it be all right if I tried to have a bath but left some clothes on which could be cleaned whilst I was in the water? That would save you having to wash them, wouldn't it?'

'Don't be silly dear.'

'Not even my swimming suit?'

'No. Not even your swimming suit. Anyway, you're always telling me that when it gets wet, it falls down and I certainly can't afford to buy you another one and anyway we haven't got the coupons. You can just grab a towel and come down to the shelter.'

'Perhaps I ought to have fewer baths? You're always saying that we mustn't waste water. I know that we're supposed to have only five inches of water. If I bathed less often it would help us win the war!'

'Now, you're being silly.'

Tim could not agree with this harsh assessment but his comments were always rejected so swiftly and almost derisively that he gave up the hope, that, one day, he might hear a reaction which seemed to treat his concerns sympathetically. No air raids coincided with his ablutions which was a testament to wartime security and the safeguarding of important information. Perhaps

Susan was informed on potential enemy raids and selected bath nights accordingly.

Many of the enemy air attacks were in the night and seemed to Tim to be timed just after he had gone to sleep. He did not know about correlations but if he had, he could have formulated a policy to assist the allies. After the raid, it was always difficult to sleep, not least as Tim wondered what damage had been caused and knew that he had to wait until daylight to see what had happened. When the all-clear sounded, if it had been a night-time attack, Tim left the shelter in the kitchen and returned to his cold bedroom and cold bed, clutching a dark brown hot water cylindrical bottle made of stone. It was heavy and his young feet were not strong enough to move it around the bed so only a part of him and a part of the bed were warm. Going back to sleep was not easy and, if the all-clear sounded before midnight, children were expected to be at school at the usual time the following day. However, if it was later, pupils should arrive in time for what was called dinner but was, in fact, lunch.

Although Camellia House was never damaged, Tim used to feel the surface of his bed after a raid, lest some shrapnel had mysteriously entered it, even although the ceiling was not punctured. If he was feeling particularly brave, he even glanced under the bed to determine whether those hideous Germans had, somehow, being spirited into his room. He had not realised that, if they had managed such a miracle, his room would not have been a prime target. Such was the impact of war on a small, innocent and frightened child who, in so many other ways was rational and sensible.

'I really don't feel well and I don't think I can go to school.'

Susan had heard this refrain before and was inclined to ignore her young son. He seemed to be unwell whenever a test was planned and as these took place often, he was frequently, and allegedly, ill.

'Do you have any pains?' Tim groaned dramatically and rubbed his stomach whilst simultaneously grimacing.

This performance seemed more genuine than his usual efforts, although his acting had improved with practice, but Susan had noted the facial grimace. She had not seen that before and decided that, this time, he was probably telling the truth. 'Well, then, I think you'd better stay in bed in the dark and I'll call the doctor.' He said that Tim should remain in bed for several days and he would decide what, if anything, had to be done when he returned within 24 hours but Susan must ring him if Tim's condition deteriorated. The urbane Dr Howard assured Susan that, if it was appendicitis, as he suspected, action would be taken immediately.

Tim was not happy at being cooped up in the dark and, immediately after the doctor had gone, asked several questions, the first of which was obvious.

'Why do I have to stay in the dark when my tummy hurts, it's not my eyes?'

'I don't know dear but that is what Dr Howard recommends and he knows best. I think that everybody has to stay in the dark when they're not well.'

'Would you, if you were ill?'

Susan, obliged to sustain her theme, agreed.

'What's the matter with me? Will I have to take some nasty medicine?'

'I don't know, dear but we must wait for the doctor to decide.'

'Why do all medicines have to taste nasty? When I'm grown up I'll invent some nice medicines which will save people all over the world and I'll be famous and rich and then I'll be able to buy a new car like the doctor's.'

The doctor returned the following day. 'Tim's got a grumbling appendix. Tomorrow afternoon, an ambulance will call and take him to hospital but you can go with him, of course. He'll be in there for at least a week. There's no need to worry, the op's routine and he'll be in good hands and you can visit him in the afternoons.'

Susan spent some time, trying to work out how to tell her young son that he had to have an operation but could not conjure up any less brutal explanation. Anyway, she argued, he's becoming a big boy and many of his school friends must now be lacking their appendices, if that was the correct plural. Even if that were true, it might not have encouraged Tim to shed his fears. After all, it was his appendix and he had but one and was about to lose it.

Inevitably, Tim wanted to know more, much more.

'Will it hurt?'

'No, dear, you'll be asleep and won't feel anything.'

'But what if I don't feel sleepy? Often I take ages to get to sleep. What if I'm not asleep? Will they wait? Does this mean that anyone can take bits of me when I'm asleep?

Confronted with these new fears, Susan sought to explain that he would be having a deeper sleep than he had at home because he would be under the influence of an anaesthetic. In his increasing fear that bits of him could be taken whilst he was asleep, he did not hear his mother's explanation.

'Who is she and how can she put me to sleep?'

'Who dear?'

'Anna whatever you said she was called.'

Susan tried again to explain but Tim still wanted to know more.

'Will I feel pain when I wake up?' He implied that he was not keen on pain, especially if something that he did not need, nor had requested, was about to be taken away.

'No, it's all very clever and you might be a little sore, but you won't be in pain and the people in the hospital know all about appendixes and will look after you and I'll be visiting you every day.'

Susan, still unsure on the plural of appendix, was at the very boundary of her knowledge and hoped that the next question, which was being forged as she spoke, was less challenging. It was more bizarre.

'How do I know that, when I'm asleep, they won't take anything else?'

'That's silly, dear, they know what they're doing and you shouldn't worry. I've spoken to our doctor and the hospital and they tell me that you'll be fine. Lots of boys of your age have their appendixes out.'

'If they take away my appendix, will I look the same?'

Susan, please to be back on safer ground, assured him that his appearance would not be affected and that he would still be her very handsome young son but her confidence was soon undermined by the next question.

'If they are going to take out my appendix and I shall be the same, why do I have one in the first place? What does it do and how can I be the same if they have taken mine away and other people have theirs still. Won't there be a big hole in my tummy?'

Expertly ignoring the first question, for which she had no answer, Susan immediately reassured her young son that there would not be a hole where the appendix had resided. She hoped that this and her next comment would put an end to the questioning.

'I think that you'll be away from school for at least two weeks.'

Tim smiled. Losing an appendix now seemed a good idea and when he was back at school, he would recommend that his chums should have theirs removed as well. Later that day, his friends called in to see how he was and Tim told them that he was going to have an operation. George was the first to speak. He was amiable but even his parents would not have claimed that he was particularly bright, especially on medical matters.

'Does this mean that you might die?'

Tim had not even thought of this and paled immediately. His mother had answered his questions but the specific matter of death had not been discussed.

James, a little older, came to the rescue.

'Of course not. Only old people die, not boys like us. My uncle was an old man and died last year just after his 45th birthday. No, young boys and girls don't die. You'll be all right.'

Edward looked puzzled. 'My cousin, Jane, never went to hospital, so she must still have had her appendix. I know that because you can only have them out in hospitals and we all have them, at least to start with.' Fending off any possible opposition, he added 'you can't have them out at home or at school or in the garden, for example' and deciding that he could offer one more venue where the operation could not take place, mentioned the beach. 'It's got to be a hospital as that's where they do operations.'

Tim was not feeling so good.

Edward continued.

'Jane was always well until the day she died suddenly, just after her seventh birthday, so you're wrong saying that children like us don't die. I know they can, so there.'

Tim, becoming more worried by the minute, was frightened to hear of Jane's death. It seemed to undermine all his theories, and those of his friends, that young people did not die. Would he be like Jane? Boldly and belatedly, but uncertain if he really wanted to know the answer, he asked why she had died.

'She was hit by a bus.'

Tim was keen to talk about something else but George said 'we all hope that you're better soon. We'll miss you at school. When do you think you'll be back?'

'I think that it'll be about three weeks.' In truth, Tim did not know but had decided that that was the minimum period he would ensure that he would be away, whatever medical opinion decreed.

He wanted to change the topic. 'What's happening at school?' It was clear that the gang had some news and Edward took the floor.

'You know Standing?'

'Yes, why what's he done?'

'Well, we were in Bird's class and he'd told us not to talk or make any noises. Poor old Standing had flu and already had a sick note that excused him from gym. He tried to avoid coughing but after a few minutes, he could not stop himself and he coughed so loudly that anybody passing would have expected an air raid warning. Bird immediately called him a naughty and disobedient boy who was trying to be clever. He then took Standing to the headmaster, Brown the bully, who gave him the stick.'

Tim expressed his immediate sympathy for Standing.

'He wouldn't say boo to a dead fly. That man Bird is a swine and so's the headmaster.' Tim did not know the meaning of swine but he had heard his grandmother refer to the Germans as swine so he knew it must be the right word. Perhaps Bird and the headmaster were Germans.

James took up the story. 'Now Standing has difficulty sitting but his mother came to the school to complain.'

'Isn't she a very big woman, built like that boxer, with a moustache, on one of my cigarette cards?'

'Yes, except that she reminds me of a rugby player with a beard. Anyway, she came to see Brown and we happened to be in the hall when she marched into the head monster's study, without knocking, and left the door open. It looked as if a major row was about to take place so we hid behind the big gong. Then the door was slammed but we could still hear Mrs Standing shouting at Bully Brown.

'She told him he was an arrogant, unthinking, sick bully, who was not fit to be in charge of young boys and that he had no concept, whatever that is, of justice. I think it means that he was very unfair. What we heard next astounded us. She said, very clearly and deliberately, "I want you to give me the cane. Now. Do you understand me? I mean now. I want the stick and I want it now". Was she raving mad?' Tim, sharing his friends' amazement, asked why she wanted to suffer like her son. This was very peculiar. He did not understand adults.

'Then there was silence. We reckoned that Brown was baffled and didn't know what to do. It didn't make sense. Why would she want to be hit by the bully? She shouted at him again. "For God's sake man, stop gaping like a thirsty goldfish. Don't you understand plain English? Pass me that stick you use on the poor little boys, you cruel, despicable little apology for a man."

'As Mrs Standing then stopped shouting, we guessed that Brown must have handed over the stick but Standing's mother had not finished. We couldn't hear everything after that but we heard her say "don't think that I've finished with you, you truly pathetic little man, oh dear no".

'Brown was silent and Mrs Standing started bawling at him again as if he'd been naughty. Then it got even more exciting. She said that her son should be given immediate compensation and that, if he didn't agree, she would be telling her next door neighbour, who was a solicitor, I think that's some kind of lawyer, and her friend who runs the local paper. 'I think that my poor little boy might be prepared to forgive your unprovoked assault for, say, £10.' We weren't sure what compensation was but it seems that she wanted Brown had to give her some money in return for her not sneaking on him.

'If you don't agree, we'll see how you like the threat of a hostile comment in the paper and then a court case. By the time that I've finished with you, you'll be lucky to get a job as a dustman. You're a grade one louse who ought to be in jail. By the way, you should know that no gentleman wears brown shoes with a dark suit.'

'After that, we couldn't hear much but, as we retreated, Mrs Standing, who was now smiling, came out and she was putting some paper money into her handbag. Then we saw her break the stick into two with her bare hands and hurled the pieces, as hard as she could, against a glass cabinet which broke immediately. I reckon she could toss a tree through a window if she really wanted to.'

Tim whistled in sheer admiration. 'The following day Standing told his friends that a rich aunt had given him some money and he was going to look for a toy train set.'

It seemed that the friends had another tale with which to regale their sick chum. Why did such exciting things happen when he was not at school? This time, it was George, who was good at English, who was to convey another fascinating story.

'You know that we thought that Allen, one of the new masters, and matron were beginning to be very friendly?'

Tim nodded. He had heard this himself and was very proud as he had dreamt up the rumour, for which he had no evidence, only two weeks before.

'Well, Kelly, you know him?'

'The chap with the small ears and large feet?'

'Well, I would have said that he had small feet and large ears but it doesn't matter because what I've got to tell you has nothing to do with his ears, or, for that matter, his feet, whatever their size. They're not involved. You know he's a border?'

Tim nodded again.

'Well, the other night, he was feeling unwell so he crept out of the dormitory to use the main bathroom at the end of the corridor. Although he knew that the floorboards squeaked, he decided against using small one next to the dorm as he thought that he might have woken up his fellow prisoners, as he put it. The main bathroom and toilet are out of bounds in the night. To get there, he had to pass the doors of the rooms occupied by Angry Allen and Mary Nurse, the matron.' Tim was listening intently. He knew the joke about matron being called Nurse but decided against complaining that the story was moving too slowly. He sensed that something dramatic was at hand and that a complaint would cause further delay.

'Kelly was just about to tip toe past Angry's door when the bully came out. Kelly leapt back into the shadows as quickly as his little feet would let him, you know he's got little feet, but they did not let him down. Kelly hid behind a curtain and was later able to report that Angry was wearing red and white striped pyjamas which reminded him of a barber's pole, like the one that our local hairdresser's got in his front garden.' Tim was not interested in Angry's nightwear and felt that if this was the main point of the story, a session watching the grass grow might have been more interesting.

'Kelly was able to see Angry do a little jig and then put his hands together and wave his arms in apparent triumph. Then he walked down the corridor and went into matron's room, which, as you know, is just a few yards further on.' Tim did not know but allowed this to pass. He was keen to hear more but first of all, he had to find out what a jig was. It might be crucial to the tale.

'A jig? Isn't that something that horses pull?'

'No, it's a little dance, but there's more to come. Kelly was really sick and it was some time before he felt well enough to return to the dorm. As he passed matron's door, and it was now very late, Angry emerged with a huge smile on his face and he did another jig. It seemed that he liked jgging. However, his smile vanished with the speed of a mouse confronted by an overweight cat when he saw Kelly who said that his face oozed with anger and fear and was so red that it matched his pyjamas. Kelly thought that he might explode. Clearly, he had been doing something naughty with matron. If he'd been ill, she'd have gone to his room and, as Kelly had seen him jig before setting out down the corridor and, for that matter, on his return, he felt that there were no medical problems on which he had to seek advice in the middle of the night. If, as Kelly put it, he could do a jig both before and after visiting matron, there was no physical problem.'

'What happened? Angry must have given Kelly gyp. I bet poor old Kelly was frightened. I shudder to think how he might have been punished. Not only had he visited a bathroom that was out of bounds but he'd seen Angry coming out of matron's room in the middle of the night. I would surmise that he did not view his immediate prospects with optimism.' Tim and his friends often practiced speaking like the adults they had heard on the wireless.

Tim's little joke about gyp, designed to hide his error on jig, was ignored.

'Kelly may not have the best brain in the country, and, although he has big ears and his feet are probably sub-standard in terms of size, his grey cells came to his aid. In a word, the word that Kelly used, incidentally, when he was telling me what happened, he had a brainwave. I think he's a genius. He pretended to be sleep walking and stretched out his arms, nearly poking out Angry's right eye, and asked, in a suitably mumbling tone, if anyone could kindly direct him to the beach as he had left his towel there and the tide was due in soon. He added that, if he did not retrieve his towel promptly, his mother, who used to play rugby, before she was banned for dangerous play, would be very angry and that would not be a pretty sight.'

'She played rugby? I didn't know that. Did she play with Mrs Standing?'

'No, Tim, Kelly invented all that.'

Tim was really impressed and when he went back to school he would reward Kelly by suggesting that he should have his appendix out and claim three weeks away from school.

'Angry, convinced that he knew nothing, returned briefly to his room and collected a towel and then offered to guide his pupil to another part of the beach, where the tide was out. He then gave him the towel and directed him back to the dormitory and assured our hero that he was now on the beach and even helped him on to his deck chair.

' A deck chair in the dorm?'

'No, it was imaginary. He helped him on to his bed which Kelly pretended was a deckchair.'

'Kelly admitted later that he nearly gave the game away as he was tempted, briefly, to say "thank you my good man" and apologise for not giving him a tip but he had no change on him as he was wearing swimming trunks. Apparently, Kelly was also on the verge of claiming that it was the wrong part of the beach but decided against risking it, partly because he was close to having hysterics. He lay on his bed, merely saying that the sun seemed to have gone in and it looked like rain. He resisted the temptation of asking if Angry could see his mother, in the hope that matron would have been summoned, to complete the illusion, but all this would have ensured that he could no longer contain his laughter so any further plans were, very sensibly, abandoned. He waited until Angry had gone and then sank beneath the bed clothes and chuckled as quietly as he could.'

The next time that he saw Angry, nothing was said but every time that Kelly saw the teacher, he imagined that he was wearing striped pyjamas.

Tim was most impressed, partly with Kelly and partly because his baseless rumour about Angry and the matron was true. If he was that clever, who should be his next victim? What else could he imagine that he wanted to come true? Perhaps bully Brown could have a serious car crash in which he killed the beastly Bird? Tim had read in the newspaper that a schoolmaster had been sent to prison because he had suggested to his pupils that Britain might not win the war. How difficult would it have been to persuade all his friends to tell their parents that bully Brown and Bird had told them that Germany would be victorious? Tim was greatly cheered by these stories but when his friends had gone home, his mood changed dramatically when he recalled that they had implied that he could soon be dead.

'Mama, will I die during this operation? I don't want to die, I've more things that I want to do.' He thought that sounded better than making up untrue stories about the staff at school. Susan, clearly concerned that her son had been worrying, said 'of course not, dear. It's all quite safe and the doctor said that it's an operation that the hospital does every week. I can promise you that you'll be all right.' He was assured and went to sleep mindful of the fact that this would be the last time he slept in his own home with his own appendix. The ambulance arrived on time and Tim and his mother were soon at the local hospital which was only about a mile from home. The first things that the young boy noticed were the powerful smell of disinfectant and that some of the nurses looked like Florence Nightingale whom he had read about in a book. The matron came over and Tim did not know if this austere person was a man or woman. He remained ignorant even after this official had greeted him.

'Well, hello Tim, in to have our appendix out are we?'

The young patient, under the impression that he was the sole owner of the appendix, paid no attention.

'What fine pyjamas you have. I've a friend who has some just like yours, but his are red-striped.'

Did this person know Angry? Had his appendix been taken away?

His bed seemed to be made of iron as Tim discovered when he accidentally banged his head on the inadequate headrest. The 'sheets' were a sickly shade of brown and smelt of rubber which was not surprising as they were made of rubber. When he screwed them up, they bounced back but he soon tired of this pastime. He was too worried to eat and speculated on what might happen the following day. What would happen to his appendix? He had no idea of how big it was but he wondered if he could have it to show to his friends or would it be given to the dustmen? He recalled the pig food bin and wondered if the pigs would like it. It could be his contribution to the war effort. There were other children in the ward, as Tim found out but they were all asleep and he was told not to wake them. If they were all in the land of nod, as his grandmother used to call it, had they all lost their appendixes?

Early the following morning a nurse, who looked like a girl, came to Tim's bedside.

'In a few minutes, we'll help you to go to sleep and then take you to the theatre.'

'Are you Anna Setic?'

The girl smiled and said nothing.

Tim wanted to go to the theatre before he went to sleep, because, as he explained, if he was asleep he would miss whatever was being performed. He was also concerned that he could not go to the theatre in his pyjamas. As he explained patiently, he had been to the theatre several times, to see pantomimes, and he had never seen anyone in the audience in their pyjamas. The nurse smiled gently and tried again to explain what was going to happen. She was replaced by another nurse, of indeterminate gender, who placed what looked like a jelly mould over Tim's mouth. He saw stars and, a few minutes later, was lifted on to a trolley and wheeled down a corridor that smelt of carbolic soap to what was presumably the theatre but he couldn't be sure because he was almost asleep. Then the surgeon commenced work, or at least, it can be assumed that he did, judging by the large scar that Tim was to carry for the rest of his life. Did this reflect the state of medical knowledge at that time or was it the handiwork of the local butcher, deputising for the surgeon? There was a war on and everyone had to do what they could to assist the war effort.

In the 1940s, an appendix operation was a potentially dangerous operation but Tim survived and also avoided death when his tonsils and adenoids were taken out, although he never remembered sanctioning their removal. Maybe it was because nobody could understand him as he had troublesome tonsils and adenoids.

Like millions of children, most of whom had a much more difficult war than Tim could even envisage, he lacked so-called 'quality time' as defined by later generations yet, somehow, still managed to avoid becoming a criminal. Susan was a great mother and a fine human being who never complained and who was always prepared to help him. She hid her worries so successfully that, for months Tim had not known that there was a possibility that his father might have been killed and he certainly was unaware that she was unwell, having given him and his new young brother some of her food ration at the expense of her own health. It was a major struggle trying to find enough food for two children, her mother and herself and queuing for hours for scarce supplies. Additionally, walking Tim to school in the early days of the war absorbed much of her time and energy when there were no labour-saving devices to reduce the number of visits to the small local shops. Regular trips to the shops were necessary, apart from the vagaries of supply, because there were only cold larders with open but grated windows. Susan was endowed with a spirit of justice, kindness, intelligence and sense of humour that enabled her to ride over worry.

She did all she could to ensure that Tim was shielded from the war and that his life was as normal as she could make it. However, one particularly serious raid on nearby Torquay resulted in more than 20 Sunday School children being killed when one of many German Focke Wulf 190 aircraft bombed the church and then hit the spire. A total of 54 humans, including some walking in the sunshine along the sea front, lost their lives. Tim knew some of the young victims and cried for them and for himself. Would he die? What was it all about? Why could nobody explain to him why adults behaved as savages?

Tim wondered if the smell from the pig food bins was why everyone had been issued with gas masks, but, if he had asked, he knew that the response would have been the traditional answer of 'don't be silly, dear'. He spent a large part of his early life exercising his imagination only to be told that he was being less than sensible. The local population was subjected to the occasional gas mask test but as the prospect of gas attacks faded, so did the remaining enthusiasm for the masks which were cumbersome and smelly. No less than 38 million were distributed in the UK and even babies had to be placed in a horrendous-looking contraption to avoid the possibility of being gassed.

Although the area was relatively fortunate in not being attacked very often, there was a surprising amount of shrapnel to be found by the assiduous hunter. On one occasion, Tim found the top of a lamp post which had been separated from the rest of the structure. It was too big and too heavy for him to manage by himself, so he enlisted Roger, a friend, and together they dragged the large souvenir home.

'And what do you think that is?' Susan demanded to know.

'We don't think, we know, it's part of a lamp post.'

It was surprising that someone as old as Susan apparently did not recognise the top of a lamp post, especially as the bulb was still visible. Amazingly, it had not broken as the structure collapsed. Tim wondered why his mother, usually so wise, did not know about lamp posts.

'And what do you think you're going to do with it?'

'We're not sure yet.'

'Well, I am, you're going to take it back to where you found it.'

Reluctantly, the boys picked up their trophy and as they plodded off, to do as they were told, which was compulsory during the war, Susan added 'remember, you mustn't pick up any toys you find in the gutter or anywhere else. The enemy have dropped some toys but, if you pick one up, it could explode and really hurt you. I've warned you about this before.' Tim and his friend did not see an immediate link between the top of a British lamp post and a German toy found in the gutter, or even on the pavement, but remained silent. Surely, it was unlikely that the Germans would go to the trouble of designing and making tops of lamp posts, which could withstand the impact on hitting the ground, just for children to pick up? Anyway, this one was safe as it hadn't exploded.

Susan had some news for Tim one summer.

'We're going to have a holiday, in Drewsteignton, near Mortonhampstead.'

Tim, not sure where Drewsteignton or even Mortonhampstead were, sought more information.

'It's about 26 miles away and we'll go on the bus.'

'How far is 26 miles?'

Susan said that it was like going to and back from school about 14 times. Tim whistled in a mixture of disbelief and excitement. That seemed a very long way and it was just as well that they were going on the bus.

'Will we come home after a few hours?'

It was apparent that Tim had no idea of what a holiday was so Susan explained in some detail. 'We'll stay in an old house, called an inn, for a few days and go for walks.'

The pub sign outside Tim's bedroom window wheezed through the night at the whims of the wind, ensuring that he had less time sleeping than Susan had hoped. The village, which would still be recognisable to its residents from centuries ago, was dominated by the elderly churchyard tombstones which confirmed the random injustice of death. One favourite walk for Susan, Ann and Tim, with Harry in a push chair, was down a steep hill to Fingle Bridge, over the Dart. This peaceful river wended its way over large cobble stones that it had dutifully polished over the centuries, gurgling cheerfully between the two sides of the valley, oblivious of mans' murderous manners. A narrow bridge, built when the only traffic was human or horse, meandered gently into the woods. Surely, there could be nothing over the other side of the forbidding hills? Was this where the real world began? Was the world really at war, were homes being bombed nightly and innocent citizens killed and crippled?

Another journey was to Chagford, a village, some four miles away, which, too, seemed so far removed from war and death that it, too, must have been in a different world. Were the whitewashed cottages, built centuries ago, and ringed with roses, in the same country that had seen such devastation of its urban population and cities? Tim enjoyed his holiday and the walks not least as the sun shone. There were no air-raid warnings and the food, supplemented by produce from the pub's garden, was more than he usually had. Was this like peace?

He and his young friends had to be self-sufficient in devising games to play. No lengthy lists of expensive and desired Christmas presents were despatched to Father Christmas and any parcels, hidden under the bed late on Christmas Eve, and sometimes covered in newspaper because wrapping paper was scarce, were gratefully received and enthusiastically unpacked in the early morning light. Tim enjoyed the innocent and enthusiastic excitement as he felt under the bed, before dawn, to determine the size and number of the parcels. In the early days of the war, companies stopped making toys and moved to producing war-related goods. For example, Lines Brothers began making gas masks, tommy guns and ammunition boxes, forsaking their manufacturing clockwork cars and trucks.

The indefatigable Susan always managed to locate something of interest for her two sons, even although it was inevitably second-hand. One treasured present that the boys shared was a magic lantern and some Disney slides which were played repeatedly. One year, after trailing around Torquay pursuing advertisements for second-hand toys for sale, Susan acquired a bagatelle table, carried it on a crowded and uncomfortable bus on which the seats had been removed to accommodate more passengers, then walked home for about half a mile and hid it until the big day.

Tim's proudest possession was a Hornby clockwork railway engine which was accompanied by some circular track, a long brown passenger coach, a red rail tank car in Shell livery and a level crossing with green gates but the engine soon ceased functioning. Other presents over the wartime years included an impressive searchlight which had a powerful light and a model field gun which could fire dead matches, a small black torch and a Schuco model car, made in Germany by a company that was set up in 1915. Ann gave Tim a black leather-covered bible for his birthday in 1943. It cost her 6/-.

Another much-loved toy, which arrived late in the war, was a box of Bayco. The set included a green base in which rows of holes had been created. Rods could then be inserted into the holes and bakelite 'bricks' or even windows, could be slid down any two side by side poles, enabling the construction of houses and bungalows. Other toys that Tim and his brother shared later in the war included an imposing fort and a garage. They also enjoyed playing Ludo, Snakes and Ladders and completing jig saw puzzles. They usually depicted an act of war, such as an RAF fighter shooting down a German bomber or, in sharp contrast, an idyllic rural scene. Cigarette cards were also popular. Tim also enjoyed the skimpy comics, curtailed because of paper shortages, and was relieved when Desperate Dan, in the *Dandy*, converted a drain pipe into a giant pea-shooter with which he shot down enemy planes.

Denied time with their parents, wartime children had to be self-reliant. Whilst it was allowed, local boys played on the nearby Preston beach and green. Eventually, the former was dominated by scaffolding, barbed wire and warning notices and the latter by a Bofers gun, which severely restricted the space available. One hobby was to make and play with bows and arrows. Bamboo canes were persuaded to bend sufficiently to allow string to be attached at the top and bottom of the sticks and arrows, too, were made of bamboo and cut at the top so that the string could be inserted. The bow was then bent back and the arrow moved through the air towards its intended target with varying degrees of enthusiasm, speed and accuracy. To his surprise, Tim found that he was good at this.

One hobby that was neither banned nor costly was the collection of conkers. The Oldway estate was generously endowed with horse chestnut trees and Tim and friends sought to hasten the fall of the conkers by hurling missiles upwards to dislodge them. Occasionally, the projectiles, usually modest branches or heavy twigs, not only failed to persuade the conkers to drop to the ground but lodged in the trees, assuming, reasonably, that that was where they belonged. There were no known instances of a pedestrian being struck by such a missile eventually obeying the dictates of Isaac Newton. The best conkers were then soaked in vinegar and put on a course to toughen them after which a skewer was employed to make a hole through the middle so that string could be threaded in anticipation of the first battle. Reputations were made or lost on the playground.

Playing marbles was a popular pastime at school. Tim's own modest supply came from a Red Cross parcel, given to children whose fathers were prisoners but, as always fearful of losing, he seldom played lest he might lose the game and the marble. The shortages of food precluded the possibility of having birthday parties but the Red Cross organised one such party for POWs' children who were given a box which included some sweets and two model cars.

On Sundays, Susan, Tim and Harry, in some form of wheeled transport, used to stroll to the beach, when it was still possible, but one favoured destination was an old and disused windmill. Another popular haunt was a cave on the Oldway estate, just a few hundred yards away, and walking for about 15 yards inside the damp and dark cave was like entering another world. Occasionally, the walks would take the family along the sea fronts at Preston and Paignton, secure in the knowledge that, if it suddenly rained, the 50 year-old shelters offered cover and, if air raid sirens indicated potential danger, the family could retreat to more robustly-constructed modern shelters.

Another 'pastime', in which Tim participated reluctantly, absorbed hours and required more much patience. He stretched out his arms towards his grandmother so that she could wind her skein of wool around them en route to creating a ball which would later be converted into something to wear for a member of the family. Borders at his school were more involved: they were taught how to knit and produce garments for the men in the forces. Tim and his friends spent some time collecting waste paper which, in a way that the boys never understood, was to help the allies win the war.

When they were feeling energetic, the boys played 'he'. The one who was called 'he' had to catch one of the other participants who then became 'he'. The fun was in avoiding capture which was indicated by just touching a player. Some time was spent in the garden, either playing or trying to encourage some plants to flower or to provide some modest food.

Tim's 'carpentry', carried out at a friend's house, consisted of finding a small oblong piece of old and unwanted wood, shaping the front into a triangle, so that it represented a ship's bow, before hammering in some short nails on to the 'deck' and weaving string around the nails to imitate railings. Old and broken toy soldiers were then melted and after fashioning out the shape of an anchor in a bar of soap, the former soldiers, poured into this mould, joined the navy as anchors which were about one tenth the size of the vessel. Another hobby was to tie string to a handkerchief which was attached to an elderly and already damaged toy soldier. The package was then thrown over the banisters at home, to the detriment of the soldier, as the parachutes rarely opened. Those soldiers who were severely damaged became anchors.

As each Christmas approached, Tim and his friends called on a few houses, singing carols. This was an instant failure and such money as the boys collected was probably given by those on whom the noise was inflicted to encourage them to perform elsewhere. The 'singers' agreed that, although they made a terrible sound, they needed cash. Tim, who had one of the worst voices, suggested that they should all listen to young boys singing on the wireless and then try to imitate them. This succeeded and the boys were able to increase their modest income.

Towards the end of the war, as Tim approached his 8th birthday, he wondered if the conflict would end before he would be forced to join the army. His limited understanding of history ceased with events around 1600 and Tim's class had spent much time studying the 100 years war to the exclusion of more relevant history. A conflict lasting less than a fifth of that time would have seen him plunged into the battle although, having been brought up decently, he knew nothing of vulgar fractions.

Another genuine worry that really frightened Tim and his school friends, especially towards the end of the war, was the prospect of contracting Infantile Paralysis. This dreadful illness struck at random and even contracting a cold induced the fear that it might lead to life-threatening problem. One friend lost the use of his arm and others died.

The Adult Life

Adults, denied much spare time, were unable to play with their children: there were no home appliances to ease the domestic burden and many hours were spent queuing for rationed but usually scarce food. Sometimes, women would join a queue without knowing what might have been available, in case something desirable was being offered. On other occasions, a rumour that bread, for example, was available in a nearby shop, would prompt the formation of a line with minimal delay. Clothes were also rationed.

Many families were divided as children were evacuated to allegedly safer areas. Some two million left London in the first year of the conflict and a number arrived in Torquay. In many instances the evacuees' different culture and way of life created major problems to add to their misery from being separated from their mothers. Some returned home but more bombing and, later, the arrival of flying bombs, induced another retreat. By September 1944, more than one million people had left London. Many Britons lived with the thought that, at any time, their homes might be destroyed or that they might be killed in the next 24 hours.

All buildings had to be blacked out so that enemy aircraft were denied clues on their location and criss-cross tape was put on the windows to reduce the risk of glass shattering and injuring the inmates. Hopes that German air attacks had ended proved optimistic when in June 1944, flying bombs, known as the V1, were targeted on London and the south of England. Between June and September, 7,000 were launched but about half were destroyed before they reached their target. As the allies reached and eliminated the launch sites, the V2, with a much longer range, was aimed at London, prompting more than 200,000 residents to leave the capital.

For civilians, mainly women, long days working, for example, in armaments factories were crippling and often dangerous. Unmarried women aged between 20 and 30 were required to be registered for industrial call up and by 1943, some 90 per cent of single women and 80 per cent of married women were involved in war work. Many women worked in munitions factories and frequently did the work previously done by men. Nevertheless, reflecting the prevalent culture, although many women were skilled, they were paid at unskilled levels. People were directed into specific jobs, to meet demand for war-related goods, and strikes were illegal, although some did take place, motivated by intolerance of very bad working conditions. Fifteen thousand young men, known as Bevan Boys, were required to work in the coal mines. Young men, many of whom were in reserved occupations, and those of a greater age, joined what became known as the Home Guard. Within six weeks of being set up in 1940, 1.5 million men had been recruited and the public had given some 20,000 shotguns and pistols to help this group.

There was little time for entertainment although wireless programmes provided some diversion for those at home and many professional singers and comedians spent time on the war fronts. Understandably, programmes that made the audience forget that the nation was at war were popular. The Forces programmes, broadcast from February 1940, were well received and one of the featured artists was Vera Lynn. Those who wanted something more cerebral listened to the *Brains Trust.*

Liverpool's Tommy Handley, in *It's That Man Again*, (ITMA) was favoured. The title of the show was aimed not at Handley but to Hitler. Listeners waited anxiously for such catch phrases as 'Can I do you now sir?' and 'I don't mind if I do', when a character was asked if he would like an alcoholic beverage. Morale, supposedly, was maintained by *Workers Playtime* and *Music While You Work* and Winston Churchill spoke, when he thought it necessary, after the 9.00 evening news on the Home Service of the BBC. A programme at 8.15, each weekday evening, called *Kitchen Front,* offered information on the availability and prices of food.

Finding time to keep the house clean, taking her young son to and from school, look after his younger brother, Harry, and queuing for food absorbed much of Susan's time although Ann helped her. Some of Peter's relatives, who lived in Torquay and had a butcher's shop, provided the occasional off-ration food which was very welcome.

Susan and her mother were talking in the kitchen.

'I've received another card from Peter. Apparently, he's received the books I sent nearly a year ago and the parcel containing soap, a few chocolates and some shaving kit has also arrived. Do you know, I sent that out to him six months ago. Still, at least he's received it and he said that it's not just what's in the parcels but a reminder of home and that he's not been forgotten. He says he's well and looking forward to seeing us all again.'

Susan was becoming tearful and diverted her emotions into a different topic.

'Do you think people in the future will realise that our lives were dominated by the fear that, any night, we could die in our beds, or that our men bravely fighting the maniacs could be killed, lose a limb or be blinded? Will they understand how we trailed from one shop to another, across the town, to queue for the chance to buy just a few items and wait ages for a crowded bus? Will they understand how we felt guilty for not being able to give our children enough to eat or to buy them new toys for their birthdays and at Christmas? Will they realise how difficult it was to sleep, always fearful that, at any minute, the siren would go, we would hear the enemy aircraft, the bangs and explosions, wondering whether any of our friends had been killed or whether we might be about to die? Will future generations know or even care about what we went through and worried about what was to become of us, despite the efforts of our brave boys?'

Ann responded.

'No, I think they'll be pre-occupied with their own lives and that what we're suffering won't interest them. I think that the sense of community, created by this war, will soon fade when the whole bloody thing is over, provided we win. If we don't, may God help us, which is unlikely considering what He has put us through so far. In a few decades time, life could be so different, for better or worse but I've lived long enough to be pessimistic. I remember what happened after the First World War, which was supposed to be the war to end all wars. What happened? Economic misery, the great depression, mass unemployment and now this bloody war which has involved civilians more than any conflict in history.

'We must remind future generations of what happened and tell them that war's not about stirring music, medals and tales of bravery. It's about the cold-blooded starvation, mutilation and slaughter of fellow human beings and the destruction of lives and property. If people don't realise this, the same mistakes will be made again and again. Humans don't learn. Just look at history.'

Susan nodded agreement and added 'One thing that worries me is that we could be starved into surrender. I know that rationing, which was imposed in 1940, has helped and that anyone breaking the law has been severely punished, but we should produce our own food. Then there's clothes rationing. I'm sick of wearing the same old clothes and looking like a tramp. It's all very well telling us to "make do and mend!" and, of course, clothes are not cheap. I noticed the other day that the maximum price of a suit was £4-18-8. No wonder we're all wearing old fashions, such as fox stoles. I've never been happy wearing an animal's feet and head.'

The nation was subjected to many wartime slogans including *Keep Mum, She's Not Dumb, Careless Talk Costs Lives* and *Coughs and Sneezes Spread Diseases*. The country was also exhorted to *Dig For Victory* and *Make Do And Mend*. Children, as well as women, were targeted in some of these campaigns, especially those relating to securing maximum benefit from existing clothes. At a late stage in the war, local children participated in campaigns to raise money for the war effort. Having contributed to a fund for the Free French, Tim acquired a smart badge, and, after donating to another fund, was given a Torquay Warship Fund badge.

Susan was worried about money. In the early part of the war, seamen captured or lost at sea were deemed to have broken their contract and all payments to the family ceased. Peter's employer was more enlightened and some money was sent regularly to Susan after Peter had been captured in the South Atlantic in March 1941.

Mrs Marjorie Green appeared twice a week to assist Susan in cleaning the house. She, the Green lady, that's her name, not an indication of her stance on environmental affairs, which had not then been invented, had a very square and kindly face, dominated by a flat nose, that suggested a serious failure to push open a medieval-sized door with her snout. She had a fine temperament and a pronounced and incomprehensible Devonian accent.

Coal fires provided the heating which was why the front room was seldom used as coal was expensive and cleaning the grate was a time-consuming and dirty chore. Fortunately, the weather in Devon was suitably considerate.

Ann encouraged Susan to spend some time out with friends. 'It's really important that you don't spend all your time in this house. You really should go out. Why don't you go out with Jean occasionally? You've got a lot in common as she used to live in London.'

'Yes, I know that I should but, come to that, so should you. Why don't we aim to go out from time to time, unfortunately not together as one of us must look after the boys. You get on well with Iris, round the corner, and I'll ask Jean if she's interested.' The women decided that, occasionally, they would visit the cinema but the first time they went, an air raid interrupted the show, prompting the management to flash a message on the screen. 'The sirens have sounded. Patrons wishing to leave may do so.' There were no refunds.

Up to 30 million cinema tickets were sold each week and although the British films were rather dour and dutiful, those from America often gave a tantalising view of what life might be like in a peaceful future. In 1942, Susan and Jean enjoyed Noel Coward's *In Which We Serve.* This was based on Lord Mountbatten's experiences in the navy and it was only after the war that Susan discovered that the wartime Ministry of Information had opposed the release of this film, claiming that it was bad propaganda. Apparently, Mountbatten appealed to the King to intervene and this was why the film was eventually released.

Brief Encounter, starring Celia Johnson and Trevor Howard, shown in 1945, told of the love affair between a suburban housewife and a local doctor and was set in a dingy railway station. Other films that were well received included *The Philadelphia Story* with James Stewart, in 1941, *Yankee Doodle Dandy* featuring James Cagney, (1942) and *Going my Way* with Bing Crosby in 1944. Some leading actors, including David Niven, James Stewart and Clark Gable, joined the forces. The popular Pathé News, dominated by propaganda in the script and overall presentation, was included in most programmes. Susan and her mother enjoyed reading which diverted their worries away from the war and towards the plots conjured up by skilful authors. They would both read the same book and then discuss it. Two favourites were *How Green was My Valley* (1940) and *For Whom The Bell Tolls.*

Ann and her friend enjoyed visits to the British Restaurant in nearby Paignton where a reasonably priced meal of minced beef, carrots and parsnips was a favourite. Just occasionally, when the Green lady looked after the children, Susan, Ann, Jean and Iris had tea together and took the opportunity to discuss the world around them. 'I don't know about you, but I'm finding it very difficult to sleep these nights' This was Iris and the others immediately said that this was a problem for them, too. Iris continued. 'I saw an advertisement for Bourn-Vita the other day. I cut it out in case it was of interest to you. I'll read it out.'

She fumbled in her large but shabby handbag, produced a well-creased piece of paper and proceeded to read. 'When you've plenty to worry about, there's all the more reason to feel equal to it. Don't walk about feeling like a blackout in a coal cellar. It hinders you and everyone else. Make sure of sound natural NOT drugged sleep. That's the best nerve-tonic that's ever been invented. MORAL-start Bourn-Vita tonight.' Iris helpfully added that it was 9 pence per quarter pound.

Susan wondered if the others had seen an item in the newspaper.

'Apparently, a woman in Barnet in Hertfordshire, has been fined £10, with two guineas costs, for allowing bread to be wasted. Her servant, who gave the bread to the birds, was fined five shillings. The woman said that she could not see the birds starve. I wonder why birds in Barnet don't like insects like other birds?' The women agreed that the fine was harsh but, presumably, it was meant to be a deterrent. Just over a year later, a factory in Barnet, making military radios, was bombed, killing 211 workers.

Ann said that there always seemed to be rumours that parachutists had landed in the country. 'I'm fed up with them but I see that AP Herbert has tried to put our minds at rest. Did any of you see what he wrote the other day? Confronted by three shaking heads, Ann, resurrecting a stage career for less than a minute, and having learned the piece off by heart, recited thus:

'Do not believe the tale the milkman tells, No troops have landed in Potters Bar. Nor are there submarines in Tunbridge Wells. The BBC will tell us when there are.'

Jean had heard that anyone who was pessimistic in public could be jailed. Did this mean that we were doing worse in the war than the government 'would have us believe?' Susan, half smiling, said that she ought to be careful as such a comment could land her in prison but felt sure that nobody would report her this time.

Invasion And Peace

As the date of an allied invasion neared, in 1944, many thousands of overseas forces arrived in Devon. Earlier, when a German invasion seemed imminent, before the Battle of Britain in 1940, which caused the enemy to reverse and then cancel its invasion plans, access to the local beaches was restricted. Initially, scaffolding appeared which was excellent for climbing. However, before long, prolific lines of barbed wire and notices to keep off the beaches deterred even the most adventurous. Pyramid blocks of concrete, designed as tank traps, were placed on strategic roads leading away from the beach to thwart any enemy vehicles that had managed to come ashore. Local signposts were removed early in the war and iron railings were taken to assist in the war effort, although some historians maintain that the iron was not used in armaments nor to build Spitfires and that the policy was more for what is now known as public relations reasons.

There were sandbags everywhere. As the war progressed, elderly local buses either had a balloon carrying gas on the roof of the vehicle, or pulled a trailer containing gas. Devon General buses were rare and loaned red London Transport buses, with winding external stairs to the upper deck, were busily engaged on Torbay roads. Parks and railway embankments were ploughed up to provide much-needed food. All food scraps were deposited in bins, the contents of which were to be fed to pigs and in the summer the bins smelt so strongly that the powerful pong might have persuaded Hitler and his allies to retreat rapidly.

Torquay, so close to Exeter and Plymouth, which had been severely damaged, was relatively fortunate. Some enemy bombers, having failed to drop their deadly cargo on the intended target, often released them over Torquay rather than taking them home which would have slowed the aircrafts' escape. Spitfires were based at Exeter airport. Some enemy bombers were shot down: a total of up to 200 aircraft may have fallen on Devon. Precise figures on the number of times that Torquay was bombed are unavailable but it seems that there were at least 650 air raid warnings and some 320 attacks on Devonian targets. The proportion of warnings whilst Tim was in the bath was not recorded.

Astonishingly, in 1944, the enemy did not realise that the allied invasion of the continent was to be launched in part from South Devon and it was a major success for the allies that they deceived the enemy. Some 80,000 American soldiers and another 35,000 navy personnel were in Devon just before D Day in June 1944. Some 21,000 were based in the Torbay area. Many were billeted in local hotels, which had been requisitioned, whilst others lived in tents in local parks. Many RAF men were based in Oldway, near the Adams house. Seemingly suddenly, the area was full of Americans and their military vehicles. Bren gun carriers, tanks, ambulances, enormous trucks and many other mechanical manifestations of modern warfare clogged the local streets and the station at Paignton and the nearby rail lines were congested as essential supplies arrived. All this was fascinating to Tim but he was intrigued mainly by the red buses and, of course, the doctor's car. Now convoys of strange and sinister-looking vehicles dominated the crowded local roads and lanes. Sadly, some schoolboys, unaccustomed to such traffic, were victims of road accidents involving heavy US military trucks driven by men not familiar with driving on the left hand side of the road and Norman, a friend of Tim's was killed.

The area between Goodrington Sands and Broadsands became a major supply dump and many open spaces were dominated by military vehicles. Slipways, some of which have been preserved, were built to allow men and materials to be loaded on to waiting vessels, many of which were anchored in the River Dart. It was possible to walk across the Dart from vessel to vessel. As the build up to the invasion occurred, the sea fronts at Preston and Paignton were adorned by Bofors guns. Apart from the massive traffic and foreign soldiers, there were exercises in nearby roads during which soldiers jumped around in the gardens, brandishing their weapons which was both frightening and exciting to the young spectators. Devon beaches were used to practice landings on the continent and the immediate area around Paignton became an exclusion zone and those living in the locality required specific identity cards.

On 6th June 1944, a teacher with mountainous hair so high that she could have concealed a secret wireless, told her pupils, including Tim, to write in their blue exercise books, which bore the legend Grafton House School, in Gothic script, on the front cover, 'Today is D Day.' Were the children told about it or the implications? No, what was really important was that their writing was to be tested. The allies might be about to try to oust a madman intent on global conquest, millions of human beings were to be killed or maimed but what really mattered was that the pupils' writing was clear and that their loops were formed correctly. No less than 130,000 men were to land on the beaches of Normandy, from 7,000 vessels, whilst air cover was provided by 12,000 allied aircraft.

Soon after the invasion, the Germans agreed that some prisoners of war should be repatriated. Many attempts had been made for some years and both the Russians and Americans had rejected proposals for varying reasons. Susan discussed this with Marjorie Green.

'Apparently, the authorities say that what matters is how old a prisoner is and how long he's been behind barbed wire. On that basis, surely, Peter must be released? He's been a prisoner since 1941 and is now in his forties.' Marjorie did her best not to allow Susan to become too hopeful. She was about a decade older than Susan and knew that good news was rare. Peter remained a captive but one man who was repatriated visited Susan and was able to confirm that her husband was well.

Judging by the strength and direction of the black arrows in the four-page newspapers, indicating the subsequent progress of the allies on the continent, it was clear, some months after the invasion began, that the war in Europe was ending. Tim heard the great news on 7th May 1945 when walking down Oldway Road, a few hundred yards from home, with his mother. They were passing the front garden of a house when a jubilant and emotional woman emerged from the house shrieking out 'it's all over. Germany's surrendered. We've won! I've just heard it on the wireless. Thank God.' Tim wondered why it was acceptable to give credit to God for peace but not blame Him for the conflict, especially if He was all-powerful. Susan immediately burst into tears of unalloyed joy and hugged her son. 'Now it means that daddy will be home again soon. Isn't that great news?' Tim, who, in practice, did not know the man, was pleased for Susan but opted to remain neutral himself until he had met his father and come to a judgement. Perhaps it was the realisation that the war with Japan was unfinished, but the boy's reaction to the end of a conflict for which millions had prayed for years and for which millions had died, was astonishingly underwhelming. 'Oh boy.'

'What's peace like?'

Susan, hastily composing herself, tried to respond.

'Well, dear, it's difficult to say but things are very different. In due course, there will be more food, we won't have to make sure that you don't have too much water in your bath, there will be more toys in the shops and, of course, best of all, daddy will be home. We won't be woken in the middle of the night by air raids and we'll always know where daddy is.' The comment about the bath made Tim realise that he no longer had to fear an attack whilst he was performing his ablutions. Peace sounded good. Susan was too emotional to continue but Tim, who wondered what would be in the newspapers as they were no longer reporting on the war, would have liked a fuller answer. Clearly, the discussion was over. His mother did not want to talk about all the painful experiences of war, so, sensing that this weak answer was all he was to receive for the present, Tim retreated into silence and decided to wait until he could work it out for himself.

He was concerned that the number of adults who would boss

him around was about to rise by half, although he did not know about fractions at this stage in his life. For example, Ann, one of his most severe critics but who could also be a close friend, frequently pointed out perceived flaws in Tim's behaviour or appearance and often sought to comb his unruly hair. 'Tim, you look very untidy. Let me comb your hair. Do stay still, what would people say if they could see you like this?' As nobody ever saw Tim, apart from when he was at school, or with his friends, George, Edward, James or Roger, this was an odd remark as the quartet never passed judgement on their appearances, seemingly well content to be seen in each others' company. Ann would then clamp a hand over his small mouth, partly to stifle any imminent objection and partly to curb the movement of his head, so she could secure her objective. What could he do to ensure that he was not ordered around by yet another adult?

What Tim did not know was that the next few years would see significant change. By the 1950's there was a determination, especially from younger people, that full enjoyment should be a key objective. There was also disillusion with the more elderly and their discredited and failed policies and a fierce determination to seek change. All this prompted a genuine belief that the hard-won peace would eventually bring benefits for its people. In 1945 and 1946, the House of Commons voted to nationalise ports, railways, road haulage, and the steel and coal industries. The coal industry was eventually nationalised in 1947 and paid holidays, sick pay and rest homes were granted to the 700,000 men who were employed in the sector in 1950. A new National Health Service was soon inaugurated and a system of national insurance was introduced. One consequent problem was that the NHS, free legal aid, the coal, steel, gas, water and electricity utilities, as well as welfare reform, had to be paid for. A third of the country's overseas investment had been used to pay for the war and the cost of the home reforms and defence of a worldwide empire meant that there was a continuous sterling crisis through the Fifties. At one time, the standard rate of income tax was 47.5 per cent and in 1950, surtax was levied on the biggest earners at 97.5 per cent.

Reflections

Some years later, Susan and Ann, now back in London, were talking about the war. Peter was at sea and Tim was busy doing his homework which seemed to take up all of his evenings and weekends. 'Do you remember that conversation we had when we were in Preston, on whether future generations would be interested in learning about what we went through in the war? On the whole, we were pessimistic and thought that once it was all over, what millions suffered would be forgotten.'

Ann nodded. 'Obviously, the worst for you was not knowing if Peter was alive or dead. I don't know how you stayed sane. Thank God we never had a visit from one of those young boys who delivered the tragic telegrams. I know Peter was a POW for four very long and hard years but at least we knew that he wasn't going to be blown up in the Atlantic.'

Susan said that so much seemed to happen once the so-called phoney war was over. 'I know that's what it was called but I always get angry as Merchant Seamen were losing their lives. It was anything but phoney for them. In total some 35,000 men and women of the Merchant Navy lost their lives and that was the highest percentage of any of our forces.'

Ann continued and picked up a book that was perched on a table. 'It all seems so long ago now but this book reminded me of so much.' She began reading from the introduction. 'In 1940, Denmark and Norway were invaded and by the end of May, Holland and Belgium had surrendered. Italy declared war on Great Britain and on France and by the middle of June, German troops had entered Paris. The French capital was liberated in August 1944 and Brussels fell to the allies in the following month.' She selected a section from lower down the page. 'Between August 1940 and May 1941, some 40,000 people were killed in London and the south east.'

Summarising another section in the introduction to the book, she continued.

'In June 1940, the British Expeditionary Force was forced to retreat from Dunkirk and some 335,000 British and French troops were ferried across the channel, aided by a fleet of small boats, manned by those brave amateurs.' Churchill hailed the operation as a triumph but argued that Dunkirk had been a 'colossal military disaster' and wars were not won by retreats. Some 68,000 men lost their lives, were wounded or missing and about 64,000 allied vehicles and other pieces of equipment were left behind.

'Do you remember, some survivors were brought to Torquay?'

'Yes. It's a pity that Hitler, Goebbels, Himmler and Goering all committed suicide. I would have liked them to die a slow and painful death, as the hundreds of thousands Jews suffered.'

Ann continued by reading a section on deaths and damage.

'Two million homes in the UK were destroyed and some 93,000 civilians, including 7,000 children, lost their lives. Some 60 million people, more than the total population of the UK, were killed between September 1939 and August 1945. That is equal to 27,000 a day. The Soviet Union lost 12 million military personnel and 15 million civilians. Germany lost six million. About 407,000 British forces were killed and the Americans lost 403,000. About 7.5 million Chinese citizens lost their lives. Nearly six million Polish citizens were killed and at least 6.5 million Jews were murdered in Europe. Some 2.1 million Japanese military men were killed and up to a million civilians died.' Ann was beginning to cry and stopped reading, commenting 'I just can't take it all in'.

'Then, of course, there were thousands of those terrible flying bombs, the V1 and V2. It must have been awful, hearing them drone overhead and then, when the engine sound stopped, you knew they were about to explode. They killed thousands of people and even when the poor devils sheltered in the underground, they were not immune.

'In this book, it says that we dropped 2.7 million tonnes of bombs on Germany and that during the war half of the UK population moved and within one month of the German onslaught on France, 8 million French people were on the move. Apparently, it was the greatest migration in West European history.

'In the battle for Stalingrad the Germans and their allies lost 750,000 killed, wounded or missing men whilst the corresponding figure for the Soviet Union was over one million, including 400,000 children. One November night in Coventry, the city was destroyed by 500 German aircraft as 75,000 buildings were ruined and 568 people lost their lives.

'Then, of course, since the war, there's been such an outcry because in February 1945, 800 Allied Lancaster bombers attacked Dresden and they were followed the next day by 400 Flying Fortresses. Up to 130,000 people were killed.

'We mustn't forget the inhuman treatment meted out to innocent citizens in the concentration camps. In January 1945, the allies found six warehouses linked to a concentration camp in which there were 348,000 men's suits, 836,255 women's dresses and 38,000 pairs of men's shoes. What kind of people were those Germans? They weren't fit to live. I'll always hate them.

'On 6th August 1945, the first atomic bomb, dropped on Hiroshima, killed 78,000 people and many more died subsequently from their horrendous injuries. Another 40,000 were killed as the second bomb was released over Nagasaki. Earlier, in March, American aircraft attacked Tokyo, dropping 500,000 incendiary bombs which killed 120,000. It says here that we saved thousands of allied lives by forcing Japan to surrender quickly and the western powers were anxious to ensure that Stalin, there's another mass murderer, was not allowed to get involved in the Far East.

'Here's something about Londoners taking shelter in the underground stations. At peak, some 170,000 were sleeping in these dreadful conditions. Some 66 were killed in the Balham station and 111 people were killed when the Bank station was attacked. It was estimated that some 50 million "person nights" were spent in underground tube stations. Starvation was a common feature of everyday life in so many cities and many were forced to eat almost anything that they could find. For example, Dutch people were reduced to eating wallpaper. At least we had rationing from January 1940 and this allowed a fair distribution of the food that was available.'

Ann pointed out that 'we all tried to grow our own food, in our gardens, and, of course, in public parks that had been converted, on allotments and anywhere else that we could. I heard on the wireless that by 1943, there were more than one million allotments in the UK.'

The mother and daughter then discussed the belated entry of the US in the war after the Pearl Harbour fiasco. Ann had spent some time reading about the Americans and their attitude to the Axis forces and produced an article neatly glued into her voluminous scrapbook.

'You know, they were reluctant to enter the war, as they were the first time, and seemed more hostile to the Japanese than to the Germans. The American public had noted the savage way the Japs attacked the Chinese and were getting worried about US interests in the area. According to this article, despite having warnings that an attack might be imminent, American military leaders in the region took no precautions. On 7th December 1941, without bothering to declare war, the Japanese bombed Pearl Harbour. Eighteen American vessels were sunk, 188 planes destroyed and another 162 were damaged. Sadly, 2,403 Americans were killed and another 1,756 were injured. America declared war immediately and within seven weeks, US troops had arrived in the UK. The United States, which had been unprepared for war in 1939, became a crucial supplier of armaments. Between 1941 and 1945, the country produced over 250,000 aircraft, 90,000 tanks, 350 destroyers and 200 submarines.'

Ann said that this had made her very depressed 'but glad that, unlike many millions, we're alive and well. I think that we were wrong when we said, all those years ago, that future generations would not be interested in the war and its impact on us all. Thanks to so many books and films and personal stories from those who were involved, I do believe that what so many surrendered for us all will not be forgotten.' Susan nodded. She, for one, would never forget the war.

Tim Goes To School

It was spring 1941. The Luftwaffe had resumed its blitz on London and on 10th May had bombed the House of Commons. No fewer than 507 bombers participated in the attacks but this was to be the last major German air raid on the capital for some time as the Luftwaffe began targeting other cities, including Coventry, Liverpool, Bristol, Belfast and Cardiff. Rudolf Hess, the deputy to Hitler, flew to Scotland on 10th May, to ask the UK to allow Germany a free hand in Europe, in return for leaving the British Empire intact. Hess was tried at Nuremburg, imprisoned at Spandau prison in Berlin and died in 1987.

'Tomorrow is miss brooks day.' Susan announced this with unaccustomed enthusiasm and the mood was heightened by Ann's observation that Tim would enjoy it and have, as she put it, 'a jolly fine day'. Tim was not all that keen on jolliness, which he treated with the utmost suspicion, especially when advocated by adults who, in his modest experience, had a different perception of jolliness. Why, he wondered why was it so good to miss something? Had brooks day occurred before and how often was it missed? Why had he not heard of it before? What was it to do with him?

Apparently, Miss Brooks was in charge of a local primary school and Tim was to visit it, as he understood, on the morrow. He knew little about schools and education, like future secretaries of state, and the prospect, as outlined by his mother and grandmother, was unappealing but, as it was only for a day, he felt that he should be able to tolerate it. Surely, it could not be too bad as his mother and grandmother had both been so enthusiastic? Uncertain of the language to be employed, and thinking that somehow, miss brooks was another name for school, he asked Susan whether she had had miss brooks days when she was young.

'Yes, dear, when I was a little girl, I went to school.' Indeed, to strengthen her case, she added that daddy, too, had been to school. It seemed that attending school was a common phenomenon in the family.

'And nana?'

'Yes, we all went to school. Everybody goes to school.'

Tim evinced no particular enthusiasm that he was about to follow what, apparently, was a family tradition but, as usual, decided against making further enquiries lest the responses be unfavourable but he did establish that Miss Brooks was in charge. The following morning, it was raining as Susan, with an increasingly damp Tim, set out for school. It was far enough away to ensure that, when the two reached their destination, they looked as if they had swum all the way. At the age of four, Tim was about to begin his education. Having said goodbye to his mother, who promised she would see him again in the afternoon, Tim wondered what would happen at lunch time and allowed himself to be led by a tall and ugly woman to a large room in which infants of both genders were playing with lumps of plasticine or with large wooden blocks of different sizes and shapes. This boded ill as Tim had had little exposure to plasticine, wooden blocks and other infants to whom he took an instant dislike.

The ugly woman clapped her hands together in an effort to engage the squealing and energetic audience to listen to her.

'Hello everyone. I want you to meet a new friend, who's called Tim. Say hello to Tim.'

The children dutifully bellowed out the requested instruction but only after their first attempt had been deemed to be inadequate.

'Now it's your turn, Tim, say hello to everyone.'

The new pupil shivered with embarrassment. He was shy and had never seen so many infants, some of whom were female, in one place at the same time. Silence prevailed.

'Come along, Tim, say hello to everyone.'

'Hello.'

'Now you can play with any of your new friends and make anything you like with the plasticine or wooden blocks. Have fun.'

Fun had not been a frequent visitor in Tim's young life and it certainly was not going to come that day if the early minutes proved typical. His new and intended friends were not to become his chums. They stayed in their little groups and paid scant attention to Tim who was equally keen not to join them. He seized some spare wooden blocks and built a small castle. Within seconds, a fat boy, who was about twice the size of all the other infants, aimed an inflated foot at the castle, which lacking any support against such hostile action, slumped to the floor. Unaccustomed to such impolite and aggressive behaviour, Tim promptly attacked the fat boy. At this point, the ugly woman returned and immediately decided that Tim, who had already been shown to be unsociable, was the aggressor and, without soliciting any evidence, rebuked him.

'Now Tim, we don't fight here and you must be a good boy and not attack your new friends. Say sorry to Colin and promise that you won't fight anyone again.'

Powered by a sense of injustice, Tim not only refused but claimed that Colin was the guilty party and pointed to the pile of wooden blocks which, until so recently, had been a modest castle. 'He knocked down my castle.'

'Is this true, Colin?'

'No, he just hit me for no reason.'

'Tim, I believe that Colin is a good boy and would not have knocked over your castle, so say sorry.'

The innocent Tim was tempted to ask why, then, his castle had collapsed suddenly but desisted. He sensed that his day at school would not be pleasurable and looked forward to the morrow when he would be free again. He mumbled 'sorry' and added, as the ugly woman retreated to arbitrate in another dispute, 'for not hitting you harder after you knocked over my castle'.

Colin sneered.

As Tim smarted because of the injustice, he saw one of his young colleagues, of the female persuasion, spit at the departing adult who, although her back had been turned, sensed misbehaviour.

'Margaret, don't do that. Nice girls don't spit.'

'My mummy does and she's very nice.'

Tim had not seen anyone spit before and decided that it might be fun to see how successful he might be but reserved this possible pleasure for when he was alone at home, in the garden. Before trying this new skill in public, he wanted to make sure that he was sufficiently competent to avoid ridicule.

Lunch was barely adequate and Tim eagerly awaited his mother's return to take him away from this horrible place. Why did his mother and grandmother say that he would like it? The day was characterised by tears of misery, annoyance, injustice and frustration so was an ideal preparation for later life. Why should he have to play silly games with other infants of both genders and obey strange ladies he did not know? He was told what to do by two adult females at home and now there were even more trying to rule him. Why were females so bossy? It all seemed pointless, boring and unfair. When he was grown up, he would have nothing to do with females.

Still, he told himself, it was only for a day. Ann had told him he would really enjoy his day and Susan had confirmed that the day was Miss Brooks day. Tomorrow all would be back to normal. That evening, he was truly horrified to learn that, from now on, he would be going to bed a little earlier each evening as he was now a schoolboy. Frankly, he had neither sought nor wanted this role and it took Tim some moments to absorb this horrific statement. This was, without doubt, the worse news that he had ever heard. He was on the verge of tears when he tried to state his position.

'I thought it was just for a day. You said that it was Miss Brooks day and nana said I would enjoy the day.' He sought further clarification. 'You mean I have to keep going to school again and again? When will it stop and I can stay at home?' Susan decided that she ought to break the news to her son and, slightly irritated by the discussion, opted, probably wrongly, for the brutal truth.

'Yes, dear, of course you will go to different schools but you will be at school for about 12 years.'

Tim reeled and sensed that he might faint. He knew that he was only four but 12 years was a very long time which was impossible to imagine. Surely, in 12 years, he would be an old man? He sought immediate assurance on this and was told that he would still be a young boy but his mother's apparently guilty expression, caused by regretting that she had been so candid, undermined his confidence. Was he sentenced to building wooden castles and making things from some smelly plasticine for 12 years? Diminishing returns had set in after just one day.

Susan calmed him down, not without some difficulty, and persuaded him that his subsequent school career would not be as disagreeable as his first day and that he would have, as she put it, 'a lot of fun', a sentiment which Tim rejected, based on what he had seen so far, and that he would make many friends. Apart from the girl who spat, he was not at all sure that he wanted friends like those he had already encountered. Apparently, he would learn how to tell the time, read and write and do sums. So far, these skills had not been necessary. There had always been someone to do these things for him. Why change? He decided that he was not going to like school and wished he was much older, little realising that time accelerates with age and that there is never enough of it.

The school, officially the Preston Preliminary School, was known locally as PPS, although few locals realised that PPS meant something rather different at Westminster. Frankly, the prospects of any confusion remain remote as it was unlikely that anyone who reached the rank of parliamentary private secretary had attended PPS and would admit this in his cv. If this seat of non-learning had survived, it may now have been known as The University of the West (Infants) Advanced Learning Academy Community University College. (UOFTWIALACUC). This title would have helped the government to claim that the UK had more universities per square mile than any country in the world. Later years would see almost everyone going to university and securing a degree, as the standards were lowered each year to ensure that nobody was ever disappointed or felt a lack of self-esteem.

The school, built at the beginning of the century, was,

effectively, a large detached house which needed painting but, of course, because the country was at war, the shreds of yellow paint obstinately remained on the rotting wood for as long as the wind allowed. It was on a corner plot, near a bridge over which trains thundered from time to time, whilst emitting that smell that often induced nausea. The sea front at Preston was adjacent but home was 1.5 miles away: there were no kilometres in the UK then. The building had started life as an ordinary residence, but, every few years there was a happy event as another room was added. The main classroom, in which forts and houses were built from the wooden blocks, smelt of plasticine. It was on the side of the house, near the railway line, which diverted attention away from the efforts of the elderly females who considered themselves to be teachers. Tim's smaller classroom was on the other side of the building and lacked a useful view but that did not prevent him from staring out blankly, wondering when his 12 years would end.

Apparently, according to one know-all boy, prisoners often received a remission of part of their sentence if they behaved. He had a question for Susan when she collected him. Initially, Tim was taken to and collected from school so, despite having little food to eat herself, she was using up precious energy walking about 30 miles a week in both good and bad weather.

'Are prisoners let out of prison early if they are good?'

'Yes, dear but why do you ask?'

'Well, does that also apply to boys, like me, if they are good?'

Susan smiled and conveyed bad news.

Tim stayed each day for what was euphemistically called lunch which was taken in an upstairs room that had previously been a bedroom. Lunch was edible but not appetising. Like everything else decreed by adults at that time, eating was compulsory as, apparently, it was good for you and everything had to be devoured, whatever the quality or quantity. Monday were the least unsatisfactory day: a minute portion of cold meat was served with some beetroot which had been doused in a pond of vinegar for at least a week. The boiled potatoes, at first as white as the children's faces when forced to consume something inedible, resembled bland islands in a purple sea.

The school was opposite a garage which was exciting as some of the few cars on the road used this site. Another advantage of the school's location was that it was near Tommy Tucker's sweet shop. T. Tucker was a kindly man, who spoke softly, slowly and gently, with an accent that could not be placed but Tim, some years later, realised that it was from somewhere significantly to the north of Torquay. He was confident in this as there was not much to the south, apart from the beach. Tommy was about 75 and his silver grey hair was cut very short which seemed to suit his apparently square head. His blue eyes shone from behind his glasses, the shape of which matched his head, and they seemed to twinkle as this kindly gentleman put his plump hand into a big glass jar and gave free toffees to his young friends. Sweet rationing was implemented in July 1942 and children were given their own allocation which was eight ounces a month. An occasional extra toffee was very welcome.

Hair grew rapidly on boys' heads during the war, doubtless because they were covered for many hours a week under a cap, which, in those days, was a form of headgear, not a maximum. Despite protests, every two weeks, Tim was marched to Mr Houseman, the local barber, who operated from a converted front room in his house near the main road. Lest anyone had difficulty in finding him, there was a long and old-fashioned striped red and white pole decorating his front garden.

Having regular haircuts was probably enforced by wartime legislation and was designed to thwart the enemy. The relevant law was doubtless the Defence of the Realm: Compulsory Hair Cuts (Wartime) Act. Anyone with long hair might have then been detected as an enemy spy. Hostile aliens might not know of the law and, even if they did, they would be reluctant to patronise a local barber. If, before they left Germany, spies intending to stay in the UK had a crew cut, not popular in the UK, they would have been very conspicuous so would have had to wear hats all the time. Consequently, being a spy in a hot English summer was inadvisable. Of course, German spies could have been accompanied by barbers, armed with clippers and combs to effect the necessary work on the enemy's hirsute crania, or, like Gandhi, they might have tried to cut their own hair. Like the Indian, they would have found it difficult so they might have been conspicuous.

The conversation with a British barber would have been difficult for a German spy determined to avoid capture because his hair was too long. 'We don't want this foggy weather, do we sir? Gives those Jerry swine a chance to slip over, unseen, and cause havoc on our coast. Did you hear on the Home Service this morning that our brave boys gave Berlin a pasting last night? Serves them right after what they've done to our cities, that's what I say. On leave for very long, sir?' What if the barber then asked 'how do you like your hair...' and the customer had instinctively interrupted 'Herr von Kreigsman Adolf Goering'.

At Miss Brooks' school, where education was not a main pre-occupation, so was ahead of its times, the infants played with the large, pasty-coloured wooden blocks, that have already been publicised, and created buildings of different kinds. Tim's work, reflecting his insecurity, would have fascinated a psychologist: his blocks were always used to construct a home that was indestructible, at least until a fellow pupil kicked it to the ground or a squealing girl fell in a heap over it. Tim's insecurity might have reflected the fact that he was not quite three when war broke out. The only life he knew was war and it had a significant but hard to define impact on his young mind. His father, whom he did not know, was away in a German prisoner of war camp and occasionally enemy planes destroyed some local houses and even killed people. This did not seem natural but he and many thousands of others, many of whom had suffered serious physical or psychological damage, knew nothing else.

Gradually, Tim became accustomed to school and even made some friends and he was fascinated by the early stages of learning how to read. At the age of five, Tim's fellow students, as political correctness now would require them to be so described, were entered into an important art examination supervised by a group well-known in the art world. The organisers, who would feel comfortable in today's world, believed that no child should ever suffer a reverse which could cause a loss of self-esteem, thus prompting them to become criminals or global dictators. Napoleon, for example, was probably very poor at art and Stalin, doubtless, was no dab hand with a paint brush. Churchill, however, was an artist and this is probably why he never became an autocratic dictator.

Inevitably, almost the entire class passed and there was much rejoicing in the PPS corridors. Certificates were brandished aloft, much in the manner of Chamberlain returning from Munich with a piece of paper and the only reason that some of the pupils did not appear on local television was that there was none. One boy was less jubilant and, possibly, feared that, as a result of his failure, he might become a global dictator. Tim was that boy. History shows the immediate impact of this reverse had on him but others must decide just how detrimental this setback was in the longer term. Courageously, trying to limit the damage, Susan and her wronged son, in a minor supporting role, challenged the teachers. Tim explained that what had been construed as an aircraft flying over a house, was, in fact, a fish leaping around a vessel. Admittedly, the fish was much bigger than the vessel, but it was a big fish and a very small boat, as he explained, puzzled that these so-called experts failed to distinguish aircraft and fish and a vessel and a house. Furthermore, he thought that the blue waves were a clue. Tim's entry was then belatedly commended so he would not have to become a global dictator.

His next venture into culture was in the theatre. In a debut that failed to impress even the most generous of critics, Tim appeared, for one afternoon only, in a Brooks-inspired pantomime in a local church. This was not for the celebrated film director, Mel Brooks, who was then only 15 years old and had not ventured into the world of theatre: it was, of course, Miss Brooks of PPS.

Food was a subject about which young Tim knew nothing. Consequently, when, as a treat, Garibaldi biscuits arrived at PPS, he was bemused and sought information from his young colleagues on what seemed to be biscuits made from squashed flies.

Unfortunately, there was collective ignorance on the composition of these strange delicacies. Tim and his young friends were unfamiliar with the name because the biscuits, like Italy before the war, had not, thus far, merited a mention in conversation. All the children except one gobbled the biscuits greedily. Tim was the exception but 'it was not done' to spurn a luxury as children had to eat everything they were given and be grateful for it. So, rather than giving his away, which could have prompted difficult questioning and being forced to eat the things, Tim crushed them and stuffed them under the edge of a rich dark blue carpet, after showing token enthusiasm for what he was told was a rare treat. When the carpet on one side of the room was full up, he then inserted them on the other side of the room. Like Italy, he changed sides which seemed appropriate for these biscuits. Eventually, those who walked on the relevant stretches of carpet, even those not of a mathematical disposition, could correlate strange crunching sounds with their footsteps. After some discussions, again involving the indefatigable Susan, Tim's allocation of biscuits was withdrawn.

Grafton House Receives A New Pupil

In January 1943, the Luftwaffe resumed its major raids on London. In the following month, the Royal Air Force bombed Berlin for the first time in daylight and in March the plot to kill Hitler, whilst he was flying to Smolensk, failed as two bombs, disguised as bottles of brandy, failed to explode and were removed, without Hitler becoming aware of the plan. A subsequent and failed attempt on the thug's life, reportedly, prompted the Red Cross to send him their congratulations on his escape. In the next month, the US rationed meats, fats and cheese, the Eighth Army made progress in Tunisia and the Royal Air Force bombed dams on the Ruhr. In July, Mussolini resigned and was arrested and by September, the allies had landed in Italy and just five days later, the country's unconditional surrender was announced.

Meanwhile, in the UK, having achieved all that could be done with wooden blocks and plasticine, Tim, now aged six and with some understanding of more advanced subjects, such as reading, joined the fee-paying Grafton House School. That should be clarified. Fees were paid by parents, not the school. This new place of learning, or, more accurately, of 'memorising', was close to Camellia House and was thus 'ideally situated'. One feature of the walk to school in the autumn was the flooding of parts of the deserted road. Leaves generously congregated around the drains, sometimes pushed there by nature but, more often, ushered in that direction by Wellington-booted young boys who then enjoyed walking through the newly-created ponds. The waves lapped over the pavements with an agreeable swishing sound which enhanced a feeling of puerile power.

There were few opportunities to express any individualism: total conformity was of paramount importance. The fact that the nation was at war was used to offset any criticism of anything. Strict discipline at school and at home effectively suppressed any desire to be different from anyone else and produced a generation of robots who only discarded these shackles much later, if at all. The disciplined, undemocratic and tedious life was all that the young and usually bemused children knew.

On dry days, denied the possibility of causing a temporary flood, the near total absence of traffic allowed Tim and his friends to kick an old tennis ball all the way to school. Judging by the ferocious evening cleaning sessions performed by his mother and grandmother, Tim inferred that it was apparently a legal requirement to polish and shine shoes each night although the name of the specific piece of legislation was unknown. It was probably the Daily Cleaning, Polishing and Shining of Males' Shoes (black and laced) (Wartime Emergency) Act. It was probably conjured up by the same person who devised legislation requiring hair to be cut every fortnight. Anyone with unpolished black shoes could well have been a spy as it was unlikely that any Germans who landed secretly would have brought shoe-cleaning equipment with them.

The boys changed their route to school when a small black and white, nasty-faced dog, of no fixed breed, which doubtless played hell with its self-esteem, decided to chase them. He celebrated having caught Tim by biting him. Tim told his friend Roger that he had worked out a plan to ensure that he would not be bitten again. Roger dutifully sought details. 'Well, I thought that I would put a juicy steak in the road as a car was approaching and the dog saw what I was doing and ran into the road and was killed.' Roger detected some problems with this policy. 'Firstly, you haven't enough money or coupons to buy a steak even if you could find one. Then there are very few cars on the road so you could have a long wait and then you can't guarantee that the dog would obligingly run into the road at the right time.'

'Precisely, that's why I shan't be trying this plan out. The dog's lucky there's a war on and I haven't any money.'

It was Tim's second serious encounter with a local dog. Soon after the family had moved to Preston, he was playing on the beach, then free of anti-tank scaffolding, and was confronted by an Alsatian. Lest you think that Tim was a very bright child who could name different makes of canines, it must be conceded that he knew that this brute was an Alsatian only because he was told later. The fact was stored just in case, one day, decades on, the story might be recounted. That moment has now come. It knocked Tim over and then, before Susan could see what was happening, the dog, doubtless thinking that the child was something that the tide had washed up, or, alternatively, that it needed to be cleaned, started to roll its victim into the water to return him from whence it thought the child had come. At this point, maternal efforts saved Tim from this environmentally-friendly canine keen to remove rubbish from the beach.

The distinctive Grafton House school uniform immediately identified its pupils. The caps were light green with the school badge, in white, prominent on the front. As an indication of collective decadence, caps were worn with the peak facing front as nobody realised that such headgear could be worn back to front. Well done, tennis players for showing, much later, what could be done with a little imagination.

The young males, no girls were allowed, wore grey shirts over heavy vests, almost yellow in colour, which were compulsory until the heat of summer, which was usually well past the date when clouts could be cast. Grey shorts were prevented from succumbing to gravity by the intervention of a cloth belt, with the two ends fastened together by a silver snake. Sometimes, braces were worn instead and Tim's fear, sustained for some years, was that there was an inviolable rule that trousers naturally fell down and that it might even be wise to use both a belt and braces. In a phrase that had not then been invented, the default position of the said bags was around the ankles, not the waist. School socks were grey and the whole ensemble was finished with black shoes, although in the summer Clarks-made brown sandals with holes in the upper part, which cooled the feet were allowed. The school tie boasted stripes of black, green and white but, oddly, no grey. Pupils wore grey jackets but in the summer, they could wear blazers with vertical green, black and white stripes that matched their ties and looked uncannily like the garments worn by aristocratic characters pilloried by the Punch magazine in earlier decades. In the winter, or on wet days, long, navy blue and belted raincoats were worn. The boys lived in fear of not just air raids but of rain so even on those days when precipitation was not considered likely, raincoats were carried, neatly folded, over the arm. In those bleak and depressing days, there were no weather forecasts or forecasters telling listeners what to wear. so people had to make their own decisions. It was, indeed, a difficult world.

One feature of wartime, which, oddly, seldom is mentioned from detailed accounts of the conflict, was the behaviour of woollen swimming trunks. As water soaked them, there was a natural tendency for gravity to do what it is supposed to do, so holding the swimming trunks up to avoid embarrassment was a common sight, not so much in cities, but certainly on the beach. It was but a further example of trousers' default position.

The uniform provoked a lout known locally, for unknown reasons, as Squeaker, to frighten younger children. His aggression might have been the outcome of jealousy or perhaps he just enjoyed being a bully. Now, doubtless, he would be diagnosed as suffering from a low ongoing self-esteem reaction. (LOSER). This meant that he could only help himself by using his superior size to inflict pain on others, all of which is quite understandable and, naturally, even desirable if it assisted his self-worth. Perhaps he harboured ambitions of becoming a global dictator or even a schoolmaster, and was just practising? One day, doubtless tired of hostile banter, he sought to engage Tim and a friend in fisticuffs. The friend, typically, legged it at speed. The thug, who was about 15, a third older than his intended victim, was wearing a cap, of the sort that was favoured later by a leading aristocratic Conservative politician in the Fifties, when he was travelling north and wanted to resemble his perception of a local. Without thinking, Tim pulled the cap down over the squeaker's eyes and ran away after punching him as hard as he could in the stomach. There was no trouble from him after that and the moral of this tale is that it's wise to remove your cap before beginning a fight with a smaller person. It might also be a useful ploy if attacked by a taller person.

The school occupied several acres. On one side, a steep wood sheltered the main building whilst on the other side of the school, there were spacious grounds where rugby, cricket and the annual sports day took place, as well as cubbing and scouting activities. The main school building, about 100 years old, dominated by giant Greek-looking pillars, could have been mistaken for a country house designed for an entrepreneur who had made his money by exploiting colonials before fleecing the locals. Many of the outbuildings were of wooden construction and, lacking heating, were cold, even in the summer. In the winter, changing for physical training, (PT) was a pleasure only for those of a masochistic disposition or those who harboured hopes of attending Public schools. Tim, who never thought about the future and who had no idea of where he was going, never enjoyed changing for any pastime. Indeed, he favoured keeping the same clothes on day and night but, despite making a spirited case was overruled by the matriarchal society in which he lived. Donning daytime clothes in the early morning in winter, when the temperature in the house occasionally induced ice on the inside of the windows, was grim.

Participating in gym 'lessons' in what was a long wooden shed, was unpleasant. Tim could see no reason for hauling himself up a rope, with great difficulty and potential damage to his hands, which he valued highly as he used them in so many different ways, just to examine the roof, which could be seen from the ground. As he complained to his friends, 'I just don't see the point of climbing up a rope and then, even if I do manage it, you've got to come down again and I always hurt my hands. It just seems daft'. The gym master, overhearing the comment, told Tim that he was being silly and that it was important to be fully fit and climbing ropes 'helped in that regard'. The young boy remained silent, in line with his policy when his mother and grandmother made similar remarks. Why was it that every time he asked what he thought was a sensible question, or made a straightforward observation, he was told not to be silly? Was that the best that they could do? If he ever became an adult, which he was beginning to doubt as he had to be in school for so many years, he would never tell children that they were silly.

Even the most detailed scrutiny of the roof revealed little of interest and certainly nothing to justify the expenditure of so much energy. Tim was unable to imagine any circumstances in later life when it might prove useful: this youthful prediction came true and he examined the most ornate of ceilings, especially in National Trust properties, from ground level. It was significant that they made no provision for ropes in their elderly houses. His reluctance to climb a rope had no impact on his life which must be encouraging to all those who have wondered but have been reluctant to admit their problem with rope climbing. Action on the wall bars was even more irrelevant. Possibly, the experience persuaded some to be window cleaners or decorators but why should the majority, who had no intentions of pursuing these occupations have to suffer for the minority? As Tim remarked to a friend, 'if a boy wants to become a coal miner, why should the rest of us be required to dig deep holes twice a week and cover ourselves with soot?' His friend stared at him blankly before revealing that he did not want to become a coal miner.

The worst exercises involved a horse but not the noble equine quadruped which has served man so well in agriculture and in other ways in peace and war. Nor was it those which had assisted in the delivery of many products, including milk, the consumption of which was then compulsory for children. Tim hated milk but bore no grudge towards the horses that brought supplies to the school gate. They were just doing their job. The object of his animosity was the exercise horse over which the boys were supposed to vault. It smelt and some of its stuffing was emerging from the once tough leather skin. The boys were intended to sprint up a short and sloping runway, jump, place their hands on the horse and vault over without sustaining any injury. Tim could not synchronise his action so never cleared the horse correctly. Happily, this had no impact on the rest of his life, so those who share his inability to vault over silly horses, and to climb ropes, can take heart.

The main building at Grafton House was dominated by the central hall where daily early morning prayers were conducted. These included the lusty rendition of a hymn and a psalm, followed by the Lord's Prayer. Then the names of some old boys who had perished in the war were announced. It was difficult for at least one small boy to reconcile the prayers with the announcement of the death of more young and innocent men. School announcements on Thursdays included the names of those miscreants whose allegedly poor work had resulted in their being placed on report. Three adverse comments from teachers over the following week would result in a painful problem for the hapless boy. The assumption was that, unless a pupil was seen to be trying very hard to understand a subject, his ignorance was a wilful act of disobedience that had to be corrected. There was never the slightest recognition of any potential failure on the part of the teacher to stimulate and teach.

The central hall was bounded by a dining hall which always smelt of cabbage, the loathsome headmaster's study, a very large conservatory, a library and stairs to the upper floor. The walls were covered with ornate boards naming those who had achieved academic standing by securing scholarships or exhibitions to Public schools. Others named head boys or those who had excelled at sport. Tim's name was never on any board which reflected his mediocrity and consistency although, as he told himself, he was younger than most of his fellow pupils. Internal access to the central hall, from some of the newer and adjoining buildings, was through the changing rooms and showers units. The latter always smelt of damp wood, which was unsurprising as the wooden trellis-like covering over the tiles was always wet as the showers lacked a clear direction. On the corner of the changing room, the sports master put up notices including the names of those who had been selected to represent the school at rugby or cricket. In vain did Tim wait to see his name.

The tunnel-like but short corridor to the central hall from some of the outer buildings was always dark. Despite this, there was not a single death over nearly five years. That said, of course, past performance was no guarantee that, in the future, young boys might not drop like leaves before a one-in-a-hundred year gale, which now occur every other year. A large allotment, tended mainly by the borders, and devoted to growing essential food, dominated one side of the main building. The sports field stretched for hundreds of yards at the back of the building and was sufficiently spacious to allow three matches to take place simultaneously. Cricket nets were available but there was no coaching. This was the age of intellectual and sporting osmosis: all that had to be done to achieve success or even understanding of anything from cricket techniques to Latin, could be achieved just by concentrating hard and, where relevant, sitting still and remaining silent for hours. Any questions to the teacher implied a failure on their part to explain their subject so only the brave or foolish risked insulting a master or mistress. Indeed, sitting still, remaining silent, memorising material and concentrating occupied many hours during the war years.

'Music' at GH, held twice weekly, bored Tim and his friends who grew to loathe, *inter alia*, *Men of Harlech* and *Camptown Races*, and *On Ilkley Moor bah tat*. The Camptown racetrack was, apparently, five miles long and the central character seems to have successfully wagered a sum on a grey-coloured horse. The song was much favoured by the ladies of the town, some of whom may have expected to be involved in the spending of the winnings. *On Ilkley Moor* (without a hat) is thought to have been a song rendered by a young lady who was concerned that her boy friend, hatless on the moor, might catch a cold with potentially serious consequences. *Men of Harlech* was based on Britain's longest siege, between 1461 and 1468. Another stirringly patriotic song, always lustily rendered, was *Hearts of Oak*, the official march of the Royal Navy, which was first performed in 1759. *Lilliburlero*, believed to date from the 1680's in Ireland and which parodies the Irish belief in prophesy, was also popular. *All things bright and beautiful, the Lord God made them all* was a frequently rendered hymn at morning prayers as were *Onward Christian Soldiers* and *To be a pilgrim. Land of Hope and Glory* was also a frequent visitor and psalm 23 was rendered at least once a week.

Tim had a question for Denis, one of his friends. It was a question that he had posed before, even to adults, but who had never received an answer that was remotely plausible. 'If God is responsible for all things bright and beautiful, who is responsible for everything else?'

Denis stared and, after but a moment's consideration, admitted ignorance. 'What's the answer then?'

Tim merely asked another question.

'As God is so powerful, why does He allow wars to take place?'

His young friend felt obliged to offer something.

'My dad says that there's no God and it's all tommy rot.'

'What's tommy rot? Does it have anything to do with tommy gun?'

'I don't know but my dad knows everything.'

Tim was less confident on the intellectual standing of his friend's father but remained silent.

Boys who were good at sport were favoured: those who lacked talent but who were keen were ignored. Tim participated in but did not enjoy rugby but liked cricket and games on the Preston sea front. Although he scored many runs when playing cricket there, before the Bofors anti-aircraft gun arrived to interrupt his progress, Tim was never given a chance to play cricket even for the house side. Membership of the elite was, like some parts of the school grounds, out of bounds. Perhaps he lacked the little match temperament? Once, in a most unimportant game, involving fellow failures, he was allowed to open the batting for his side and scored a single before the game terminated within minutes of his innings commencing. He conjured up the scorecard:

Adams (T)	not out	1
Bloggs (F)	not out	0
Extras		0
Total (for no wicket)		1

Summer sports at Grafton House were disastrous for Tim. Only in later years did he discover that he was better at running long distances and revelled in keeping going whilst others capitulated to common sense. Such events were not on the menu at GH and he had to struggle with hurdles, 100 yard, 220 yard and 440 yard races and the high and long jumps. The only metre then known in the UK was a gas meter. The boys refrained from throwing things and it was only years later that he discovered that he was no good at the javelin or putting the weight. Simply, he was a failure at rugby, athletics, climbing ropes, vaulting over stuffed horses and cricket unless it was on the sea front. As first class inter-county cricket matches would never take place there, his hopes of becoming a professional cricketer were fading.

The school excelled at rugby and some contemporaries went on to play for Devon but Tim could never summon up the energy or the will to fling himself at a fellow pupil in the mud just because he was carrying an odd-shaped ball, about which he was less than enthusiastic to take for himself. If he enjoyed running past Tim, carrying this strange object, why try to relieve him of it? It was not Tim's and, frankly, his opponent was welcome to it and Tim baulked at the prospect of wrapping himself physically around a fellow male. It all seemed rather rude and pointless which was usually what his team achieved.

Boxing was compulsory at the school. Later, Peter, back from the war, and keen on the sport, wanted his son to learn how to box. He bought Tim a pair of boxing gloves which was not gratefully received. The only pleasure the gloves gave him was their smell and if someone had punched him on the nose with his own gloves, he might well have even have requested a second blow as he so liked the odour, although of course, if he had been struck on the snout, it might have adversely affected his olfactory senses and thus his appreciation of the aroma.

In early 1947, there were explosions in Texas City which killed 377 people, a nationalist uprising against France in Madagascar and the British government decided to partition India. Henry Ford died and Princess Elizabeth married Philip Mountbatten. However, the main event in Tim's young life was the annual boxing competition which saw him matched against one of the best boxers in the school after a very lucky win against a boy who had marginally more pugilistic ability. This opponent was a square-faced, nasty and aggressive little chap, at the best of times, and this was not the best of times. He slipped after one of Tim's feeble efforts to hit him and the underdog anticipated terrible retribution but survived without serious injury. Meanwhile, his modest stock soared as his friends believed that Tim had knocked the leather-faced lout over. It was naively thought, usually by those of a certain age who had grown up with a sense of fair play and observing rules, based on a chap called Queensbury, that boxing was a useful skill if one was attacked. It might have been if the aggressor observed some basic rules but, on the two occasions Tim was attacked in public by some aggressive louts, boxing was as much use as an ability to play canasta, although he did not put this theory to the test, as, when confronted, he did not have any cards with him.

During the war, GH boys used to go out for organised walks occasionally. This was decades before the age of obesity and, as gym lessons were a main feature of the curriculum, presumably such additional exercise was taken so that the teachers were spared the challenge of teaching, on which they were singularly inept. The crocodile of young boys, sometimes hand in hand, long before such behaviour might have aroused comment, used to wend its way around the nearby lanes. Everyone behaved perfectly, of course, but Tim was very peeved when, on one occasion, a sudden check revealed that he was innocently carrying a small maroon penknife, a treasured birthday present. He was required to surrender it and never saw it again. That was but one small example of injustice that he and many thousands of others of similar age were to see in their formative years.

Most of the teaching staff at Grafton House had little idea of how to stimulate young minds. Doubtless they could not recall being young and only understood the grim culture they had experienced themselves, decades before, although it was difficult to imagine that some of them had ever been young. Indeed, the principles of teaching were those that had been laid down in the 19th century. The teachers were too dim to even consider that there must be an alternative to merely forcing children to memorise material. Furthermore, society favoured total control and could not see the benefits of training children to be questioning and inquisitive when total obedience without questioning would be required when they joined the forces or went into paid employment.

Many teachers, old, tired and incompetent, relied on creating fear and forcing parrot-like learning, bereft of understanding, rather than inspiration. Even after the war, although one or two younger men joined the staff, the standard of 'teaching' remained poor. The women 'teachers' were no better than the men and few were qualified. Those who wore gowns probably had created them from some spare blackout material. One looked as if she had given up an unsuccessful career as a wrestler several contests too late and spoke with an incomprehensible Irish accent. Another resembled the before part of a two-part advertisement for improving on the lot that nature had allocated and showed no imagination or desire to teach. Her main feature was her head. Her hair was coiled up high, taller than a chef's hat, which denied her the opportunity of working in a kitchen. The temperature of her topmost hair must have been different to those that occupied a more lowly position and might well have served as a home for some displaced birds.

The 'teachers', full of their own importance, revelled in being dominating and domineering giants in a world of pygmies. They rushed around, feigning urgency, so that their gowns billowed out behind them and one sadist, in particular, endowed with a beak nose and a streamlined head, looked like some bullying bird of prey that had not quite made the evolutionary transition to becoming a human. It was possible to imagine him tucking in to a late night meal of lightly-fried small boy. He was contemptible in every way and lacked any human qualities. The headmaster looked like a well-groomed vole, but few people realised this as their knowledge of voles was sadly lacking. His white hair was always coated in some form of hair oil and any flies intending to land on his shiny bounce would have slid off immediately so his head became a no-fly zone as word circulated in the insect world. His face was lined and his eyes peered out from below bushy eyebrows. He was short and very fat and clearly enjoyed exerting power over his charges and inducing fear. A collective sigh of relief was almost palpable when this head monster, who terrorised pupils on history and geography, went out in his large black and blue Humber. Those were the colours he favoured for some allegedly difficult pupils. However, after Mrs Standing had exchanged views with him, and extracted some financial compensation after he had cruelly attacked her son, he was marginally less brutal.

Despite the teaching staff, the school had a good academic record and made some attempt to interest pupils in the world outside but fear and the requirement to memorise large chunks of history, geography and all the other subjects, off by heart, rather than through understanding, was crucial in this record. 'Teaching' usually consisted of reading text books and then being tested on what the boys were supposed to have read. Few members of the staff accepted even the desirability of explaining topics and stimulating young minds. Many on the GH staff sought to find fault so that punishment could be exacted rather than taking the trouble to find out why a pupil failed to understand a particular lesson. The smug self-satisfied pompous idiot who 'taught' maths was totally incompetent and assumed that those boys who failed to understand his subject, who constituted the majority, were being deliberately hostile. Tim was deeply unhappy but, knowing nothing different, assumed that this was all part of growing up. He considered complaining to Susan but did not as she always was telling him that he was lucky to be at such a fine school. His efforts to disagree were swatted aside.

When the sirens sounded, the entire school marched in an orderly fashion, of course, there was no alternative for such well-drilled and fearful automata, into the cellar. The boys sat on wooden benches in the whitewashed 'rooms' and wondered what was happening outside. One in five schools in the UK was badly damaged during the war but GH was unscathed.

In early 1944, American bombers had begun daylight bombing of Berlin, Rommel had been forced to commit suicide and an allied invasion was expected shortly. In the Easter term, Tim, oblivious of all this, was placed 3rd out of 15 boys in his form, despite being ten months below the average age of his fellow pupils. He was aged seven and three months and was an unimpressive three stone 13 pounds and just four feet and a quarter inch tall. He finished first in Divinity, a good position for someone who subsequently was a life-long agnostic. 'He has taken a keen interest in the stories.' Was this why he joined the Crusaders? This was a Sunday afternoon event in nearby Paignton and was, effectively, a Sunday School. However, the real reason for his patronage was that he liked the badge, which was given after attending ten sessions.

He was also first in English Literature and English Grammar. 'His English both oral and written is excellent.' The same cannot be said for the teacher who does not understand the correct use of commas. Tim's position on Writing was second but 'he must take greater care with his writing'. What, then, of all those who finished lower in the rankings? This was offered by the same woman who did not know about commas, so her comments can be ignored. Tim was second in Reading and first in Nature. 'A little more attention is needed in Gym.' Quite. Just concentrate hard. That's all that was required: an inability to do the necessary co-ordinated leaping around, even after the most dedicated attention, was not even considered. He was ninth in Geography, where his work was 'average' and 10th in History, after a 'disappointing' examination. He was 12th in Drawing which was 'a rather weak subject at present'.

One term later, showing their facility in Arithmetic, the staff noted on Tim's Summer term report that he was four months older, had gained no weight but that his height was a quarter of an inch more. Happily, this rate of growth was not sustained as he would now be over eight feet tall so that any efforts to climb ropes would be unnecessary. Despite being nearly a year younger than the average of the form, Tim managed to maintain his position of being third overall. His position in English Literature and Grammar was sustained but he became first in Reading and soared to number three in History. He was only second in Divinity, although, showing a lack of imagination, the 'teacher' noted that he had a 'very good knowledge of the stories'. Sadly he was last but one in Drawing which made him wonder how bad one wretched fellow pupil must have been. Apparently, his prowess at Gym was 'quite good throughout the term' which suggested he had been mistaken for another boy.

Despite the war, the school contrived to organise an impressive range of available activities. These extra-curricular interests were doubtless very influential in the development of young and impressionable boys when it was so easy to restrict activities because of the war. Debating, on Saturday evenings, was a stimulating aspect of school life and Tim enjoyed listening and was often keen to contribute but desisted for fear that anything he said would be described as silly. Topics, suggested by the pupils, included state control of schools, the suppression of vivisection, which had to be continued, and the 'portioning' of Germany after the war, no, thank you, I'm full and I've really enjoyed what I had. This debate ended prematurely because of an air raid, so the generals and politicians had to decide what to do for themselves and history shows what problems that caused.

Other topics included the release of boys of 14 from school for war work, the superiority of the air for transportation and the disadvantages of explosives, presumably, when they were used by the enemy or when they went off accidentally in the UK. On balance, it was thought that the discovery of explosives was more of an advantage to mankind than a curse. Was electricity better than coal for domestic purposes? Yes, it was but did anyone mention that coal or, indeed, any other primary fuel, was necessary to produce electricity? Despite a spirited performance by the teachers, the motion that manual workers were needed more than teachers was carried. Perhaps the boys had shrewdly decided that some of their 'teachers' were best suited to mentally undemanding jobs. Tim did not doubt that the verdict was correct. Ships were preferred to aircraft and the boys also discussed whether the wireless had rendered newspapers unnecessary and whether road transport was better than rail. Unsurprisingly, it was agreed that the school leaving age should be reduced to 12 and the minimum age at which youths could be called for military service be raised to 20.

There was a Scouts' troop and a Wolf Cub pack, run by the teachers, who, although failing to stimulate the pupils during lessons, nevertheless devoted themselves enthusiastically to these activities. In 1944, Tim and some of his friends received their First Stars and were rewarded by having a trip to Shorton Woods where they played games and cooked their own teas. One Saturday afternoon, the wolf cubs, charged with imagining that they were newspaper reporters, walked to Paignton Sea Front to conjure up an article. Tim had no knowledge of the teams playing football, the individuals or even the score but, nevertheless, 'filed' an imaginative report which suggested that, one day, he could become a successful tabloid journalist.

He and his friends spent much of their spare time collecting for various wartime charities and the school Savings Group and were particularly successful during the Torquay Warship Week between 7th and 14th March 1942. Admission to the school sports day, in 1943, was granted only to those who bought a savings certificate. £92 was collected. The target for the current year was set at £2,000 as the school had raised £1,800 in the previous year. In Salute the Soldier Week in 1944, the school raised nearly £3,500. (To achieve the same spending power today would require well over £100,000.)

Tim did not relish the annual sports day. He came last in all the sports for which he was entered, compulsorily. Nevertheless, he was cheered on by Susan in a female-dominated crowd. Because of wartime restrictions, the competitors wore an interesting but diversified range of clothing and there were no medals or prizes. The headmaster merely gave the successful children certificates which could be exchanged for medals after the war.

As the end of the war approached, the school mounted a series of talks on different occupations, although it would be many years before the boys entered employment or even had to decide which subject to study before leaving full-time education. Over some weeks, the boys heard presentations on what it meant to be a chemist, doctor or dentist. Tim was not planning to be involved in any of these presentations and still harboured doubts on whether he would ever become an adult, let alone a professional. Despite the activities in the gymnasium, there was no talk on how to become a window cleaner.

The boys staged plays and concerts but managed well without Tim but he, with the rest of the school, saw films, played at the school, in November 1944. The programme included *A voyage across the Sahara*, *How to play golf* and the ever-popular Charlie Chaplin. The entire school visited the Pavilion Torquay to see *Where the rainbow ends*.

The headmaster, a pompous, self-important, pedantic and verbose writer, even judged by the grotesque and extravagant standards of the day, always made a speech at the end of each term. It was Christmas 1943 and the boys were gathered in the cold central hall, awaiting his profound thoughts. As he approached, Tim and his friends fell silent.

'You boys may not know it but Herr Himmler, of whom you have heard.' At this point, some brave boys expressed feigned ignorance but the headmaster, who, fortunately had not seen their facial expressions, continued. 'says that anyone who is not jolly and bright is an imbecile'. Some boys, implying that Tim was rarely jolly, turned towards him and nodded like ignorant donkeys. 'Mr Himmler intends to reinforce his "apophthegm" with punishment for those who fail to look happy'.

How the pupils must have rejoiced at the use of the word 'apophthegm'! Doubtless, the head monster had noted that the pupils used this word in the playground when they wanted just one word to convey a short clever saying which expresses a general truth. Arguably, the bully, that's the headmaster, not Himmler, although, he too, was a bully, had used the wrong word.

'We Graftonites have no need to be threatened with punishment if we're not happy, because we're always happy here.' An astute observer might have commented that many of the boys were deeply unhappy because they were frequently and unfairly punished. 'We've every cause to be cheerful when we review our activities over the last few months. We've won most of our rugby matches, our academic record is the best in the area and we've more pupils than ever before. As well as that we can now look forward to what we must hope will be the year when the allies mount a long-awaited invasion against the brutal enemy. The allies have occupied Palermo and German Field Marshall Paulus surrendered at Stalingrad and Italy, having decided that it had been wrong to support Germany, like the Soviet Union, has declared war on its former ally.

'However, it would be remiss of me and totally unacceptable, if I did not mention that no less than 150 old boys are now serving in the war. Sadly, I must tell you that some have made the ultimate sacrifice.' Here he read out a list of names and Tim shuddered. If this war lasted much longer, his name might be read out.

'Some of you will be moving on to Public Schools and we all wish you well. Here you are the bloods but you will soon be microbes.' Tim and the gang, having heard this comment and, having an approximate idea of what a microbe was, pondered requesting an explanation but this would have been interpreted as a major and punishable offence, so remained silent. Soon the headmaster had finished and dismissed the actual bloods and potential microbes, expressing the hope that they would all have an enjoyable Christmas and would return in the new year, refreshed and keen for another term's successful work and that the new year would bring peace to a deeply troubled world.

When would the boys turn into microbes? Later, Edward had looked up what this strange word meant and he reported back at the gang's next meeting. He read from a very fat book which said that 'microbes are microscopic organisms which could be a disease-causing bacterium'. He had asked his grandfather who assured him that he would become a man, not a microbe and that whoever had said he would become a microbe was a fool. On hearing that it was the head monster, he smiled, nodded and said 'I might have guessed. He's an idiot and he wears brown shoes with a dark suit'.

At the end of the Christmas term in 1944, the headmaster, noting that the invasion had taken place and that the end of the war was in sight, confirmed that another 25 old boys had lost their lives in the war so, sadly, their families would not be able to welcome them home when victory was achieved. Tim was not alone in thinking that this was an odd comment. Moving on to more local ground, the headmaster noted that the life of the school, which had not been seriously disrupted, was beginning to return to normal but 'we mourn the loss of another of our pupils, killed in a road accident by an American lorry'.

Peace returned but there was no spare time for hobbies, as the boys attended school for six days a week. Bullying was rampant: the boys who were bigger than their younger colleagues imitated the teachers who took pleasure in bullying their pupils. A few years after the end of the war, the school closed and was demolished and the miserable memories of Tim and hundreds of other boys were obliterated.

Peter's War

Peter was doing his best to keep sane in the POW camp but there was so much to upset him that he wondered if he would be normal after the war, whatever normal was. He did not feel normal now: it was unnatural for innocent adult humans to be caged like dangerous animals. What would the world be like when the fighting stopped? He was living, no existing, with hundreds of men whose life, culture and, indeed, habits of hygiene were so different from his own. Everything, absolutely everything, was done in the sight of others and it was a sustained struggle to avoid descending into depravity.

He and Alf, a marine engineer who was about the same age, had developed a strong friendship over the years of incarceration and, as both originated from the north of England, a bond had been established. This enabled each of them to give voice to whatever angered them at a particular time which was important as it meant that frustrations would not be allowed to fester and grow, and worries could be shared. Surrounded by deprivation, consumed by worry about their families and fearful that they might never again taste freedom, many of their conversations inevitably, were repeated frequently. There was not much that was new to either man but repeating previous thoughts was almost like sharing worries and each tolerated the repetition as it helped to release key emotions.

Alf, like Peter, had been captured in the Atlantic but whilst Peter and his crew had been taken on board their captor's vessel, his friend's colleagues had been less fortunate. As their ship sank, the Germans had machined-gunned them in their lifeboats. Alf and several of his mates had avoided detection and had spent several days on a raft before an enemy vessel rescued him and just one of his friends. The other five had died during the ordeal. Understandably, Alf had total contempt for the Germans and, now, if he could help a fellow prisoner cope with the misery that hung over the camp, it was a small way of retaliating.

Peter felt particularly low. A few days ago, the Germans had shot one of his friends, in cold blood, and then had the effrontery to attend his funeral, join in the prayers and say that it was an accident. It had taken all Peter's resolve not to attack his tormentors and, as he observed to others attending the service, it was difficult to believe that they were, allegedly, human beings. Somehow, that incident was a harrowing summary of what war was about. The innocent suffered and the guilty triumphed. Where was God and why did He allow all this? Peter had been a believer but his faith was being challenged daily.

Now, today, it was Peter's wedding anniversary and this kindled memories of the happiest day of his life. Ironically, it also reminded him, so poignantly, of what he was now missing. His own childhood had been unpleasant and dominated by his cruel mother. His apprenticeship had proved harsh, with little humanity or understanding being conveyed to him and his young colleagues. Then, when the family life he had craved for decades became possible, he was captured and was now unsure if he would ever see his wife and sons again. This review of his life took him close to tears and he found a solitary area, some distance from the barracks, sat down on the dusty ground, fumbled for a handkerchief, bent his head forwards between his knees and cried.

After some minutes, he began to regain control and his weeping gave way to powerful sobs. There were hundreds of men in the camp and, fortuitously, it was Alf who found Peter. 'Are you in pain or do you feel ill?' Peter shook his head. Alf, sensitive and intelligent, sensed that Peter, whom he knew as a kindly and caring man, had been overcome by a tidal wave of anger, worry, fear and frustration. He had himself succumbed to such attacks occasionally and knew that talking was the only way to ease the immediate pain.

'Tell me what's upsetting you.'

Peter was grateful to be able to speak candidly to his friend. They had long since exchanged confidences and both men knew that there was little new that they could discuss but talking always seemed helpful. 'It's my wedding anniversary today and that day, the happiest of my life, brought back so many memories. It just made me profoundly unhappy as I know that I may never see Susan again. That led me to think about my life and, without being too self-centred, I realised, not for the first time, what a rotten life I've had. Here I am, in my forties, and, apart from periods of leave during my few years of marriage, the only happiness I've had was when I was a Boy Scout. My parents ignored me, apart from making me work and run errands and, do you know, when I was taken on as an apprentice, they couldn't even be bothered to visit me, just a short bus ride away from my ship.'

Aware that he was on the verge of a long speech, he asked his friend if he had the time to listen. Alf looked at his watch, grinned and said that he was not going anywhere soon as far as he knew. Peter wiped away a tear, smiled and thanked him.

'I know that millions of other children had an unhappy childhood. My brother was the favourite and it was always me that had to do the household chores. My parents never took me anywhere but they always seemed to have time for my brother.' Hearing himself, Peter paused and apologised for this opening and self-pitying salvo but said it was true.

'Carry on.'

'As I just said, they did not even see my ship when that rotten company offered me an apprenticeship for a miserable £10 per year. Three of the ships I was on during the Great War were mined, torpedoed and involved in a collision, when I had to jump for my life. By the time that the war was over, I was still only 17 but I cannot forget what millions of young men, just like me had to face during the war. At least I was alive. What a waste of life and for what? The war to end all wars. Bloody rubbish.'

Alf had heard all this before, but wanted to help his friend by just listening.

'Don't misunderstand me. As I just said, I know that other boys of my age suffered and, of course, many lost their lives in that awful war but all I remember from my apprenticeship is hardship, poverty, exploitation, constant danger and a total lack of consideration from the shipowner and from most of the captains and officers who I served under. Admittedly, it was wartime but, surely, somewhere, there should have been some kindness and just a glimmer of a happy, carefree youth? After an unhappy childhood and a difficult time as an apprentice, I was beginning to feel that life was going to pass me by but then there was a miracle. I met Susan, who was to become my wife. My world changed so radically that each day, when I woke up, at home or at sea, I had to persuade myself that I had not imagined it all. Then, in 1936, I had a son. I had always dreamed of being part of a family and now, at last, it seemed that my prayers had been answered. Despite my pleas, my employers put me on vessels that never reached the UK so I did not see my son for three years and then Hitler intervened. My second son was born in 1940 and I still haven't seen him and there are times when I wonder, as we all do, whether we'll ever see our families again.'

He choked back the tears again and Alf took advantage of the pause to ask if his friend had received any news that had made him so depressed.

'No, as I said, it's just that today is my wedding anniversary and although it was the best day of my life, it also reminds me of my cruel and greedy mother who did her best to undermine the marriage. I never knew why and I shall never find out now as she died last year. I shall never be able to tell her how much I hated her and still do. That makes me very irate.

'Once all these memories come flooding back, they make me realise how angry and impotent I feel, cooped up here like a wild animal. What really upsets me and, you too, I'm sure, is that we can't do anything to support our brave boys and that makes me feel very guilty. I also feel guilty when I think of the thousands who've given up their lives and I've done nothing.'

Alf said he felt the same way and added a thought of his own. 'Yes, and assuming that our men sort out these thugs one day, just think of the casualties that they'll experience just fighting their way here to liberate us.'

Peter mentioned that, in the last few days, he had learned of the deaths of some more of his old colleagues. Both men fell silent, feeling guilty although they knew there was nothing they could do except score a few verbal points off their captors.

Peter was already beginning to feel better for being able to articulate his thoughts but there was more he wished to say. 'Marrying Susan was the best thing that ever happened to me and now, stuck in this place, I wonder if my happiness has gone for ever.'

Alf was sure that he and Susan would be reunited and happy before too long.

'Yes, that's what I hope and pray for but it'll all be so different. When I was last at home, I had a small son. Now I have a young boy and my other son, whom I've never seen, isn't an infant any more. How will they react to me? What if they don't like me and will Susan's love be divided between all of us? Will she still care for me as she did when we had no children? Then, think of my life in recent years and what I have experienced. I'm frightened that I've become a very different person and my biggest fear is that Susan will not even like the new me, let alone love me. I know that I've become much harder and, in some ways a worse person. I worry that, having been with adult males for so long, I shan't adjust to living with my wife and mother-in-law and two small boys who might resent me and see me as a stranger and an intruder.

'I don't know how to react to two children. I've been accustomed, as a captain, to having my orders obeyed. I'm sure that my two boys won't like that and, if I ever get out of this place, I'll have to be very tactful. I just hope that I can manage it. I had a rotten upbringing and I am desperate that my own sons have a much better beginning in life. That must include their education and I don't know if I'll be able to afford to send them to a decent school. In fact, I worry now about money but it seems that Susan is managing. God knows how. I've always worried about money and I don't suppose that'll ever change.'

At this point, Peter seemed much calmer. Alf made a few positive and encouraging comments, put his arm around his friend's shoulder and suggested that they should prepare for, as he put it, another dinner at their own Savoy. Peter smiled, his worries temporally dormant but aware that his fears were real. Only time would tell what might happen. His life was in others' hands.

Peter Returns

Tim wanted to know what was happening. He knew that victory in Europe would be declared officially on 8th May and that, at 3.00, Winston Churchill would confirm that the war was over. The king was due to speak on the wireless later that evening.

'Please can I listen?'

'Of course, it's going to be part of history.'

Tim's life was changing fast. Peace, whatever that was, was imminent and his father, a prisoner of war in Germany for four long and harrowing years, would soon be back in England. Before then, Tim was to attend a party in Torquay. He had only been to one or two but had not enjoyed them. He was unsure about girls, of whom he knew nothing but they seemed rather different, which flummoxed him, the games, which seemed pointless, and the bossy women who always seemed to be in charge. Everywhere he went, females told him what to do and what not to do. What was worse, everyone always seemed to be enjoying themselves, judging by the shouting and laugher, and all this pushed Tim, a natural introvert, further back into his shell.

Susan met him at the hotel, to take him home and dutifully asked him if he had enjoyed the party.

'No, not really.'

Susan tried another approach.

'What did you have to eat?'

Tim was more expansive on this and admitted that he had enjoyed the sandwiches, cake and jelly and cream. Feeling that he ought to add a little more as his mother had generously organised his attendance, he volunteered that the magician was 'very funny but he was a thief'.

'A thief, how was that?'

'Well, he put his hand behind a girl's ear, found a half crown and put it in his pocket. I mean the half crown, not her ear.'

'Why does that make him a thief?'

'Well, it's obvious that she was keeping it there and he had no right to take it from her.'

'No, dear, it was his and he put it there and he was clever because nobody saw him. It was definitely his. Do you know anybody who keeps their pocket money behind their ears? It would fall off.'

Tim was tempted to comment on the availability of glue and the absence of regular pocket money so was ignorant on where he might keep it if he had any, but continued with his summary of the party. 'I asked him to see if he could find a threepenny bit behind my ear but he just laughed. Anyway, what happened later was really funny.'

Susan, required to ask for information, duly obliged.

'Well, he produced a pigeon, a real pigeon, out of an empty box and it flew around.'

'That's not funny. That's what pigeons do.'

'Yes, I know that, but made a nasty mess on his top hat and he was very cross and, as we laughed he got even more cross as he couldn't catch it. It was like watching a dive bomber.'

Tim knew that he would be meeting his father in just a few days time and was worried and excited. What sort of man was he? Would he be friendly or would his stay in a prisoner of war camp have made him bitter? Would he like his son? What if they could not be friends? It would be a long time before he was grown up. Some of his friends hated their fathers, who had already returned from the war and shouted at them. Even some of the mothers, who used to be kind and gentle, were now hard and strict and one of his best friends was now ignored by both parents. What would happen when Peter returned? Tim was tired of being bossed around at home and at school, mainly by females. He resolved to do all he could to ensure that his new father would not dominate him. If necessary, he would just ignore him.

As he plied his mother with questions, he noticed that she seemed nervous. Tim did not realise that six long and challenging years had passed since she had seen her husband. Even if he had, six years was a meaningless term to him as it represented about three quarters of his life.

Tim's efforts to find out more about his father were not entirely satisfactory. Susan said that he was kind, gentle and generous and that he really loved them all and had missed his family more than he could ever tell. 'In all his postcards to you and to me, he's always said that he's looking forward to seeing you again and playing with you. He's very keen on cricket, so I'm sure he'll take you to matches. That'll be fun, won't it?'

Tim recalled that his mother's definition of fun never coincided with his. Some of his friends' fathers, who had been too old to be involved with the war, were austere, strict and rarely smiled. They were as devoid of personality as a wet sponge whilst lacking its mobility. They were the sort of people who could easily have been substituted successfully for waxworks at an exhibition and if Tim had known about human reproduction, he might have observed that it was difficult to imagine that they had ever found the passion which gave them a family. In fact, the more he thought about it, the more depressed he became. It seemed that all fathers were strict and, if they had been in the war, they disliked their children. He vowed afresh, that, if necessary, he would keep his father at a distance.

'Is he tall?'

'No, he's not very tall but he's dark and handsome, just like you.'

'Is he fat?'

Susan knew that the sustained lack of food in the camp meant that he was not fat. The last photo she had received, some months before, had revealed that he was gaunt but whilst she wanted her son to know the truth, she did not want to frighten him.

'He was never fat, dear, but we must remember that, like us, he's not had much food whilst he was a prisoner. I expect he's quite thin but he'll soon put on weight. Do you know, I read the other day, that the Red Cross sent 90,000 food parcels a week to our prisoners in Germany but, of course, when we started bombing parts of Germany, it was more difficult for the POWS to receive the parcels. Without those parcels, daddy would have been even more hungry.'

Even although Peter had never seen Harry and Tim seemed keen to accompany her, Susan had decided that she must be alone when she met Peter. She had not seen him for six years and wanted to be alone with him for what was likely to be a difficult and very emotional meeting. Anyway, it would be too late for the young boy and the train was bound to be late. She knew that the war had made her into a different person and, she argued to herself, as she had changed, how might being a prisoner for four years, starved and deprived of freedom, have altered her husband? She tried to guess but soon gave up but she was as nervous as she had been on that day, many years ago, when, as a teenager, she had met Peter at Kings Cross. Now they were to meet at Paignton station.

Her elderly taxi moved sedately along the streets which were crowded with people, keen to be outside in the early warm evening and determined to celebrate victory. The shops, with little for sale, were dominated by welcome home signs, union jacks and bunting. Some went further and indicated their owners' hatred of the Germans and celebrated 'our glorious victory'. Other posters reminded the passers-by "Never forget those who gave everything so that we could live". Everywhere there were union jacks, fluttering from flag poles, dangling from lampposts, telegraph poles and quivering in the modest breeze from windows on the upper floors of offices, homes and shops. It was as if everywhere had been painted red, white and blue.

As she stood on the station platform, in the warm May evening, she shivered with excitement and fear. They were husband and wife but they had become different people. He had seen brutality, had confronted the possibility of death and the reality of starvation and been denied freedom. She had brought up two boys, coping with a lack of food and doing her best to shield her children from the

125

impact of war. She had remained loyal but, not for the first time, she wondered if it would be possible to rebuild her marriage. Was it possible to fall in love again with a man who must have changed so much? When they were last together, they had just one infant. Now the infant was a small boy, aged nearly nine, and his brother was five. What difference would this make to her own relationship and how would the new Peter react to having two sons neither of whom he really knew?

The authorities had told Great Western Railway officials that this train was carrying many former prisoners and military personnel so the small station was decorated for the occasion. The woodwork had been cleaned and the elderly officials, most of whom had served in the First World War, had tidied the station. The two platforms had been decorated with Union Jack flags and bunting and a large sign said, simply, WELCOME HOME AND THANK YOU.

The station was crowded as anxious relatives awaited the return of their men from the war yet there was near silence. The occasion was too important for words and the only sounds came from the rustling flags and a few children who were playing on the pavement outside the station or on the platform. Several were standing on the bridge so that they had an early view of the train which would come into the station from the left. All adult eyes were focused on the track beyond the level crossing just outside the station. An announcement on the crackling loudspeaker system said that the train would be five minutes late. Susan, whose heart was thumping, growled inwardly and then smiled to herself. What, after a wait of six years, was five minutes?

Clouds had gathered over the town but now the sun was fighting back and a strong beam illuminated the track as if determined to emphasise the significance of the moment. The five minutes rushed past and the sun broke through, just on time. There was a warning message and then a clanging noise as the level crossing gates closed and the few buses and cars came to a halt. The crowds on the platform and on the adjacent pavement turned to look up the track. The wind was blowing the steam from the approaching train in the direction of the station and the familiar but unpleasant smell which reminded her of other reunions, was the most welcome that Susan had ever experienced. Hissing, chuntering and clattering, the train that was bringing her husband back into the real world and to her, something that, in her darkest moments she thought might never happen, was coming ever closer. The crowd swayed to the left, anxious to have an early glimpse of the advancing train. As it slowed, hissing furiously, as if reluctant to admit that its role was over, and then halted, there was a spontaneous cheer, followed by a rush to greet the passengers many of whom had returned from hell. Susan was sobbing quietly. The moment was one for which she had prayed for so many years and now it had arrived. She was overcome and she was not alone.

She looked up and down the long platform. There were hundreds of men, some hobbling because of their injuries, propped up by colleagues, some in uniform and others in ill-fitting demob suits. She could not see him. Where was he? Surely, he hadn't missed the train? Then she saw a familiar but very slim figure, as dapper as possible in bulky demob clothes, at the other end of the platform. Was it British to run to greet each other? After a moment's delay, as if neither could understand the new reality, both ran to each other and Peter dropped his small suitcase in his anxiety to greet his wife. They hugged, much in the manner of two old friends, rather than man and wife, and kissed gently. There was no immediate conversation, just cries of 'oh my god' before emotion ended any intended sentence prematurely. There were no words that were adequate and other couples up and down the platform, were similarly silenced by emotion. The only noise came from the few squealing children on the platform who seemed more interested in the engine than in its passengers, at least until their brothers, uncles and fathers emerged from the crowd.

After a few moments, with both struggling and failing to hold back the tears and unable to speak, the newly-united couple asked each other, awkwardly how the other was. Both responded that they were well but Peter thought that Susan looked thin and wan and she thought that Peter looked emaciated and haggard. The conversation was stilted and limited but, after a few minutes, Peter asked why his sons were not there to meet him.

Susan smiled.

'It's past Harry's bedtime and I thought that it was best that you met Tim in less emotional circumstances.' She grinned again and found it difficult not to keep smiling. This was a scene she had played over and over in her mind, especially during the six long months when she did not know if Peter was alive or dead. 'Anyway, I wanted to meet you by myself. Sorry if I'm selfish.' Peter smiled and nodded understanding. Susan then took his hand and led him out of the station to a waiting taxi. Mr Hawke, the elderly driver, had been engaged to meet many returning military personnel. Susan had told him that Peter had been a prisoner, after being captured in the Atlantic, when master of an oil tanker. Taking the retrieved case, he shook Peter by the hand and said 'Welcome home, sir, very glad to see you back'.

Peter looked back towards the station and was not surprised to see that the platform was almost as crowded as when the train groaned to a halt some minutes before. Few passengers had left. They were too busy becoming reacquainted with relatives and friends. They had begun a process that could take months, and, which, in some cases, would never be concluded satisfactorily.

The short journey home from the station was punctuated only by sporadic and failed efforts to say something sensible that matched the occasion. Peter's first wish, after greeting Ann, who was waiting in the front garden, was to embrace his elder son. Tim, standing silently by the side of his grandmother, was very confused. He and this rather austere man were strangers and he did not know what his own future would be. He was pushed forward. Tim had been rehearsed to say 'hello, daddy, it's good to see you, how are you?' but was overwhelmed, forgot his line and remained mute, squirming and uncomfortable. Peter was too choked to say anything profound and, suppressing his emotions, struggled to say 'hello my boy, it's great to see you again. It's six years since we last met and I must say you've grown a lot.' Both smiled at this trite observation and Peter took Tim in his arms and hugged him tightly. He would not let him go for some moments and the boy, totally unaccustomed to such parental intimacy, tactfully made no effort to escape. He might have been young but he was beginning to have an idea of what separation from his family must have meant to his father.

'Now I'm home again, there's so much I want to hear about you and we must play cricket together and go for walks and you can be my guide and you can tell me all about school.' More seemingly inconsequential but simple chat followed but Tim thought he understood, partly because he had been given advice, in advance, by both Susan and, more particularly, by his grandmother.

'Now I must see my other son.'

Susan said that he was asleep but, providing he did not make a single sound, he could peep into the room. Peter obeyed dutifully but retreated swiftly as he burst into tears. At last, denied a family life when young by poverty and then by his life at sea and subsequent imprisonment, he was about to have something which he wanted more than anything else and for which he had yearned for many years but feared that he would never experience.

Tim's mind was in turmoil. Some of his friends had told him that they had been ignored by their returning fathers as their parents tried to get to know each other again. Would it be different for him? How would he get on with this new father? How would his relationship with his mother change, especially if her main concern was to rebuild a relationship with Peter? Ann had warned him that he must not feel neglected as it was important that his mother and father got to know each other again and that could take some time so he must be a good boy and not become upset or angry. Tim was already feeling overlooked as Harry was his mother's clear favourite and now it seemed that the little attention he had received might vanish. He knew he had to be self-reliant and try to ignore being ignored as his parents became re-acquainted, as Ann had said. He tried to understand but was hurt by what Ann had told him and frightened at the likely consequences. Was he not part of the family and what about his relationship with his father, whom he had not seen for virtually all his life? Would his father ignore him or boss him around? Couldn't he try to get to know him? Could adults only work on one relationship at a time? He decided, at least for the present, to be very quiet and acquiescent but, if he was bossed around by this stranger, he would fight back. He had had enough of always being told what to do.

There were so many questions for a confused boy of eight and no answers. Apart from his relationship with his mother and his new father, he still wanted to know what peace was like. What would be on the wireless and in the newspapers? Susan had shielded her children from the news very successfully. There would be no barrage balloons, which had fascinated him since 1941, no air raid sirens and no houses being demolished and the people living there killed. He had heard on the wireless that more than three million properties, mostly homes, were destroyed during the war. Hopefully, there would be more food and less dried egg, which always made him feel ill, and more cars on the roads.

As Susan and Peter grew together again, it was clear that Peter did not wish to tell her, despite her entreaties, about how he had been captured in the Atlantic and taken into a prisoner of war camp. 'Please understand, I don't want to re-live it. One day, I promise, I'll tell you everything but not just now.'

'Well, tell me about your journey home.'

Peter smiled.

'Yes, that's the good part. On 10th May, we were flown from our base in Germany to Brussels in a Dakota. As you know, it was the first time I'd ever flown and it was really exciting, especially as, at last, I was coming home. The plane took off so quickly that some of us were still trying to find somewhere to sit. The RAF pilot took us over the recent battlefield and we saw the destruction on the banks of the Rhine. We had little idea of what our brave crews had done to hasten the end of the war and everywhere I looked there was rubble. It was hard to believe that, not so long ago, there were towns and cities where people, like us, lived. I'm sure that many of them didn't want war but Hitler and his thugs intimidated them. I couldn't help feeling sorry for the men and women who had lived in some of the large cities that had been flattened and I thought of what had happened to our own people.

'Then, when we landed in Belgium, we were told that we'd missed the last plane back to the UK. That was very depressing and after so long out of the country, one more day shouldn't have mattered but it did. We were going home and I felt ashamed of being so selfish. I'd been spared. Millions of others, ordinary men and women, who had left home years before would never see their families again. I felt very humbled, privileged and guilty and I still feel guilty. Why had I been spared? So many of my colleagues were killed at sea and have no monument except their rusting ships.

'The following day we took off in a Lancaster bomber for home. We sat in two long rows, facing each other, and I tried to think what it must have been like, being over enemy territory, being fired at by guns on the ground and in the air and then being hit. What a strain it must have been for the crews. I don't know how they managed it, day after day, knowing that the more raids they flew, the greater the chance that they would be shot down. It must have been awful for them when they heard that some of their friends would not be returning, having been shot down over Germany or over the sea and then, perhaps later in the same day, having to take off again as if nothing had happened. We must never forget what those amazing men did for us. I know I would have preferred to be on a tanker loaded with crude oil.

'We landed smoothly at Dunsfold, a little air strip in Surrey, and my heart was beating so fast I was surprised that my shirt was not moving up and down. It was the moment that I had wanted for years and I must admit that there were many times when I feared it would never come.'

Peter wiped away a tear and, after a brief struggle, continued.

'I could hardly believe it. Now I was nearly home and I wasn't the only one struggling to keep back the tears. As we left the plane, another one was preparing to land and disembark its cargo of former POWs. The planes were coming in so fast after each other, it was like watching buses in the West End of London. I asked an official about this and he told me that by the time that the operation was completed, 45,000 returning POWS would have landed at Dunsfold. Somehow, it seemed a very English and appropriate place to be where we first stepped on to home soil after so long.

'One of the signs on a hanger said simply WELCOME HOME. We were then deloused and moved to a large hanger where we were given real tea, with milk and sugar by kindly and attractive WRAF personnel. What a treat that was after years of foul ersatz drinks! We also had swiss roll and other cakes, for the first time for years, and sandwiches. I could hardly believe my eyes. I know that some of our boys, who were in worse camps than mine, had some trouble adjusting to good food again.

'We were all badly dressed and emotional as we waited for lorries to take us to our reception camps but all that mattered was that we were in England again. Our lorry took 14 of us to a country house near Chalfont St. Giles, where we were to spend the night but the journey took longer than it should have done as the driver lost his way and all the signs had been taken away. As we drove through Surrey into Berkshire and then Buckinghamshire, it seemed that the fates had decided to give us a memorable homecoming. I couldn't help comparing it to the scenes of total devastation that I had seen, just a few hours before, as we flew over Germany. Was this really part of the same world? Thank God, this region seemed to have been spared although, of course, I know how so many of our cities had suffered cruelly.

'The sky was blue, it sounds as if I'm about too burst into song, doesn't it, but I'm not, the sun was warm and the countryside truly beautiful. The neat fields, confined by low stone walls, seemed unbelievably green as nature came back to life after sleeping through the winter. It was as if some film producer had conjured up the ideal weather and backcloth for our return. I remember thinking that we had all been deprived of colour when we were in the camp. All that we had known for years was khaki, dark blue, grey or black. Of course, the sky was blue sometimes but our lives were drab in so many different ways and there was so little to cheer us up, especially when we thought about the slaughter going on all around us.

'We passed through typically English small towns and villages and saw some thatched cottages, narrow cobbled streets, ancient churches and village squares, the small gardens with their trim privet hedges and a profusion of colourful flowers and shrubs. It was like looking at a series of colourful postcards. So many scenes reminded me of happy pre-war days with you. Smiling people waved at us as we passed and some even cheered. They knew that we were going home and were happy for us but I couldn't help thinking of the millions who would never go home. I'll never forget them nor their families in their grief, now as we rejoice.

'We skirted around Windsor and the castle, dominating the landscape, looked marvellous in the distance. Somehow, it was so British that it confirmed that we were home. We reached our destination in early evening and had a short speech of welcome in which Lord somebody or other explained briefly why the allies hadn't been able to arrange more repatriations with the huns. Then we were given drinks and a meal and allocated to individual rooms. I went to sleep in a bedroom that I had all to myself! For many years I'd slept in cramped, cold and unpleasant quarters with many other men, who practised varying levels of hygiene, and now I had a room of my own. I was so excited that it was difficult to sleep and I kept telling myself that, in the next 24 hours, I would be seeing you again. I even repeated it out loud as if somehow, that confirmed my wish and that I wasn't dreaming.

'The following morning, I tried to ring you but couldn't get through so I phoned Rosemary who then called you. After a medical exam, we were given some more clothing, most of which did not fit very well, but this didn't seem to matter, especially when someone gave me some safety pins for my trousers, which were much too long, as you must have noticed when we met at the station. We were also given a small suitcase as well as some money, so we could buy a cup of tea on the way home, a ration card, an identity card and a rail ticket to home. Rosemary met me and thoughtfully brought some spam sandwiches and an orange. What a luxury! I'd almost forgotten what an orange looked like. I don't know where she got it or how she persuaded a friend to drive her to the station, using up so much scarce petrol.

'Then it was on the train to Paignton. Most of the people in the compartment were in uniform, but nobody spoke: we were all immersed in our private thoughts. I just sat silently, staring at the countryside as it flashed past, trying to absorb what was happening to me. Watching the scenery reminded me of being taken in a wagon, with 30 others, through Vichy France and then on to Germany but this time I wasn't going into a POW camp. I was on my way home, my beloved wife and sons. It was like a dream and I was afraid that I was suddenly going to be woken up by a guttural German command.'

In the next few weeks, as Peter and Susan began the task of repairing and renewing their marriage, the relationship between Tim and his father did not develop satisfactorily, partly because Tim felt unwanted so implemented his policy of virtually ignoring his father. He had learned to cope with his brother being given favourable treatment but he was now number three in the queue for his mother's affections and he began to retreat inwardly which was construed as arrogance. He certainly conveyed a sense of superiority which was his way of retaining some self-respect.

'Why does that boy always misbehave? Susan assured her husband that Tim, on the whole, was well behaved but was struggling to accept that, for effectively the first time in his life, there was a man in the house and that he might feel neglected as they tried to rebuild their relationship. 'Please try to be lenient with him.' Furthermore, she suggested, being tactful, that if Tim had some understanding of Peter's background and some of his wartime experience, he would doubtless be more sympathetic and less argumentative but he was not prepared to discuss any aspect of his own life.

'It was too unpleasant for me to re-live it now.'

Peter, knowing that Tim's life was so much more comfortable than that which he had endured, felt that his son should show more respect and gratitude for having parents who looked after him. All this perplexed the young boy who did not know what to do or say and who had assumed that most parents looked after and loved their children. Consequently, to Susan's chagrin, there was frequent shouting as her husband tried to treat her son as a young and disobedient apprentice. Like Tim, she did not know what sin he had committed, apart from seeming aloof, and he, inevitably, became sullen, unhappy, silent and more introvert. Occasionally, he argued, sensing that unless he defended himself, matters might only deteriorate further but eventually he resumed his policy of silence.

'You must remember, Peter, that he's only a small and nervous young boy who hasn't had a father for virtually the whole of his life and he doesn't know what you want from him. He's confused and I think that you really ought to have a quiet chat with him.' Such advice was ignored and a very sympathetic Ann tried to explain to Tim that Peter needed time to adjust to not just freedom but to his family and, especially to Susan. 'You must realise, Tim, that they've become different people because of the war and daddy has been a prisoner for four long years. He doesn't understand small boys.'

'Yes, I can understand that but why is he always shouting at me and bossing me around? He obviously hates me but I tried to help Mama during the war, especially when I heard that daddy might be dead.'

'How did you ever know that he was missing for so long?'

'I overheard her crying one night and saw you trying to comfort her.'

Ann, impressed that he had kept the secret to himself, felt great affection for her grandson and put a friendly arm around him. She knew that Susan rarely showed him any physical assurance and felt genuinely sorry for Tim and told him that he had been a very brave and thoughtful boy. 'I'm sure that it will soon be all right and that you and daddy will be great friends but it'll take time. He really doesn't hate you: he loves you and you'll have to be a very good boy and wait until daddy has adjusted to his new life. Will you do that for me?'

The disputes with Tim, over very little, continued and he started to defending himself vigorously, which, inevitably, led to further ructions. Susan sensed that the rift with his father was increasing but did not realise that strict discipline at home and at school had made Tim determined to rebel against any new attempt to discipline him unfairly, as he saw it. Indeed, the more that she tried to explain Tim's behaviour, the more likely, it seemed to her, that she was endangering her relationship with Peter. She decided to be less confrontational with her husband and to persuade Tim to be a good boy as 'daddy has suffered a lot in the POW camp and is still trying to be your friend so please do try to understand that'. Tim tried at first but was thwarted frequently by a father who seemed to him to resent his very presence. The young boy retreated to within himself and just hoped that, one day, he would be released from his own developing misery. Occasionally, he was really aggressive, partly because Susan was now taking Peter's side, prompting Ann to intervene on Tim's behalf. There was nobody at school in whom he could confide so all that he could do was to play with his few friends, work hard at school, do the best he could not to upset his parents or teachers and to ignore Harry's mischievous attempts to get him into trouble. One day, surely, all this must end?

A few days after an intervention from Ann, Peter started shouting at Tim again, accusing him of being supercilious, superior and ungrateful. Tim did not know what supercilious meant but decided against asking for a definition: it sounded bad but, not knowing what he had done wrong, he was unaware of how he could change. Yes, he did convey superiority, partly because he tried to bolster his own self-image by using long words which, he thought, wrongly, might have been unknown to his father. He was certainly supercilious when he tried to defend himself. This was the worst row so far and it prompted Susan to risk her own relationship with Peter, once again, by insisting that they discussed what was becoming a very serious rift in the family.

'We must do something, together, to ensure that we don't lose Tim for ever. I tried to explain to him the other day that he was a lucky little boy, being brought up by two parents who loved him and that he lived in a comfortable house. I pointed out that both of us were not so lucky and that family life for you, Peter, was very difficult. I thought that I got through to him and this strengthens my view that, if we try to talk to him he'll understand. At the moment, I know that he seems ungrateful and superior. He assumes that his life is just like anyone else's and does not know the hardship you faced as a child. If he knew, things might be different. I know he seems to think that he's superior, but that's just his defence.'

Peter admitted that he was finding it very difficult adjusting to peacetime and family life.

'I'm sure that you are but your, our, innocent son is totally bewildered and unhappy. A few evenings ago, I heard him crying in his bedroom. Are you proud of that?'

Peter exploded.

'Of course, I'm not. For God's sake, what sort of man do you think I am? I don't think you understand what I've been through over the five years and how it's affected me. Well, I'm not a machine. I'm a man with feelings and I've seen and heard things that no civilised man should ever experience. Do you really think that they didn't affect me? Can you even begin to imagine what it's like when you suddenly see a bloody great German battleship and you expect to be drowned any moment? Then when you're taken off your own vessel, at the point of a gun wielded by some madman, and then, later, stuck in a wagon and transported, for four days, with very little food or drink, across Vichy France to a concentration camp where you see holes in the roof to allow gas in? Do you know what it feels like to realise that you could die at any time without the chance to even say goodbye?'

Susan was close to crying but realised that, at last, Peter was speaking about what had happened to him. Both of them knew that it was not directly linked to his behaviour towards Tim but it was something that he had to get out of his system.

'I've seen men so hungry that they've fought for potato skins, I've lived in acute discomfort, surrounded by men who rarely washed, forced to stand for hours on a parade ground, in deepest winter dressed only in underclothes, I've been so angry at it all, for so many years, unable to speak out, denied freedom and forced to listen to those bastards claiming to be so damned superior. I've had few friends that I could trust as we knew that some of the prisoners were spies. I've seen men lose their sanity and we've all been forced to do disgusting work at the point of a pistol. At one stage, the names of those who were about to be repatriated were announced and then the German swine changed their minds. How do you think the men felt about that? I've had to share lavatories with hundreds of others and everything we did was always in full view of everyone else.

'I've seen men shot dead, in cold blood, for some alleged misdemeanour, I've spent years wondering when, if ever, I would see you all again, I prayed to God to end it all but He did nothing and even more millions were slaughtered. I've been forced to listen to those German murderers boasting about how they killed thousands of our innocent citizens, day by day, I've wondered if you were still alive, especially when I found out that Torquay had been bombed. I've seen simple and innocent German citizens, living on a farm near the camp, trying to make a living off the land, blown to smithereens when the RAF dropped a bomb nearby. One of their legs was blown into the camp and an arm was caught on the barbed wire. I've seen so many of our own boys killed, near the camp, as they fought to liberate us. They died so that I and others could live. That made me feel so guilty.

'Do you really think that I can forget all this and live a quiet life as if I was some bank clerk who avoided the war? You've got to understand my own background. I was ignored by my own parents except when I was ordered to do some work, such as collecting lumps of coal from a nearby tip. We were a large family, living in a very small and damp house, sharing facilities and, if you wanted a bath, which was allowed once a week, the tub was filled up in the kitchen. Then, when I went to sea in the First World War, conditions were grim and we had to work 77 hours a week in circumstances that often were very dangerous.

'Then, years later, I was captured and thought that I would never see you again. I longed to see you and my two sons and then, when eventually I come home, I find that my elder son takes everything for granted, as if by some divine right, and treats me like a stranger. For so many years, for so many reasons, I wanted to experience family life and now that I'm home, I find that I have a son who shows no understanding for what I've been through and, although it's us who are paying for his education, seems to think that he's so damned superior. It's very difficult for me to take as I remember how hard I had to study and all the hardships I had in my early life. He's not had any of this but assumes that, somehow, it's all his basic right. I want him to love me and me him, but there's no respect. I don't know what to do. He won't even speak to me.'

Susan, now sobbing openly, put her arm around Peter.

'I could not begin to imagine what it must have been like for you and I'm so, so sorry but now you must understand that I've spent the last five years, trying to shield Tim from everything about the war and your captivity. Of course, he knows very little and if that's wrong, it's my fault, so blame me. I wanted to protect him and preserve his childhood as far as that was possible. He always did his very best to help me and, although I didn't know it then, he heard me crying when you were missing and I thought that you might be dead. At that time, although he was so young, he became the little man of the house and helped me in so many different ways. Now his role has changed and he sees you as yet another adult determined to boss him around and he's had no explanation. He showed an understanding well beyond his years when I wasn't able to give him much at birthdays and, unlike other children I know, he never asked for much. If you tell him something of what you've just told me, I'm sure it'll help. Please, please, I can't stand these rows, so will you talk to him? I know he can seem superior and insensitive but I think that's just part of growing up. I'll have a quiet word with him about that.'

Matters did improve but for Tim it was too late. He had become introverted and silent and his imaginative sense of humour vanished. Occasionally, he reacted to his father's verbal attacks, by being deliberately provocative which ensured the resumption of hostilities at a more intense level. When Peter was away at sea, as he was for many months at a time, Tim confided to his friends that he wished he would stay away for ever.

A Holiday In London In 1946

Susan had some news for Tim.

'Whilst daddy's still on leave, we're going to have a holiday in London. You'll remember that I told you that we have a house in London and that, one day, we'll be going back? This'll be just for a week and we'll be staying in a hotel. Won't that be exciting? '

Tim was unimpressed and excitement was far from his mind. What he knew about London was that it was a big city with millions of people, that it had been severely bombed during the war and that there was no beach or countryside. He preferred Torquay and, unhappy at home and at school, he did not want to leave his friends, who were like a substitute family, for even for a week. He knew nobody in London and was distressed to hear that the family would, one day, return to the capital to live. He could probably manage one week without being accused of being a misery, which was the usual charge when he was not very jolly, which was for most of the time.

However, staying for what he saw as the rest of his life made him very depressed. To add to his troubles, although his relationship with his father had improved, it still seemed that much of what he did was wrong, from putting too much jam on his bread to failing to comb his hair sufficiently frequently and omitting to polish his shoes. He felt a failure. The only person who seemed to understand him was Ann who tried, unsuccessfully, to intercede with Peter, only to be told to mind her own business.

Susan, sensing his less than ecstatic response to the news, continued.

'You'll like London. You really will. It's a busy city and you'll see the Houses of Parliament, Buckingham Palace, Nelson's column in Trafalgar Square, the Thames and Downing Street, which is where the prime minister lives. We can go to the museums and we'll ride on the tube and the trams and trolleybuses as well as the buses.' Her son remained unimpressed. He had seen pictures of some of these places in one of his books about London and thought that Oldway, at the end of his road, not only provided him with conkers but looked better than Buckingham Palace. Nevertheless, despite his misgivings, Tim, now nearly ten, was, inevitably, soon accompanying his parents and younger brother on the train journey to London. They arrived at Paddington station and Tim was immediately disenchanted. It was so much bigger than Paignton. The station was noisy, crowded and foggy as the unpleasant smelling smoke from the steam trains tried to escape through the partially open roof. The area around the station was dominated by open spaces, some of which were littered with rubble that had once been sturdy buildings. German bombs had demolished shops, houses and other buildings. Some of the open spaces were used as car parks, but there were very few cars. Recalling that his doctor in Devon had a car, he wondered where all the London doctors were. There were many buses and crossing the road required great care. Above all, there were so many people. Where did they all come from? Where were they all going? Why were they in such a rush?

Peter had booked accommodation for the four of them at a hotel in Tavistock Square. The hotel had avoided the bombing which had devastated so many other nearby buildings. Within minutes of his arrival, Tim, confronted by a dingy, dirty and old-fashioned building where the furniture and carpets should have been replaced many years before, wanted to go home. He even wished that the Germans had bombed this hotel providing there was nobody staying there.

On the first morning, Peter asked his unhappy son if he had slept well.

Tim knew nothing about diplomacy and the problems his father had experienced in trying to book rooms for the family. He still knew very little about the conditions Peter had been obliged to tolerate, for four years, in a prisoner of war camp. So much could have been different if he had been told. His honest answer was that it was awful and he had hardly slept as the 'mattress seemed to be made of wood and I think I saw a mouse or it may have been a rat in the room'. This answer riled Peter, who had more evidence of his son's lack of gratitude. Peter also recalled that rats resided permanently in his barracks but his angry expression prompted Susan to calm him down before a verbal torrent was unleashed. Quietly, hiding behind a newspaper, she reminded her husband, once again, that Tim was only a little boy and did not really understand what had happened during the war.

She turned to Tim and, unusually, put a friendly arm around his shoulder. 'You must realise that there's been no new furniture for some years as all the country's efforts have been devoted to defeating the enemy. Things will improve but it'll take time. Meanwhile, we must all think how lucky we're to be alive and in London, so soon after the end of the war and can see the sights. Many children would be very happy to have this opportunity.' The same argument, that other children would appreciate food that Tim did not want, was often paraded and diminishing returns had long since set in.

Suitably silenced, Tim decided against commenting on the quality of the sausages served at breakfast which he had planned to mention next. He even refused himself permission to consider what was inside these black and indigestible containers. He began speculating, but only to himself, what the impact on Germany might have been if these sausages had been dropped on Germany during the war. 'This is the BBC 9.00 o'clock news and John Snagge reading it. Last night, in a daring raid, a large number of allied bombers attacked Berlin with a new weapon, based on the concept of a sausage. Millions were dropped and it has been confirmed that substantial damage was caused. Allied casualties were described as light.'

Tim allowed his imagination to roam a little more freely before being aroused by his father asking when he would emerge from his daydream and honour his parents with his presence. Tim had heard about Bomber Harris and speculated that, if he had been involved with the sausages, he might have been re-named 'Banger Harris' and some newspapers might have carried a headline 'Berlin fries under night banger attack as Allied bombers roast military targets. The raid was described as successful.'

The London pavements were crowded with happy civilians and forces personnel, from many different nations, still trying to adjust to the fact that the conflict in Europe was over and to determine what the future would bring. Large areas were wastelands but some sites had been converted into allotments, during the war, in an effort to increase the supply of food. Harry, now five years old, seemed bemused by it all. The boys had never seen a tram and were intrigued by their distinctive clanging sound and the bell that warned of their approach. Tim enjoyed riding on the red underground trains, with their distinctive but not unpleasant smell. Until Susan told him, he was totally oblivious of the role that the stations had played during the war when thousands slept in total squalor on the platforms trying to escape the consequences of enemy action.

'You know that we told you that Bounds Green is our nearest underground station?'

Tim did not know but thought it wise to say yes.

'Well, it was very sad, many local people were killed when taking cover there.'

Tim was glad that he had not been in London during the war. It seemed that it had been a very dangerous place and now it was dirty, damaged and dusty. Why would anyone want to live there?

One of Peter's many but modest hopes, when incarcerated, was that, one day, he would be able to walk around London again, in peace and with his family. That time had now arrived. They strolled around the West End, relishing the freedom and the atmosphere although Tim's interest in the Houses of Parliament, Big Ben and Trafalgar Square took second place to peering at the red London buses. Some very elderly specimens had been despatched to Devon during the war and it was strange seeing the same type of vehicles, with their open staircases to the upper deck, prowling the streets of London.

A large area in Oxford Street, previously the site of a departmental store, was dominated by a full size Wellington bomber which attracted significant interest because of its crucial role in the war. Alongside it was another plane that immediately engaged Tim's attention. Recognising the aircraft and its German marking, he shouted out triumphantly that it was a Fucker Wolf FW 190. Aware that he had suddenly attracted an audience, although he did not know why some of them were smiling, he added that it was a single-engined, single-seat fighter. 'I know because it's in my book of aircraft' he added, in order to sound more authoritative. Peter, suppressing a smile himself, said that it was not a Fucker Wolf but a Focke Wulf.

'That's just what I said. It's a Fucker Wolf.'

Peter decided that no more should be said on the correct name for the enemy aircraft and diverted attention by suggesting that it might be time to have an ice cream. The two boys had already shown more interest in this new food than in the sights. This was a new and exciting luxury but, being unaccustomed to this delicacy, Harry and Tim were unaware of its propensity to melt in the sun. 'Look, you have to lick all sides of the wafer in turn, to stop the ice cream from melting and making a mess on your clothes.' Peter then generously offered a brief demonstration before checking to see if Harry had mastered the necessary technique. His efforts were monitored to the obvious satisfaction of his teacher. However, Harry suddenly erupted into childish giggles. His own wafer was under control but, during his peroration, Peter had forgotten to manage his own ice cream and it was tracing a neat white line down his smart new navy blue jacket.

Some months later, Peter, back again at sea, bought as much food as he could whilst in the West Indies and sent it home. Susan, because of worry during the war and too little food, as she gave so much to her children, like so many mothers, had developed tuberculosis and was booked to go into a sanatorium. Fortunately, the imported food restored her and the stay in the sanatorium was cancelled. Gradually, but much more slowly than anticipated, food supplies became easier. A friend of Peter's, who lived in Canada, had sent food and clothing parcels to the family during the war and had generously given Tim a dark blue lumber jacket with a zip, a device unknown to him at that time. This garment became his favourite item of clothing and, indeed, remained his only non-school item of clothing for some years.

In 1946, for the first time, the family hired a hut on Preston sea front where they changed to sit or play on the beach. The wooden beach hut, just a few yards from the beach, always smelt of metholated spirit, used for boiling water for tea on the small Primus stove. A competing odour, that seemed to last the entire summer, was that of burned milk. Tea was then the national drink as coffee was favoured mainly by foreigners. Food remained in short supply but Susan and the redoubtable Ellicombe, the gardener, grew tomatoes in the back garden which meant that one luxury, whilst idling in the hut, was munching tasty and soggy tomato sandwiches, seasoned by a modest touch of salt. The floor of the hut was seldom free of sand, shed by spades and buckets, essential for working on the beach. Some deck chairs, accompanied by a small folding table, also lived in the hut.

Sand castles were built to challenge the incoming tide and deep holes were dug to the vexation of parents who complained that excavation and construction efforts were always within yards of their deckchairs whilst 'you've got the whole of the beach to choose from'. In the circumstances, Tim, who took pleasure in his pedantry, ignored this serious example of ending a sentence with a preposition and, doubtless recalled the comment attributed to Churchill who once criticised something 'up with which I shall not put'. Somehow, even although it was Harry who had chosen the location for a new hole or castle, it was always Tim who was blamed for irritating the parents.

The boys collected shrimps and the occasional crab from the small pools left by the retiring tide and sought shells and coloured glass, washed smooth by years of caressing by the sea. The pools between these rocks could be dangerous as Harry discovered when he stepped into what appeared to be a very shallow pool, only to find himself sinking fast. Tim saved his life. Other entertainment was provided by the occasional Punch and Judy show, always popular as violence was the main ingredient, and docile donkeys could be hired for a few minutes for a few pence. During the winter, some vessels finished on the rocks, attracting considerable attention whilst they continued to be battered by the relentless tide before becoming wreckage. One attraction was visiting a friend of Susan's for tea. Tim used to stand at the back of the house, on a veranda, and watch the trains thundering past, belching out smoke and creating an unpleasant but strangely seductive smell. Inside the house, the crockery rattled in sympathy with the engines. Whenever Susan caught but a whiff of the smell, she was reminded of her reunion with Peter at Paignton station.

The relationship between father and son, although still difficult, had improved. Tim remained largely ignorant on the deprivations that Peter had suffered during the war but one incident frightened him and gave him a better understanding of his father's behaviour. The two were walking near Preston sea front and Peter saw a German prisoner, identified by his uniform, in close proximity to a local girl.

'What on earth do you think you're doing?', Peter snarled at the girl.

Even Tim could see what they were doing. She was being cuddled and kissed by the prisoner and, as she was not resisting him, he concluded that she was enjoying it. Tim's doubts on why his father had exploded were soon explained. Peter, manifestly having difficulty in controlling his anger, continued his verbal attack.

'Millions of decent, ordinary, people have been killed and many millions more injured and had their lives ruined and their homes demolished because of the activities of the Nazi scum like this man. I saw German swine shoot innocent prisoners and they allowed fellow sailors to drown. Don't kid yourself, the ordinary soldiers were no better than their leaders and were responsible for so much hardship, cruelty and murders. They could have stopped it if they wanted to, but they didn't. How can you even think of touching this man? I spent four long years in a prisoner of war camp, not knowing if I'd ever see my family again and it makes me feel sick to see young and ignorant girls like you fraternising with the enemy. If you'd behaved like that in France, during the war, you would probably have had all your hair cut off when the country was liberated or you might even have been executed. You're no better than him. You're scum too.' He then spat at the pair with, what Tim noted, was impressive accuracy.

The girl had remained totally silent and still during this savage verbal attack. The German, one of the thousands in the UK, occupied on farms or helping to rebuild properties that their countrymen had bombed, who probably knew little English, nevertheless realised the gist of what had been said and smiled. Tim thought that his father was about to hit him but desisted at the last moment, muttering that he was not worth hitting. Instead he spat at the pair a second time. As father and son walked away, the girl resumed her clinch, which she had abandoned whilst being rebuked, smiled and kissed the surprised prisoner with renewed passion. 'Ignore him. One day, your country and mine will be friends again. It's not your fault you were in the war. You had no choice.' The German had looked worried momentarily but soon resumed his amorous attentions. Tim was worried at what he had just seen and was frightened that his father could become so angry so quickly but it did show just how badly he felt about the war and his imprisonment. He made a mental note to take account of this in future. He recalled that the only other time he had seen anyone spit was at Miss Brooks and that he had intended to practice this art himself but had forgotten. If his father could do it, perhaps it would not be so much fun to do it himself.

As food supplies gradually improved, local children were invited to parties. The man who lived opposite to the Adams, widely believed to have profited from the black market, arranged one for his children and their friends in a hotel in Paignton. Tim and Harry were invited and the latter was given an orange. It lacked the necessary instructions and the young boy, never having seen one, ate the skin, prompting complaints about the sharp and unpleasant taste. Why should grown-ups moan about the absence of this strange fruit? Tim, offered a banana, which he had never seen before, was unimpressed by the taste but he had read about them, so, when asked what he thought of the fruit, replied pompously that it tasted like breadfruit which he had neither seen nor tasted. Nobody commented on this shrewd observation, doubtless fearing that any remark could reveal their ignorance.

At another party, in a hotel in Torquay, one young girl, possibly aged 14, about 18 per cent older than Tim, seemed interested in cuddling him, presumably in the erroneous belief that he was her brother. He was puzzled but not wholly disenchanted.

The absence of regular pocket money and, usually, something to buy, meant that children continued to rely on their own company and imagination in devising their own entertainment. Tim's gang, consisting of George, Edward and James, was flourishing and their headquarters were the shed in George's father's garden. He was an austere and pompous man and nobody had ever seen him smile. The shed always smelt dusty and the ancient carpet on the concrete floor probably weighed more than twice its original weight because it was home to so much dust and deceased insects. It might have been wise to wear the discarded gas masks.

Cricket on Preston sea front was resumed. Susan's brother, Brian, visited the family and joined in the cricket. Had Tim heard of the disaster with the *Lancastria*? He had not. 'I was on that vessel. It was a 16,000 ton liner belonging to the Cunard company and the government had taken it over to be used as a troopship. There were up to 9,000 of us on it, nobody knows just how many, including soldiers, women and children leaving France as it seemed that the country was about to fall to the Germans. We'd reached St. Nazaire, on the west coast of France, when the ship was bombed. It was absolute hell. There was little hope for most of us as the ship sank in 20 minutes and I was very lucky to be one of about 2,500 survivors and it's thought that between 4,000 and 5,000 people were drowned. The fuel oil from the vessel was set alight and many men who drowned were weighed down by the oil or because they refused to dispose of their rifles as losing a rifle was a punishable offence. It was the worst marine disaster in UK history and, as the news could have seriously undermined the country's morale, Prime Minister Churchill censored the story. But the *New York Times* reported what had happened and revealed that more people had been lost than the total who were drowned on the *Titanic* and *Lusitania*.' Previously unaware of all this, Tim was no longer irked by Brian's opposition to his insistence on wearing his shirt collar inside his jacket collar when he was tie-less. This fashion, of course, was adopted decades later.

Harry and Tim enjoyed occasional coach tours not least as the family did not own a car. A 'mystery' tour, inevitably in a Bedford coach, was popular initially but its attraction faded when some passengers realised that they had visited the mystery location before. Widecombe, on Dartmoor, was a popular destination and the family made forays to Brixham and Paignton Zoo. Most coach trips in the late Forties cost 12/6. The family also patronised some itinerant circuses and fairs in the area. Zoos had been closed during the war, reflecting staff shortages, and only 14 were open in 1945. Some 20 million people had been to the seaside in the last year before the outbreak of the conflict and, now that workers had two weeks of paid holiday annually, Torquay and other parts of Devon soon became very popular resorts.

Tim and his friends liked to inspect the speedometers of parked cars, most of which were pre-war but, apparently, even a modest ten horse power car could exceed 100 miles per hour so what speed could more powerful cars manage? The boys had assumed that the top speed indicated on the gauge was the maximum speed that could be achieved by the car, but eventually, looking at the *Motor* and *Autocar* magazines in the doctor's surgery, the mistake became apparent. The absence of many cars on the streets prompted Tim and his friends to collect engine numbers. It was free and occupied some of their spare time. Later, this 'interest' would be transferred to noting the numbers of London buses of which there were then a fascinating variety of makes and models.

Soon after the war Tim was delighted to be given a second-hand, maroon small Royal Enfield bicycle. Later a new black bike, a Phillips, appeared and, years later, this was eventually sold, together with some other possessions, to fund the purchase of a BSA Golden Wings. Having a bicycle when there was so little traffic was a massive privilege and Tim not only enjoyed cycling to school, and, especially, home again, but also to local villages. Roger and he ventured to Dittisham, some 14 miles away, one afternoon in the school holidays: their prolonged absence caused some consternation.

One new hobby was stamp collecting. A friend of Susan's gave Tim an album and some stamps and he used birthday and Christmas present money and occasional pocket money to augment his collection. Stamps could be bought, relatively inexpensively, from Stanley Gibbons in London and Tim specialised in stamps from India. He also spent some time 'sailing' his yacht, made by one of Peter's sea-going colleagues, in the small lake in Victoria Park in Paignton. Occasionally, the yacht became becalmed in the middle of the lake, so two people, with some long string, had to walk around the pond, in the hope of catching the mast and then dragging the mischievous yacht to the side. Another summer occupation was catching butterflies. The insects were trapped in a net and then carefully transferred to a glass jar containing laurel leaves at the bottom and cotton wool on top. The gas killed the butterfly which was later pinned into the valley of a small board with its wings stretched out on either side.

Post-war interests were modest and simple. Apart from inventing games, young boys collected Dinky toys, which returned to the shops gradually, priced between 1/6 and 2/6, but which were rationed. They also wrote to football clubs for their players' (printed) autographs. Making models with balsa wood, at 9 old pence for a piece about four inches wide and 30 inches long, was another hobby. Tim made a football ground stadium, using spent matches as seats. A more ambitious project was to create roads on a large wooden base and then build shops by the side of the pavement.

For many years, Tim had to be self–sufficient in his spare time. Occasionally, he would spend a few shillings on model aircraft kits. The planes were made of balsa wood and construction required some tissue paper, which covered the fuselage and wings, and some unpleasant smelling dope for sticking the parts together. Unfortunately, as soon as the plane was invited to fly, it usually crashed, causing irreparable damage. Tim was given a second-hand and very small billiards table which gave him hours of pleasure as matches were played between his left and right hands. This might imply some versatility but the reality was that such slender skill as he had became shared between the two hands. He also enjoyed Table Soccer, known as Subbuteo, priced at 10/6. This became a major passion and Tim organised leagues and played for both sides in each game. Records of all matches were kept and Arsenal, by an odd coincidence, the team that he supported, finished each 'season' in first place. During the school holidays Tim played cricket in the local recreation ground with two of his friends, Robert and Brian. Cricket was a salvation for young Tim.

Just after the war, in 1946, professional footballers threatened to strike unless they received a minimum wage of £7. Tim knew nothing of this but, before the family moved back to North London in 1948, he had became a regular supporter of Torquay United, despite, or perhaps because, the winter sport at Grafton House school was rugby. Like many small boys, he would join the queue in Paignton for the bus to the Plainmoor ground and, when he could not attend, occasionally spent a few pence on a local sporting newspaper which appeared on the Saturday evening with all the results and reports. Support for the club was noisy as the boys had wooden rattles, a relic from the war when such fiendishly loud devices were used to give warnings of danger. In the 1946-47 season Torquay finished 11th out of 22 clubs in the Third Division South.

Despite disliking school rugby, Tim often went to Queens Park in Paignton to watch the local rugby side but he spent much more time there in the summer watching cricket and selling scorecards for the club. He was such a regular visitor that he knew the players by name and, in particular, always enjoyed watching the professional all-rounder, Reg Routledge, who went on to play first class cricket, with some success, for Middlesex. At the end of each season, the

151

local club played the Cross Arrows team from Lords. The latter included some mature players one of whom was the legendary Patsy Hendren, then aged 58. Tim was in the ground early and anticipated the arrival of the great man at the crease. Unfortunately, he was run out without facing a ball but the large crowd was disappointed as he was not invited to return to continue his innings. In 1948, Devon played Gloucestershire, who included some first class cricketers, including two who had played for England, at Torquay. Tim was suitably excited. Notwithstanding his lack of opportunity and success, he still wanted to be a professional cricketer. Driving a train did not appeal and his brief desire to be a doctor was only because the local man had a new car which was assumed was a perk of the job. School, if it had taught Tim anything, encouraged him to believe that success in any given field could be achieved by concentration. That was all that he had to do: ability was never mentioned.

Visits to the cinema or theatre were limited. In 1946, a third of the population was visiting the cinema at least once a week but Tim was not in that group. The family used to see the annual pantomime, usually featuring the legendary Clarkson Rose, an actor whose name was synonymous with pantomime, at the Torquay Pavilion. There was a cinema near the Oldway complex, and one memorable film was based on the First World War and a character called the Black Ace. It was frightening and Tim was not the only child to hide behind a seat. Another film that made him uncomfortable, even at the age of 10 in 1947, was *Green for Danger* with Alastair Sym. It was described by a New York film critic as a 'humdinger of a baffler' which says more about the critic than the film.

This was the golden age of radio and Tim was always keen to hear the latest editions of popular shows. Indeed, he owned several crystal sets over the years which gave him enormous pleasure at minimal cost. One favourite programme, which was broadcast five nights a week, from October 1946, was *Dick Barton, Special Agent*, introduced by the memorable signature tune, the *Devil's Gallop*. Mr Barton and his loyal chums, Snowy and Jock, managed to put themselves into the most bizarre and seemingly hopeless situations, only to extricate themselves the following day. At its peak, when paper for comics and newspapers was in short supply, the programme attracted an audience of 15 million. Once, when technical problems prevented the programme from being broadcast, the telephone lines into Broadcasting House were jammed and many children arrived at the studios to help Dick Barton. For the younger children, Uncle Mac on *Children's Hour* was a favourite.

In 1949, favourite songs included *Ghost Riders in the Sky*, *Powder your face with sunshine* and *Dear Hearts and Gentle People*. The lyrics were simplistic and sentimental but they could be heard and the tunes were, well, tuneful. Other popular artists and programmes included Arthur Askey and the Lyon family in *Life with the Lyons, Educating Archie, Have a Go* and *The Goons*. Later, in the Fifties, despite the arrival of commercial television, *Much Binding in the Marsh*, with Kenneth Horne, Richard Murdoch and Sam Costa, demanded attention as did *Take It From Here* with Jimmy Edwards, Dick Bentley, June Whitfield and Bill Kerr. The comedian Tony Hancock, who later committed suicide, became a very popular figure on radio and television: in 1954, the government decided that, if a nuclear attack on the UK occurred, his programme should be broadcast to improve the nation's morale. In the same year, 1954, the soap opera, *The Archers*, an everyday story of country folk, attracted an audience of 10 million who tuned in to listen to the 800th edition of the programme.

Television returned on 7th June 1946 but only 10,000 sets were in existence. In 1949, there were some 90,000 in the UK: by early 1953, they cost about £80, which was about eight times the national average weekly wage. Independent television commenced on 22nd September 1955 and the first screened advertisement was for Gibbs SR toothpaste. Advertisements were restricted to just three slots of two minutes each every hour. One very popular television programme in 1956 was Dixon of Dock Green. Jack Warner played an amiable local policeman and violence was a rare visitor. There were 434 episodes and the audience was often around 14 million. Vera Lynn had been a popular and successful singer during the war and her song, *We'll meet again, don't know where, don't know when*, remains well-known. She was the Forces Sweetheart but failed to engage the enthusiasm of the BBC Board of Governors, who, commenting on her show, *Sincerely Yours*, observed 'popularity noted but deplored'. Much later, Tommy Steele, partly because of his 1956 hit, *Singing the* Blues, was touted as the UK's answer to Elvis Presley.

Tim's musical interests were determined by the availability of some old 78 rpm, that's revolutions per minute, records and a very ancient gramophone that Peter had owned and used on his ships which explained why it was covered in canvas. Its age meant that it had to be wound up continuously whilst the record was still playing. The modest record collection included some from Uncle Mac, the children's favourite, and various classics including the *Warsaw Concerto*. One record featured the comedian Sid Field, who was learning how to play golf. He was recommended by the coach to stand behind the ball. He whined pitifully, 'how, it's round all the way round?'

When more paper became available, publishers took advantage of the great interest in radio and film with regular editions of *Radio Fun* and *Film Fun*, as well as other magazines such as *Picturegoer*. Pocket money was not paid regularly and Tim had to rely on the occasional generosity of his parents and even grandmother who kindly gave him some money from time to time out of her very modest pension. That said, he was supplied with sweets free of charge and was given up to three quality comics, *The Rover, The Hotspur* and *The Wizard* each week. He also had the monthly *Boys Own Paper* and the *Meccano Magazine* which contained information on the latest Dinky Toys. Previously, Tim had been an enthusiastic reader of *The Beano* and *The Dandy*. Another favourite publication was *Children's Newspaper*, edited by Arthur Mee. These well-written and intriguing tales in the comics and articles in the magazines had a profound impact on Tim's subsequent life. His love of reading and studying even extended to buying history textbooks that were used at school, from the two bookshops in Paignton, so that he could read them during the holidays. A favourite author was Captain W.E. Johns who wrote about the exploits of Biggles and Gimlet. Tim liked the Just William stories from Richmal Crompton and an eagerly anticipated event was the arrival of the Rupert Bear annual. The Ward Lock collection of Wonder books were also popular and his favourite was that on the RAF. Children of different ages enjoyed the works of Enid Blyton, who was publishing up to 30 books per annum.

Having returned to sea, Peter, when visiting New Zealand, bought Tim a watch with luminous hands and this was announced, immediately, as his favourite possession. Another present was a ball pen. This was in 1949 when such instruments were rare: the first Biro, which became a synonym for ball pen, was on sale in the UK for £2.15.0. Imported copies of the *Saturday Evening Post* fascinated young Tim who was mesmerised by the colourful life that these magazines portrayed and, in particular, the vast range of products that were unavailable in the UK. Even in 1947, there were US advertisements for mopeds which consumed one American gallon every 125 miles and there were bewilderingly colourful and attractive-looking sleek and streamlined powerful cars offering 'more style, more economy, more go and more comfort' when the few car owners in the United Kingdom had to be content with polishing pre-war cars and coaxing them into action. In 1949, there was even an advertisement in one American newspaper for a 'Stereo Realist' camera 'that puts 3rd dimension on film' and which 'sees the same as you'. The price of $182.25 included tax and a viewer. Portable television and radio sets were available: the radios cost just under $20.

These advertisements and illustrations by the incomparable Norman Rockwell in the *Saturday Evening Post* suggested that there was another way of life, a colourful existence and not the black and white one that dominated the UK. Austerity and concentration on exports, to the detriment of domestic consumption, apparently, need not dominate UK lives for ever. Tim was seduced by the apparently easy way of life and the plentiful availability of so much, not least food. Whilst the UK was still subjected to food rationing, which had started in January 1940, it seemed as if there were no such shortages in America and sweets, which Tim's contemporaries regarded as a treat, were plentiful in the US.

The US portrayed in the *Saturday Evening Post* was part of another and significantly and different world: it was a country that Tim was determined to visit one day. The contrast between the nation shown in the *Saturday Evening Post* and the UK's admirable but different *Picture Post* which had been first published in 1938, and *Weekly Illustrated* was startling. The UK seemed a small, congested, black and white and austere country but the US was a spacious and colourful land where so much was available for those with a few dollars to spend.

Tim remained unhappy at home and, although he had no close knowledge of other families, it seemed to him that other boys were treated differently. Whenever Peter was on leave, his life became more miserable and when his father was away, Susan made little attempt to disguise the fact that Harry was her favourite. Ann tried to comfort her grandson who, she knew, was significantly less than perfect. She agreed that he seemed superior and unwilling to compromise, and explained, to Tim's astonishment, that she thought that Peter was probably jealous of his own son.

'You see, dear, his parents worked hard and ignored him, apart from giving him jobs to do in the home. For example, he had to go to local coal tips and find lumps of coal that had been left behind by the owners of the mines. Their house was old, cold and very small and, of course, lacked electricity. There was no bathroom or indoor toilet and money was always tight so they did not eat well. He had a tough time at sea, as a young apprentice, and his ships were mined, torpedoed and involved in a collision and he had to jump for his life. Then he was captured in 1941, as you know, and spent years in a grim prisoner of war camp, not knowing if, at any time, he might be killed. Now he sees the relatively comfortable life you are having and he feels that you ought to show how grateful you are that your life is so much better than his when he was a boy.'

Tim listened intently but reminded his grandmother that he had been blown down the stairs when a bomb dropped nearby. Ann smiled and suggested that, although that was frightening, it was not quite the same as being at sea.

'Thanks, nana, I do understand and promise that I'll try to be better towards daddy but why couldn't he tell me all that himself?' Ann could only suggest that it had been so grim that he did not want Tim to worry about it and that he did not want to re-live it.

In 1946, Simon, a new brother, had arrived but, at the age of 11, in 1948, living in a sadly-sisterless family that consisted of his mother, grandmother and two young brothers, Tim was beginning to realise that not all young people were males. Those who were not boys looked rather different and were, according to some of his male friends, for he had no relevant experience himself, not wholly undesirable. That, of course, was not meant in the carnal sense.

The war, the lack of toys, the absence of fathers, and mothers pre-occupied in working hard to keep families together, forced boys to unite in gangs but they were totally different to modern gangs. They were neither hostile nor confrontational. Members just enjoyed belonging to a small group of friends and devising their own simple and innocent games. Girls were excluded, not on principle, but because Tim's gang members did not know any and knew nothing about them. They were an alien species so membership made no provision for the admission of females. Some of Tim's less immature schoolmates, significantly at least ten per cent older, boasted of their 'girl friends' but they, the girls, were more for prestige as they were friends who happened to be of a different gender. Relationships were totally platonic but Tim's two adult bosses at home, increased in number by 50 per cent after Peter returned in 1945, somehow implied that speaking to a friend who happened to be a girl indicated a major character weakness that had to be overcome. Any tendencies in this unhealthy direction had to be eliminated before they developed so any relationships had to be secret if they were to be sustained.

Keen to show some innocent defiance and interested to find out what being friendly with a girl meant, Tim become acquainted with a blonde, blue-eyed girl called June who was the sister of Graham, one of his friends. Tim did nothing to disabuse his warders of the view that, when he went to the house at the top of the hill, and spent some time there, he was visiting Graham. This was partly true but Tim realised that telling the whole truth would result in the immediate dismissal from his life of the young June. He liked her and she was different to his other friends and, in some ways, better company. She was not only a girl, which meant she was less immature than Tim but was also one year older and had a slightly different and welcome perspective on the very innocent relationship. Just as the friendship was developing, but still within blameless boundaries that would now induce a contemptuous sneer from even infants, Tim had bad news as the family were having their tea one Sunday.

'You know that daddy and I want to return home to London and that we have had trouble with the tenant of our old house, who's refused to move, well, there's some good news now.' Tim anticipated what was coming and knew that, for him, it was very bad news. He had been dreading this for months. He had learned over the years that whenever he was promised fun or that some good news was about to be released, he should expect the worst.

'Well, the tenant has now agreed to move after daddy promised him some money. He's going very soon and that means we can go back to London just as soon as all the arrangements can be made.'

Tim glanced at his feet to confirm that his whole being had been converted into cold water which had drained to his shoes. He knew that his opinion was irrelevant but felt that he was obliged to voice some thoughts although it would not be wise to mention his new female friend whom he might never see again.

'When will that be?'

'We don't know yet, but it will be within a few weeks, all being well.'

'I hate London. It was so crowded when we had a holiday there and I'm sure it's worse now. There was so much traffic and there're no beaches. I'll have to go to a new school where I don't know anybody and I'll lose all my friends down here. Do we have to go? Don't you like it here? Please can we stay?'

Susan tried to console her son.

'I'm sure that you will make new friends and, even if we stayed here, you'd have to change school before too long anyway. We'll have holidays at the seaside and that'll be fun, won't it?'

Tim did not share his mother's enthusiasm. Going back for a holiday and then knowing that he had to return to London might be worse than not returning to Devon at all. She continued. 'Perhaps you can stay with some of your friends for a holiday, if it's convenient to them?' Tim remained silent but his mother's attempt to placate him had given him an idea which might just change his life. He lost no time in implementing the first part of his master plan. The following day, the gang assembled in their dusty hut headquarters. Tim said that he had something important to say and his chums immediately fell silent.

'You know that, before the war, my parents bought a house in London?'

His friends nodded.

'Well, in the next few weeks, we're going back as the man who lived in the house during the war has agreed to go.' He added, somewhat unnecessarily, 'that means I've got to go with them'.

The gang members absorbed this shocking news and George, as usual, had something to say.

'I went to London once and I didn't like it. Everyone bumps into you and there weren't any beaches. There were too many people and it was very noisy. If my parents said they were moving, I'd stay here.'

'Where would you live and who would look after you?'

'Well, it hasn't happened yet so I haven't got any details, but I wouldn't go.'

Tim was disappointed that nobody had said that they would miss him, so he told them that he would miss them, which had the desired outcome.

'I think that we may be back for family holidays occasionally but my mother says that I might be allowed to have a holiday with a friend if someone down here invites me.' The immediate response was profoundly disappointing. Clearly, none of his friends could commit their families to having Tim to stay but there were not even any offers to open discussions with the parents. He was not prepared to accept defeat so, in the absence of any invitations or even interest from his friends, he would modify his plan.

The family was fortunate in that the London home had not been damaged. During the war, many homes were demolished or damaged and schools were used to provide accommodation for those who had been 'bombed out' and who could not live with relatives. Immediately after the war, German prisoners of war in the UK were required to assist in building pre-fabricated houses which could be constructed in three days.

To London In 1948

In 1948, although holiday makers flocked to the west country, only half of all families went away for their holidays which was unsurprising as the average wage for skilled men was only £1-7-6. Thousands may have been heading for Torquay but the Adams family was going in the opposite direction. On 27th July 1948, two days before the Olympic Games began, which meant that the pre-occupied press failed to report the family's plan, the Adams returned to North London. Just a week later, the Olympic yachting events were held in Torbay, which, hopefully, went some way to alleviating local residents' depression at the news that the family had left the area.

Some days before the move to London, Simon, Tim's younger brother, now two years old, developed whooping cough. Peter and Susan were discussing what to do and their eldest son had an idea which he knew would be rejected instantly but felt that he ought to make the point once again.

'Why don't we stay here in Preston and continue as we are? I don't want to go to London, our friends are here and we all enjoy going on to the beach in the summer.' He then added darkly, as if such a crucial fact had been overlooked, 'and there aren't any beaches in London'. Such was his sense of despondency, he even borrowed two of his grandmother's expressions and suggested that 'people don't like London, you mark my words'. He knew it was futile but he had to say something. Then, such was his desperation, he suggested that as Simon was ill, it would be illegal to take him on a train and that severe punishment, possibly including a jail sentence, might be meted out to offenders.

'If you both had to go to jail, what would we all do?' The thought that Ann would have to take over by herself prompted him to suggest that only the father, in such circumstances, would be imprisoned. He realised too late that he had been particularly clumsy and tactless but, before he could apologise, as he intended, Susan's sharp rebuke reminded him that Peter had been in a POW camp so Tim, who had only been guilty of being careless, not malicious, generously reduced the penalty for taking a child with whooping cough on to a train to a substantial fine. His wild imagination never went down well with Peter who glared fiercely at him for several seconds whilst seemingly on the brink of cuffing him.

Tim made one final and desperate attempt. 'I think that I saw in the newspaper, last week, that someone with a nasty disease was fined a lot of money for going on a train. Just imagine if hundreds of people got whooping cough and then spread it around London. It could become very serious as if bus drivers caught it, there could be no transport and then people could not go to work and everything would stop, all because of Simon being on the train.'

Susan enjoyed Tim's rambling imagination occasionally but this was not one such occasion. 'Don't be so silly dear. But you're right. It would be difficult to go to London by train. Apparently, we would have to book a whole compartment and that would be very expensive.'

Tim knew it would be wrong to be even mildly optimistic and did not have long to wait to hear dreaded news.

'Daddy's hiring a car and driver for the long journey to London.'

Tim was about to be plunged into a new world of which he knew almost nothing and one where he knew nobody. This was an unpleasant prospect for a very shy and socially-retarded 11 year old.

The family had to vacate their home in Preston a few days before their journey to the capital and stayed with a Mrs Owen in her small bungalow. It may have been that the place was full of Owens, so it is important that it is emphasise that the Owen in question resided in Oldway Road. She was in late middle age, round-faced, short, fat and had a fringe. Ann had remarked to Susan that she resembled her dogs and the likeness had been noted by the perceptive Tim, who announced that he didn't want a dog any more.

'Why is that dear?' Susan enquired, although she was happy to hear this, 'you've wanted a dog for as long as I can remember'.

'Because if you have a dog, your face changes and you look like your own dog.' He then looked pensive. 'If you had a bulldog and then he died and you bought a spaniel, what kind of face would you have? Would you look like a mongrel?' Ann assured him that very few people grew to look like their dogs but this merely encouraged Tim to raise the issue of why owners did not resemble their cats or, seeking to be very imaginative, their goldfish. Peter, who neither enjoyed nor appreciated his son's inventive imagination, intervened. 'Don't be so silly.'

The bungalow belonging to this particular Owen was significantly less than capacious and her two unfriendly chow chow dogs roamed around at speed, creating the impression that the bungalow was even smaller than it was. It seemed as if there were dozens of the brutes and Tim soon realised that they regarded new but temporary residents with less than overt enthusiasm. Possibly, they suffered from an inferiority complex, reflected in their determination to be recognised by repeating their name. Who has heard of a spaniel spaniel and does a bulldog need to repeat its name just so it can make an impression? No, these chows needed counselling. At least they did not bite Tim and he denied them the opportunity of repeating history by rolling him into the sea simply by not going to the beach. The family had never owned a pet so perhaps the dogs were seeking revenge for the failure to give a home to a fellow canine quadruped.

The journey to London was on the day when Australia scored 404 for three at 3.58 runs per over to defeat England at Leeds, just 15 minutes from the end of the match. Don Bradman scored 173 not out and Arthur Morris contributed 182. Such was England's plight that Hutton and Compton were required to perform with the ball, and, together, they bowled 19 overs for 112 runs. Perceiving Tim to be an expert on the noble game, the Owen lady asked him on the morning if an English defeat was likely. The idea was ridiculed but, fortunately, having not seen her in the intervening six decades, Tim has been spared her scorn. England lost the series 4-0 with one match being drawn. At the Oval, in the final test, in their first innings, the home country managed to accumulate 52, of which Hutton contributed 30.

The 'new' terraced home in North London, built around 1900, had been bought by Tim and Susan in 1932. Detached houses, with much larger front gardens, on the opposite side of the quiet road, enhanced the appearance of the immediate neighbourhood but the dejected and depressed Tim, who felt as if he had been parachuted into a foreign land, was unimpressed but remained comforted by his plan, the second part of which he hoped would be successful in the next few weeks.

Despite the absence of garages for most of the houses, there were few cars parked in the tree-lined road, which led to the Alexandra Palace grounds and the railway station. The Palace was also the site of the BBC's first-ever television station and such was the strength of the signal that, in 1948, Tim could pick up the sound of television programmes on his crystal set, long before a television set was acquired. This enabled him to be well-informed on programmes, which enhanced his reputation at school, years before the necessary set was purchased.

The Palace grounds included a horse racing track, a cricket club ground, a garden from which early television gardening programmes were presented, a lake and parklands. On a good day, it was possible to see London in the distance. When the wind was in the right direction, Tim claimed that he could hear Bow Bells, so he was officially a cockney and his efforts to speak like one provoked such mirth in the family, allied with the inevitable injunction not to be so silly, that he ceased to be a cockney.

Alexandra Palace Station had been opened in May 1873. Just 77 years later, in 1950, when Tim used the steam train service to go to a school near Highgate, which, according to the time table, was but seven minutes away, despite stopping at Muswell Hill and Cranley Gardens. The engines and rolling stock dated back to Victorian times so attracted the interest of railway enthusiasts. The antiquated coaches, which lacked corridors, had very elderly and old-fashioned sepia photographs of seaside resorts in each compartment above the string luggage racks. Unlike society, it was a classless train but elsewhere, third class was abolished only in June 1956. The service was for passengers only but some coal was carried occasionally for use in the adjacent Alexandra Palace building. Between October 1951 and January 1952, all through services to Kings Cross were suspended to save coal. Tim left Hudson Hall School near Highgate in December 1953 and his withdrawal of patronage proved fatal. The line, which then terminated at Finsbury Park, was closed the following July. The local station became a community centre and the rails were removed.

The Adams' terraced house had a short curved path, bordered by a lawn on one side and a flower bed on the other. It led to a very solid and impressive front door, the top of which had an ornate glass window. A modest lobby, separated from the small and narrow hall by glass doors, was where, years later, Tim kept his 98 cc Corgi motor scooter. Peter probably tolerated the whiff of petrol as he knew that his son used GOC petroleum products and he was keen to ensure, that, when the time came, this company, his employer, had sufficient funds to pay his pension. When he was older, Tim had thought about buying a pale green BSA Bantam 125 cc motor cycle but the blue Corgi was cheaper and fitted in the lobby which was a marketing problem that BSA never addressed with a consequent loss of sales.

The glass doors opened into a hall which had a small gas fire which, like its fellow fires, was only used in the coldest weather. Coal fires were lit occasionally, mainly in the one room employed for eating and lounging and, occasionally, a black circular paraffin heater was brought into action. It emitted a strong smell and this, coupled with the whiff of gasoline from the lobby in later years, suggested that the house was a small refinery. Susan was an enthusiastic smoker but the refinery never caught fire. The paraffin heater also created substantial moisture so parts of the house always seemed damp. A single bar electric fire was used although its output was inadequate. If it was really cold, a double-bar fire was employed but, because it was seldom used, the extra warmth was only felt after the dust on the bars had been burned off. The house was usually smelly especially in the winter.

Although the house was large, socialising with friends was rare. Peter was usually at sea and Susan, trying to bring up three boys, almost on her own, and denied the modern domestic appliances now regarded as essential, had little spare time or, indeed, energy to make and maintain friendships. Similarly, Tim was never encouraged to invite any of his friends to visit which embarrassed him and, doubtless, was a factor which reduced the number of his potential friends significantly.

It was years before the family had a car: Harry and Simon were to win scholarships but nobody, least of all Tim himself, gave any consideration to his achieving similar academic status. So, to finance his education, his parents generously denied themselves a car until the late Fifties. A small black and white Murphy television only arrived many years later. It lived in the dining room but was not always reliable as Peter discovered when he attacked it with a screwdriver and the machine reacted to his hostile approach by taking up smoking. Exclusive phone lines were rare and, when a phone was allocated, linked to the Tudor exchange, the line was shared which meant that each party could hear conversations held by the other.

The hall, so narrow that now it would present a challenge to a standard-sized obese child, led to a lounge, a dining room, the kitchen and a scullery. The lounge was seldom used for lounging and, although it would have been costly to heat it during the winter, it was not used even in the summer, being reserved as the 'best' room. It had been the venue for the wedding breakfast in 1932. The room had a lush green carpet on which Tim used to mark out a football field, in white chalk, for his table football, Subbuteo. The pile of the carpet had an adverse impact on the standard of the game and all matches were cancelled after efforts with the chalk were discovered by senior management and the room reverted to its role of being effectively out of bounds for most of the year. Instead, armed with a bat, he practised cricket shots, by looking at numerous photographs in a book, costing 2/6, written by the phenomenal Sir Donald Bradman. There was no damage to the room as no ball was involved and his shots were mainly defensive, which reflected his essentially timid character.

The dining room, at the back of the house, was rarely used for dining as the family was ahead of trends because meals were eaten in the small kitchen where a coal-burning boiler offered precious heat. The dining room backed on to a conservatory but neglect and the repercussions of wartime bombing in the area had caused such severe damage that the glass roof and the rotted wooden sides were soon removed, leaving just a floor of red tiles and some steps down on to the garden. These were useful for Tim's cricket practice: he would hurl a tennis ball at the steps and, depending on which step it struck and at what angle, the ball would fly back at surprising heights and direction. He was becoming competent in catching but predictably protracted parental protests prevented practice permanently.

The small kitchen was dominated by a deep brown dresser with open shelves on which the crockery lived, collecting dust. Food was stored in a pantry near the door which led to the back garden. The presence of the boiler meant that the kitchen was the warmest room in the house: a clothes horse, known as a clothes pulley, that could be propelled to the ceiling, helped the clothes to dry but washing up was done in the adjoining dark scullery which concealed a downstairs lavatory behind the wooden and very elderly draining board. The scullery had no window and relied on a small glass panel in the side door. Like millions in those days, the family lacked central heating, a refrigerator, dish washer, washing machine, freezer and double glazing.

The drains outside the back door were always smelly and the narrow side path to the pavement, which was shared with the dour next-door neighbour, became progressively narrower as an unchecked tree did what healthy trees do. Presumably its development was not adversely affected by the smell.

A large shed, used to store coke and garden tools, and a smaller shed, which housed coal, were to the right of the steps leading from the kitchen into the back garden. As the house was terraced, the only route for the coal from the road to the shed was via the narrow and smelly path and then through the scullery and kitchen. The imminent arrival of the coalmen was indicated by the presence of newspapers spread out all over the kitchen floor. The steps from the kitchen led to a small and mangy lawn, the condition of which was rendered even mangier by Tim's desire to play cricket on it, with his co-opted brothers, without any regard for its condition or their dislike of the game. The garden was small so the most modest of shots was liable to propel the ball over the bramble-covered fence into the neighbour's garden.

Upstairs there were four bedrooms, a separate lavatory and a bathroom. Each room had a gas fire but they were used rarely. The bathroom lacked any form of heating and it was often necessary to scrape ice off the inside of the windows before making a heroically masochistic gesture in favour of hygiene. Tim occupied the very small room at the front. This room had a gas fire but its main use was as an earth as he connected a wire from his crystal set to the fire's black pipe. The fire was so close to the bed that it would have been dangerous to ignite it. Furniture was sparse.

One aspect of his room puzzled Tim and he sought information from his mother.

'Why does my bedroom have bars across the windows?'

'I don't know dear, as far as I can remember, they were there when we bought the house many years ago.'

'Why would anyone have done that? Was it to prevent people climbing in or to stop people falling out?'

'I've no idea but, for the time being, we've more things to think about than removing bars.'

Tim was not satisfied. 'But it makes me feel like a prisoner.'

The answer was, of course, totally predictable. 'Don't be silly, dear, nobody thinks that you're a prisoner.' Despite further occasional protests, no action was taken.

Ann, whose original sympathy for Tim had persisted as the relationship between Peter and his son improved, thanks to her explanation of Peter's background, may have felt that the bars were an omen. Despite her help, Tim used to rebel against her for rebuking him, prompting her to claim that she 'would swing for that boy' or, alternatively, 'that boy will end on the gallows'. Fortunately for 'that boy', the death penalty in the United Kingdom was abolished on the 9th November, 1965. However, she tired of complaining about Tim's behaviour and the two developed a much closer relationship.

By peering out of an upstairs window, Tim could just see the traffic on the distant main road. He did not like London but one factor that did appeal was the wide range of different types of buses, trams and trolleybuses. The last London tram route was eliminated in June 1952. Trolleybuses, uniform in appearance, were silent but they offered the free spectacle of their conductors, manipulating a long pole, trying to coax the vehicles' arms back on to the overhead cables after they had sought freedom from remaining where their designer had intended.

For some years, after the war, transport was dominated by trains, trolleybuses, buses, trams, cycles and motor cycles. The average journey to work, immediately after the war, was five miles so, as cycling was cheap and real wages so low, this was a favoured mode of transport. For more than a decade after the war, 30 per cent of employees went to work by bicycle, bus or on foot whilst only 16 per cent used a car. Motor cycles were both relatively cheap and popular. More than 400,000 BSA Bantam models were sold in just 23 years, despite being too big to fit in the lobby at Tim's home.

At the end of the war, petrol was still rationed and cost around 2/1 per gallon and travelling from London to Torquay took a day. There were just two million cars on Britain's roads and the total had only reached 3.6 million ten years later. In 1948, there were more than 32 motor manufacturers in the UK but few new cars were seen on the roads because production was mainly for export and fulfilment of an order for a new car could take two years. If a new model of a Ford Popular could be found in September 1953, it would cost the buyer £390, including £115 in purchase tax. It lacked most modern features and many that were widely available on other cars. There were no glove compartments, heaters, warning lights, radio or sun visor. In 1954, the Mini arrived and survived, under the British Motor Corporation and its successors: by 2000 more than 5.3 million had been sold. It played a significant part in making family motoring more economic and attainable. In 1956, the Hillman Minx convertible cost £848, of which £283 went to the government in tax. By the 1960s, 28 per cent of UK households owned a car.

The house to the right of the Adams residence was occupied by a permanently grumpy and humourless father. Seemingly, he had been denied the ability to smile at birth and was married to a long-suffering but kindly woman, who bravely ignored the fact that nature had given her an extraordinarily large triangular snout. They had two sons, one of whom played cricket with Tim in the Alexandra Park grounds, and one remarkably plain daughter. The other neighbours were the Barnes family. There were two sons and a mother, Anthea, whom Susan had known before the war and who had lost her husband in the conflict. Opposite lived an elderly lady named Drinkwater, who, according to local legend, favoured a stronger brew than her name indicated, and her almost equally elderly spinster daughter.

A New Life

The summer of 1948 was not the happiest period of Tim's young life as he faced the unknown. He was unhappy at Grafton House, but, lacking any comparisons, assumed that the school was just like any other and that this was something that had to be endured en route to maturity. Crucially, he was about to lose close friends with whom he had spent time during the war, and, with commendable imagination, had overcome the lack of time spent with parents, having few toys and the imposition of harsh standards of discipline imposed by the school on the pupils who lived in constant fear of the teachers. The 'gang' had created a substitute family that had filled a vacuum. He would also miss his new friend June, who, totally innocently, was beginning to compensate for the lack of a sister. Now he was alone and it was difficult to make new friends.

Peter had made an effort to understand Tim who, thanks to Ann, was also more understanding. Rows between the two were significantly less frequent but total peace had not broken out. Tim decided, as far as possible, not to argue but the phrase 'that boy' was still heard from time to time during the confrontations which continued for many years. Tim's unhappiness was also fuelled by the fact that Susan still favoured Harry who took occasional delight in ensuring that Tim was rebuked for an alleged offence on his person, when he was in a different room. 'Leave that boy alone' was a familiar order and Tim's protests that he was elsewhere and thus could not have been guilty of whatever crime Harry had invented were dismissed immediately. 'Timothy, I'm not interested. Don't tell lies.' This favouritism, always denied, but patently real, faded over the years but it contributed to Tim's unhappiness.

In 1948, when Tim realised that he was to be deported to the capital, he had suggested to June, his casual friend who happened to be a girl, that she might like to come to London for a holiday. Knowing that she enjoyed tennis, he even speculated that they could go to the Wimbledon tournament but June pointed out that the Wimbledon Singles Finals had already taken place, won by Robert Falkenburg and Louise Brough. Another attraction that might have encouraged June to visit, although it commenced only 48 hours after the family's return to London, was the London Olympic Games, which were staged between the 29th July and 14th August at a time of such deep austerity that competitors had to provide their own towels. They were accommodated at 30 different sites, including army barracks, schools and colleges. Rationing was still in force but overseas athletes were granted rations allocated to workers in heavy industry and could also have two pints of milk a day and half a pound of chocolates or sweets. British athletes, who failed to win a single gold medal, even had to sew the national badge on to their clothes. The USA won 38 gold medals, which, unsurprisingly, were not made of gold. The event, which attracted 80,000 spectators to Wembley, was opened by King George V1 who was aided by 2,500 pigeons which were released as a gesture of peace. Cynics may feel that as they had been captured in the first place, this adversely affected their basic avian rights.

June promised to ask her mother to approve her having a holiday in London. Tim had not discussed his high-risk initiative with Susan, fearing that it would be vetoed with the speed of a politician, guilty of a stupid remark, claiming that the had been quoted out of context by the malicious and mendacious media. He hoped that if Mrs Foster accepted the invitation for her daughter it would be difficult for Susan to withdraw an offer she had not made.

One morning in August, Susan was visibly angry and shouted at Tim.

'Timothy, what do you think this is?'

Tim was tempted to say that, at a range of several yards, it was difficult to be precise but was reasonably confident that it was a letter. However, seeing his mother in what seemed to be a unique rage, he decided, wisely, to remain silent, in line with his policy of not defending himself or challenging an accusation.

'I'll tell you what it is. It's a letter from a Mrs Foster. Apparently, she is the mother of a girl called June, whom you invited to spend time with us in London. That's the first I've heard of it.'

Tim, who now realised that his plan faced problems, considered mentioning that Susan had suggested that Tim might spend a holiday with any of his friends and that he knew June's brother, but remained silent. It seemed best not to add fuel to what was fast becoming a conflagration.

'Mrs Foster says that, rather than June having a holiday here, you might like to spend time with them.'

This, of course, was the first that Tim had heard of the counter proposal and, as far as he was concerned, it could have been a welcome move as he could spend some time with his other friends in the summer holidays. His hopes were cut short.

'Well, I can tell you that you have absolutely no chance of spending time with this girl. I'm disgusted about the whole affair.'

Her son came close to denying that it was an affair but remained silent. Why was his mother so angry? Admittedly, he had not mentioned the proposal to her in advance as he knew it would be rejected. 'It's disgusting and depraved that a small boy would even consider having a holiday with a girl. I think that there must be something wrong with you. I really don't know what your father would make of all this. It's very peculiar. Say something!'

On the grounds that, confronted with such violent and sustained anger, silence was his best tactic, Tim remained mute, although he was anxious to know why, apparently, there was something wrong with him. Some of his fellow pupils had friends who were girls and they seemed quite normal. It was clear that he would not be going to the west country and that London would not be seeing June.

Susan ignored his silence and continued.

'I've got a letter here, addressed to Mrs Foster, and, as part of your punishment, you must take it to the box at the top of the road and post it.'

Tim took the proffered letter and, gloomily and ten minutes later, left the house.

Oddly, the front door was already open but his thoughts were on the cruelty of ordering him to initiate his own execution. As he reached the post box, he took a lingering look at the letter, debated whether it was preferable to destroy it and then, after a few seconds' pondering, entrusted the communication to the Royal Mail. As he turned back, he happened to glance further up the road and, to his intense anger, he saw Susan, who had hidden behind a tree. She obviously did not even trust him to post the letter and, this hurt almost as much as the fact that he would not see June again and that, apparently, there was something wrong with him. Why was his life so unpleasant? Later that evening, mother and son were home. Ann, who knew nothing about this crisis was away, spending a few days with a friend in Hastings, so could not mediate.

Susan was still angry. 'I'm really disgusted about what you've done but we'll say no more about it.'

Tim, having decided to request an explanation, started to deliver the composed sentence but was immediately silenced.

'I don't want to hear any more about it. Is that understood? And I'm going to punish you by cancelling your pocket money for a month.' As Tim never received regular pocket money, he smiled inwardly but still wondered why Susan had been so angry and accused him of being odd. Some days later, he discovered that Harry apparently received regular pocket money and he took great pleasure in telling Tim that 'I've got more now as Mama says I'm such a good boy'.

Had he been saved from some terrible fate by a considerate mother? Nothing unpleasant happened to other boys who had girls as friends. Why should he have been different? Susan must have resented being deceived but, given the chance, Tim would have contended that her policy of refusing to discuss having a friend who was a girl gave him no choice. Presumably, Susan was motivated by her concern for Tim's welfare but an explanation might have helped to ease the overwhelming pain. In those days, a normal relationship between two young people of different genders was very different to that which prevails now. The total innocence that characterised such friendships would be ridiculed by most young people today, if they could even understand it.

Three years after the June non-affair, Tim met the daughter of one of his father's crew when he visited the vessel in dock. Mary, then in her mid teens, was totally innocent, like Tim, and wrote to him suggesting a stay with her family in Salisbury. Amazingly, lightening had struck again in the same place. If he had known the phrase, he might have muttered something about *déjà vu*. Again, the heavy hand of the censor intervened, making Tim wonder afresh why it was so wrong to be friendly with a girl even although his male friends were not so restricted and that there was no evidence that knowing girls had ruined their lives. Tim was never treated to an explanation. Elders knew what was best and explanations were unnecessary because, by definition, parents were both older and wiser. All that Tim had to do was to obey.

In the late Forties and early Fifties, most of the family enjoyed the occasional holiday when Peter was granted leave. In 1949, the year after the family had returned to London, the Adams had a holiday in Preston but, a cowered Tim did not even attempt to see June. He saw her parents' elderly Ford but she was not in it and he knew that he had seen her for the last time which made him very sad. Subsequent vacations were taken in Bournemouth, Lyme Regis and the Isle of Wight. The island holiday proved a failure which prompted Peter, volubly and unambiguously, conveying to the manager of the hotel some of the faults that he had perceived and then being surprised that the brothers knew what he had said. Few on the island would not have heard his comments. Before launching into a memorable speech, he muttered, as if to motivate himself, 'am I a man or mouse?' Clearly, homo sapiens triumphed over the rodent.

Peter and Susan generously paid for Tim to attend the local preparatory school, Sandgate. Harry, patently brighter, eventually attended the junior section attached to Hudson Hall School and Simon followed some years later. Tim had disliked most of the bullying staff at Grafton House but at least respected them for their efforts in extra-curriculum activities in very difficult circumstances but he had only contempt for most of the staff at the new school. It was situated in a very old house, in a busy road, not far from home which was fortunate as heavily-laden and multi-buckled satchels, containing homework and games clothes, had to be carried.

One feature of the period was the dense smogs that obliterated everything for weeks but enlivened the walk to school. The familiar became alien, even where its outline shape could just be discerned, and some skill was required when crossing the road. It was impossible to see your own hand in front of your face, however keen you were on examining it, but the main memory was the smell that was lodged in the boys' snouts. The smog was caused mainly by the widespread use of coal so any exposure to it made the boys and their raincoats dirty. Eventually Clean Air Acts curbed emissions and dense smog became a thing of the past. In December 1952, when smog persisted for five days, some 12,000 people died prematurely. In the same month, patrons sitting in balcony seats at the Festival Hall could not see the stage and some people, walking along the banks of the Thames, fell into the river.

In 1948, the impact of the war was still partly responsible for the abysmally low standard of teaching but this private school was run for profit with little apparent regard for academic levels. Judging by their performance, most of the 'teaching' staff were cheap. One master was a 50 year old, with the energy of a frail octogenarian, who had no concept of teaching and found it impossible to communicate. Simply inarticulate, he merely exhorted his pupils to read the text books, leaving him to keep discipline and he failed in this too. He was always dressed in baggy old brown trousers and a battered green sports jacket, probably bought, second hand, before the war. Clothes rationing, which had been introduced in the UK in 1941, ended on 1st February 1949 but there was no change in the poor man's apparel.

A former vicar was in charge of sport. He was a black-suited blatant homosexual who parted his hair down the middle which, in itself, seemed odd to the boys, as did his clear dislike of sport. They did not know about homosexuals. He did nothing to hide his keen interest in little boys, relying on their total innocence and the apparent inability of the headmaster to detect or take action on any deviance. He left suddenly, for reasons that were never explained, merely saying that he was going to California. This was announced with all the gravitas with which an impending journey to the shops in nearby Wood Green would have been revealed. He was a fundamentally unpleasant man and, in later years some of his charges must have wondered what might have happened if even one pupil had been brave enough to recount the odious man's apparent fondness for slapping small boys' legs. The abhorrent vicar was replaced by a younger man, Swinford, who showed similar tendencies.

What provoked two seriously deranged men to apply for and secure jobs as 'teachers' in a boys' prep school in the late Forties? The new man was more discreet and seemingly more discriminating in his choice of little friends. Thankfully, Tim was not in this band and Swinford formed a school scout troop for reasons on which it would be wrong to speculate. Despite his previous experience in the Wolf Cubs at Grafton House, Tim was not made a patrol leader, so resigned in protest. This, one of his first acts of defiance, was not well received.

There was one genuine teacher on the staff. Aged about 60, Robertson, bald as a billiard ball and with a head shaped much like an Easter egg, was a kindly man and stimulated an understanding and appreciation of English that played a significant part in the rest of Tim's life. Indeed, he was the first real teacher that Tim had experienced and he made him realise the inadequacies of the others even more clearly.

The gym master, who would have failed to hold down almost any other job, was full of his own-self importance and enjoyed making young boys leap around in any way he wanted. Jones was an ignorant, sadistic and nearly hairless man and his lack of imagination in the matter of his name extended to his day-to-day clothes. He always wore an elderly black polo-necked sweater that, to judge by its appearance, had provided a long-term home and restaurant for moths who were not too fussy about the lack of a varied menu. Lest there be any doubt about his role, his feet were permanently encased in some tired gym shoes. Wearing gym shoes all day, every day, does not a gym teacher make. Like most people, he looked older than his years and sported cheap ugly glasses that detracted from the youthful and energetic personality he was keen to present.

The headmaster was a reasonable teacher, despite his lack of formal training, but his main pleasure seemed to be applying corporal punishment to his charges, often for the most trivial of reasons. Almost hidden in a huge gown and sporting a beard which, presumably, was intended to make him look like an academic, the man should never have been allowed to be in charge of a school. His ignorance of or acquiescence in the homosexual activities of two of his staff should have immediately disqualified him for life. Did he have such inclinations himself?

When Tim arrived at Sandgate in September 1948, it was too late to take part in cricket matches, not because the match had started but because the season was over. To his surprise, not having played soccer, he secured a place in the school first eleven which suggests that the standard was very low. Previously, his winters had been spent playing, no, that's wrong, participating, in rugby matches and, although his dedicated following of Torquay United in the Football League Division Three, South, had given him some ideas on what the game was about and how to play it, he was not fully conversant with all the rules. His fame soared when, from left back, he scored for the school second team as it succumbed to a local school in a 12 goal thriller that was lost 11-1. The side would have been lucky to score nil.

The next year, 1949, Tim developed as an opening bowler, became vice captain of the cricket team and won the school bowling cup. His batting average, of just over six, was about five more than his ability warranted but only a few behind the leading batsman. He was awarded his colours and his impressive blazer, of which he was immensely proud, was navy blue and edged with gold which resembled the England cricket team's blazer. Furthermore, under the school badge, on the breast pocket, to save anyone querying the reason for such a colourful garment, the legend was 1st XI cricket. Tim missed the whole of the 1950 season, having had his right arm badly twisted by some thugs in a nearby wood.

One aspect of Sandgate life was the Christmas play. Inexplicably, Tim was selected to play the role of the Mad March Hatter in an ambitious production of Alice in Wonderland. Bizarrely, the hatter was required to have a Lancashire accent which was odd as it was years before having an impenetrable regional accent was favoured by the BBC and long before any gardening experts hailed from the north. Acquiring such an accent proved beyond Tim and, in a move that spelt disaster for the future of British drama, and, possibly, televised horticultural work, he was relegated to the role of a mere gardener. He was allowed to use his accent-free voice when offering his immortal single line. He blamed a fellow gardener for some minor problem, or should that now be issue, claiming that 'Seven jogged my elbow'.

The play was rather unusual. Not only was the mad hatter required to have a Lancashire accent, but, in the interests of regional equality, other actors had to have Scottish, Birmingham, Liverpool and Devonian accents. Predictably, this meant that much of the play was totally incomprehensible as the boys tried, and failed, to oblige. Indeed, some accents seemingly owed more to Australia and Germany, for example, than to parts of the United Kingdom. The audience, understandably, was baffled but lacked little in their loyal praise for their brave boys who tried their best.

However, even as a mere gardener, Tim was involved in a serious incident on the first and only evening performance. The horticulturalists, and the number suggested that Tim was not the only boy who failed to master an alien accent, had to sit cross-legged and motionless whilst a few long but sadly unintelligible speeches were made. Determined to resurrect his career in the theatre, or, to be more accurate, in a converted class room, he stirred not and could easily have been mistaken for a statue. However, there comes a time when even young gardeners must stand up. At the right moment, Tim failed this elementary move. Pins and needles had set in to such an extent that his feet could have been sawn off and he would not have felt anything or noticed until trying to don footwear. 'I say, has anybody seen my feet?' His fellow gardeners hauled him to his feet and propped him up.

Before the play started, some boys had placed the unpleasant gym master's long and shabby raincoat on a hanger and then draped trousers on the rung of the hanger. The model had been completed when a football, adorned by a hat, had been stuck on top of the hanger. The completed work, facing inwards, was then draped over the inside of a long window which backed on to the street.

Eric Wilkins, the local constable, was ambling down the road, bemoaning the lack of crime which might have given some impetus to his stalled career. On the other hand, he was happy not to have much responsibility and, on balance, preferred life as it was. Frankly, he would have liked more pay and status but unaccompanied by more work or responsibility. Suddenly, he was jolted out of his reverie. He happened to be glancing towards the large window on the front of the school, when he saw, no, it couldn't be, what seemed to be a hanging body gently illuminated by the modest light inside. He peered again and was convinced that he was not wrong, even although he was in his own peaceful patch and local crime, in his view, would not afflict the area for about another four decades. He happened to be near a public phone and, surprisingly, the phone was in working condition.

'Sarge, I think that I've found a body.'

'Wilkins, I've told you before, you must not drink whilst you're swanning around on duty. Now pull yourself together and don't bother me whilst I'm trying to fill in the station's football pools coupon for this weekend. I'll say no more about this call now but don't give me cause for complaint again, otherwise your career will be cooked, like a dead goose.'

Wilkins never understood his sergeant's apparent and wonky obsession with birds but had more on his mind.

'No, I'm sure that there's a body hanging up in the local school.' Sergeant Dickson replied.

'I know that some bullies work there but murder does seem a little hard to believe and rather final. Now, stop mucking around and get back to work.'

'I tell you, I'm not joking. I want some backup before I go in.'

The sergeant swallowed hard and pondered his next move. Should he give his colleague the bird? Could he afford to chicken out of the situation? He was not making much progress and he was not all that confident that Arsenal might manage a draw with Manchester United.

'I'm busy doing the pools. Do you think Arsenal might draw at Old Trafford?'

Wilkins opined that the north London side had too many foreigners. This provoked an outburst.

'They don't have any.'

'They certainly do. The goalie is a Welshman and they even have Scots and Irishmen.'

'Yes, perhaps they do need some more Englishmen.'

The sergeant looked at his scribblings, before continuing to fill in the coupon that, if successful, could ensure that the local police force all resigned simultaneously. It was time to stir his remaining grey cells in another direction.

Wilkins, increasingly concerned about the body, felt that this was not the right time to discuss Arsenal's prospects.

Dickson responded. 'If I do come and this proves to be a wild duck chase, you'll be back on traffic duty for the rest of your career. If I remember rightly, there is no back entrance and ….'

'Don't ring off, sarge, I haven't any more change and the pips will go any minute.' As he spoke, the pips duly obliged, neatly confirming his forecast.

After deciding that Arsenal's multinational team would lose, Dickson, having thought that he ought to visit the school, walked around the corner to see what the problem was, or, as people now say, he headed, you know, like, for the school to sort out the issue. Wilkins, unsure if he was to receive back-up, was pacing nervously up and down outside the local centre for education, wondering what to do. He was greatly relieved to see the man, whom he reluctantly called his superior, approaching.

'Look, here, the body's hung up on that window.'

Sergeant Dickson did as he was bidden. 'Yes, it certainly looks like a body. Well done Wilkins.' The sergeant took decisive action, which was admirable as, in his 35 years with the force, he had yet to see a body but he had listened to many crime programmes on the wireless so he knew what to do.

'There's no back entrance to this school, right?'

'Yes, I'm sure of that.'

'Right, we'll break down the front door and charge in. I want you to ensure that nobody, I repeat nobody, leaves. We must surprise them. Got that?'

Wilkins, who was both short and thin, confirmed that he had got that and, beckoned by his bulkier superior, planned a hefty physical assault on the front door. He lowered his shoulder to overcome the door's resistance, took a run and promptly fell in a heap in the hall. The door was not only unlocked, it was not shut. He picked himself up and, using his remaining supplies of immediate energy, stormed into what had been converted into a theatre, followed swiftly by his superior.

'Right, nobody move, stay just where you are.'

Wilkins tried to sound authoritative to overcome his nervousness but something went wrong and he sounded like a small boy whose voice had not quite broken. The audience, already baffled by the proliferation of accents that had resulted in the most unusual production of Alice in Wonderland that any of the parents and friends had ever seen, was puzzled by the arrival of two policemen. Presumably, it was all part of the play although nobody seemed able to recall the police being involved in Alice. However, a German and Italian, for example, who had appeared in the first few minutes of the play, had not figured in the original story either so the injection of two English policemen did not seem necessarily incongruous.

The arrival of the police coincided with another totally impenetrable speech from the mad hatter whose Lancashire accent had mysteriously been supplanted by something that sounded vaguely Spanish. This, according to some perceptive members of the audience, was one accent that had not been heard in the first hour of the dramatic production. The sergeant's wish to take the audience by surprise was fulfilled. The mad hatter abruptly ceased his peroration and looked appropriately shocked. One man, sitting in the front row, commented favourably on the young actor's very professional reaction.

'He looked genuinely surprised. He'll go far in the theatre.' The drama lover turned to his female friend and observed 'it's remarkable what they can do with makeup. Did you notice that policeman's moustache and his face which looked as if he was about fifty? The only flaw was when that first copper told us that we shouldn't move. His voice had not broken, poor lad, and no makeup could make up for that.' The audience, now fully accepting that this was a most unusual production of Alice, began to laugh. It seemed that the police had more than a silent role. The boy who was wearing a sergeant's uniform, barked out an instruction to his fellow thespian.

'Wilkins, it's on that window. Check it.'

Wilkins, who had inspired this event, knew precisely where the body was and promptly proceeded in the correct direction to examine what he had seen. If it was a body, then he would be really involved and that would be a welcome change from checking road fund licences. If, on the other hand, it was not a body, he might be in trouble. Then again, on the other hand, he might be praised for being alert. He realised that he now had three hands so approached the body. Meanwhile, thinking about the audience's reaction to his command that they should remain where they were, he was less than happy because his order had induced guffaws. The boys, who knew about the body, prayed that the coppers would arrest the headmaster for wasting police time. Suddenly, rousing himself from his temporary bemusement, the head, surprisingly employing a southern English accent, demanded to know what was going on but met with no response. The audience welcomed his participation in the play which, according to one woman in the front row, confirmed that he was not 'too stuffy'.

Wilkins, having investigated as ordered, returned to his superior with the news that it was not a real body. As the audience continued laughing noisily, the sergeant asked his subordinate to repeat what he had just said as he could not hear him. 'I said, sarge, it's not a body, it's just some old clothes on a hanger.' Then he added, gratuitously, 'They're really old, filthy and smelly. Only a real tramp would wear rubbish like that.' Jones, who had recognised them as they had mysteriously vanished from his locker two days ago, displeased to hear this description of his outfit, wisely decided to defer claiming possession.

The audience, having given up trying to work out how all this impinged on Alice or any of her friends, laughed afresh as the police beat a hurried and, apparently embarrassed retreat, as fast as their boots would allow. It had all been so realistic but it was not clear how it fitted into the plot but, somehow, it did not matter. One person in the audience, Hugh, the father of one of the pupils, was the editor of the local newspaper. As he had seen such an unusual version of the play, he decided to write a few words. If he did it almost immediately, it could be in the weekend edition.

Local school's challenging interpretation of Alice in Wonderland

School plays usually reflect hard work and genuine endeavour. All involved, including the teachers who devote so much time to the productions, and, of course, the pupils, apply themselves with an enviable enthusiasm in an effort to impress parents and friends but the common factor is that the dramas are always predictable. No such charge could be levied against Sandgate School. In a memorable version of Alice in Wonderland, they defied convention by, inexplicably requiring many of the actors to speak in what appeared to be attempts at regional and foreign accents. Unfortunately, not all the pupils succeeded. This unconventional approach bemused the audience but the boys deserve praise for their efforts.

However the highlight of the evening was when two boys, clearly the best actors in the show, appeared as policemen, apparently determined to find out why a body was hanging over a window. As one member of the audience told me, 'I'm not sure how they fitted into the play but their make up and enthusiasm was most real. Even the headmaster had a modest role when he demanded to know what was going on. I respected him for his imagination and unselfishly taking only a tiny speaking part. The 'police' soon realised that the 'body' was a fake and left to much applause. They were the best part of the show and we all thoroughly enjoyed their participation even if we don't know how all this was relevant to Alice.'

Many West End 'sophisticated up-market' productions puzzle audiences. This small school, with its unconventional approach to a well-know play, deserves our congratulations for their courage in following a worthy tradition and the audience, albeit bemused, enjoyed the experience.

The editor's son, Jimmy, was chatting to his father two days later. The latter suggested that the two of them should visit White Hart Lane football ground on the Saturday, to see Spurs but first of all, he wanted to know why the 'police' had become involved in the school play. Apparently, their arrival was not in the script and the so-called body had been created by some imaginative boys who, of course, had no idea that their prank would involve the real police. The headmaster had not seen the joke and had told those who had 'perpetrated this act' that they must own up. Fearing severe retribution, nobody had, so the headmaster decided that all those in the two senior classes would have to be in detention on the Saturday afternoon.

'So, you see, dad, I can't go to the football.'

'That's very unfair. Hasn't the man got a sense of humour?'

'Apparently not.'

Hugh picked up the phone, introduced himself to the headmaster and said that he had been in the audience and had enjoyed the participation of the police. 'I understand that, contrary to what we thought, they were not boys acting but the real police and they turned up because they thought that there was a body hanging up. In a word, they were doing their job.'

'Yes, but.'

'No, let me finish.'

The headmaster acquiesced.

'Now, I understand that it was but a simple prank by some boys who have decided not to own up. Frankly, I'm not surprised, given your reputation for harsh punishment, but I don't want to go into that just now, but perhaps another day I might well investigate that and the sudden departure of some of your rather queer staff, especially that odd chap who was going, allegedly, to the US. Apparently, many boys will now be in detention next Saturday afternoon as nobody has owned up. That's not justice. As you'll know, I wrote a friendly piece for my paper. I shall follow that up pointing out that my investigation now shows that the involvement of the real police was the result of a prank by some of the boys, not because you had written the police into the script. As the police scene went down so well, I think that my readers will think that your sense of humour and justice have deserted you and that your judgement was lacking. They'll think it odd that you didn't admit what actually happened, before the end of the evening. Obviously, you knew that they were real police but you didn't explain that to the audience. Frankly, it doesn't show you in a very good light.'

The headmaster, who, like some of his pupils, knew when he was beaten, had listened carefully, struggled to say something and eventually managed it. He knew that he was about to lose so sought to reduce the damage.

'I can see now that I have over-reacted to what was a silly prank. I'll apologise to the police for wasting their time and cancel the detention.'

Then, trying to sound as casual as he could, he continued.

'Is there any chance that you might forget a new article about this business?'

'What article?'

'Thank you.'

Hugh told his son that the detention had been cancelled and that they would be watching Spurs that Saturday afternoon but the headlines came from Old Trafford, where Arsenal had triumphed 4-

0.

All pupils had to partake of the mid day 'meal' at least twice a week, doubtless in the school's quest to increase profits and to justify the employment of she who did something to the food before the brave boys tried to eat it. There was no dispute on the quantity of food made available: the portions were generous. Would that they had been smaller as the main problem was the lack of quality.

The person masquerading as a cook, Mrs Salmon, was, hopefully, unique. Her facial features would have justified a permanent hatred of mother nature who had decided that, as she was to become someone involved with food, she ought to have a face like a raw, earthy and creased potato. Trying to imply that she was a cook, she sported a chef's hat which occasionally slid down over her eyes which may have explained why she did not always add the right substances, not all of which were food. Salmon was an inveterate smoker and ash frequently dropped into a large bowl of what was, before she became involved in its future, described as food. She enjoyed lobbing potatoes into the huge container from distant parts of the filthy and old-fashioned kitchen. Her skill fell short of her ambition, especially when her headgear succumbed to gravity and reduced her vision. Many of the spuds were picked up from a filthy floor and dropped into the receptacle. Despite daily practice, she did not become more accurate.

Fortunately, the staff were served with the same 'food', although doubtless they generously insisted that the growing lads should have larger portions than they in those days of austerity. Cabbage was a Salmon speciality. If criminals had been forced to eat a few bowls of her cabbage, crime rates would have plunged and recidivism would not have become a problem. It is difficult to describe the outcome of her efforts with a well-known and much-liked veggie. One theory was that she had used carbolic soap to clean the leaves and had omitted to wash it off before further preparation. This was unlikely because cleanliness was an alien concept in this kitchen. Whatever the processes inflicted on the hapless leaves had the most dramatic impact and the Royal Society for the Prevention of Cruelty to Animals would, surely, have banned it for non-human consumption. Pigs would have opted for starvation during the war if offered this material and humans compelled to eat the foul substance could now invoke Human Rights legislation. If it had been exported to the United States for prisoners to devour, the lawyers could have justly argued that this constituted a cruel and unusual punishment that violated the Constitution. It was certainly no good for Tim's constitution. In a word, lunches were inedible.

One challenge for the boys was how to avoid consuming Salmon's muck: her main efforts were devoted to ruining cabbage, and, in this, it may be doubted if anyone in the country could have challenged her, but she deployed similar skills on much else that had been purchased as food. It was not possible just to re-organise the provisions around the side of intending consumers' plates and, commenting on how delicious the meal was, claim to be full up with appropriate apologies that you just couldn't manage another mouthful.

Sadistic and toady guards, volunteers to a boy, who had generously forgone their own meals, were positioned on either side of the door to the kitchen, to check all the plates being returned and the amount of rejected material on each. Only clean plates or those that did not hide much rejected material, were allowed in to be placed on a kitchen worktop. Tim had a bright idea. There was no set procedure for the collection of plates of food from the staff. Sometimes one of the masters would oblige, doubtless in an effort to ingratiate himself with the headmaster. One day, when Tim could not eat any of the infamous cabbage and the rest of the main course, which was even more distasteful than usual, he noted that the staff had arrived at a similar view. He rose and chose Jones, the horrible gym master and then Swinford, the sadistic homosexual.

'Can I help you, sirs, by taking your plates away?'

Each immediately agreed and, very carefully, Tim added his own rejected muck. Equally cautiously, he clambered up the stairs to the room where good ingredients were converted into inedible material. As he had anticipated, the juvenile food police wanted some basic information.

'Who's left all this food?'

Before Tim could say anything, including challenging the view that he was returning food, the older guard intervened. 'Take this food back to where it came from and tell the owners of the plates that they must eat everything.'

Tim had placed his rejected 'food' on the top two plates so that his was empty.

The older guard resumed. 'Look, someone enjoyed his lunch. Leave this plate and take the other two. Tell whoever left all this food that it must, repeat must, be eaten. There are millions of children, all over the world, who are starving and would wolf this down.'

Tim's plan was working rather better than he had anticipated but he realised that he must reveal that the rejected sustenance came from the staff. His attempts were immediately brushed aside.

'Take them back, do as you're told and don't interrupt.'

Tim felt that he had no choice and approached Jones and Swinford who looked up in surprise as what appeared to be their lunch, albeit in a disgusting heap, rather larger in volume than that which they had rejected, was being returned. Before Tim could begin his account, he was asked why he was presenting them with the remains of their sustenance. His return, with full plates that, seemingly, were now being returned to two members of staff, had attracted the attention of some fellow pupils. One obsequious and temporary teacher, unaware of the identity of the criminals, expressed surprise that so much good food had been rejected and voiced the view, loudly, that they should be forced to eat it as thousands of children around the world were starving.

Tim was about to deal with Swinford's wish to know why his meal had been returned, 'albeit in an even more repellent form, piled up like some old and smelly socks'.

'As you know, sir, two boys outside the kitchen check all the remains on the plates as they are returned and they always insist that if there is more than say, a few spoonfuls, it must be returned to what they call the 'ungrateful boy' to eat.'

'Yes, we know that. Didn't you tell them that the plates came from the staff?'

'No, sir, I tried but they wouldn't let me speak and just ordered me to return the plates and to tell whoever left the food to eat it up and be grateful as there were so many starving people around the world who were starving and who would be grateful for anything that prevented them from starving as they were starving.' Tim, now aware that most of the school was now listening, had obligingly increased his own volume but was becoming nervous and felt that he had not expressed the views of the food police in a very articulate form.

Jones spoke next.

'Take these plates back and tell them that they are plates from the staff.'

'They won't let me, sir, they refused to let me speak.'

'Right then, Adams, come with me and bring the plates.'

As the plates, accompanied by Tim and Jones left the room, there was a buzz of more intense conversation. Characteristically, the headmaster remained impotent and silent. A few moments later, conversations ceased as they heard Jones giving voice.

'You two boys, were you here a few minutes ago, when Adams brought in some plates?'

'Yes, sir.'

'Did he tell you whose plates they were?'

'No, our orders, from the headmaster, are that all food must be eaten and we must reject any leftovers.'

Jones exploded and even allowed himself to swear.

'You stupid boys, I don't give a damn who gave you the orders. If you think that I'm going to eat this flaming muck, that's not fit for animals, let alone humans, you must be mad. The food here's bloody disgraceful and I'm amazed that the brave boys who do eat some of it aren't ill. They must be either desperately hungry or frightened of the headmaster. That blasted Salmon woman must be a relative of his. I can't think of any other reason that she's got a job here. She's a magician, she changes good ingredients into inedible muck.'

At this point, Jones marched over to the dustbin into which the remnants of the food were tipped. 'There's only one place for this and it's the dustbin. I just hope that it's not given to pigs. I rather like pigs.'

The blasted Salmon woman, who had been cowering in the corner, burst into tears, pulled off the headgear which suggested to the uninitiated that she was professionally involved in cooking, picked up her coat, slipped on a potato still on the floor, kicked a cabbage which hit the window, walked down the stairs and marched into the temporary dining room. She approached the headmaster, who had heard what Jones had said but had remained silent whilst pondering what to do. He need ponder for no longer. Matters were moving fast.

Salmon, clearly deeply angered, addressed the congregation.

'I've never been treated so badly in my life. I don't come here every day to be insulted.'

Someone muttered that he wondered where she did go to be insulted but was silenced by a glare from the headmaster.

'I've always done my best and nobody has ever complained before.'

Another critic suggested that might be because they died of food poisoning.

'I don't really like this place and some of you boys are always rude to me. I only work my fingers to the bone here so I can support my sick mother.'

'No wonder she's sick if she has to eat your food.'

This critic, too, was silenced by a glance from the headmaster who was still trying to work out his response.

'Well, you can all go hungry for all I care. I'm leaving now.'

So saying, she picked up a dirty and gravy-stained potato from one of the boy's plates and threw it in the general direction of the headmaster. It was, for once, an accurate lob and it hit his jacket and proceeded to trace a neat brown line down the lapels of his light grey suit. The boys were spellbound and silent. They had never seen such an exciting incident. A few minutes later, the headmaster, now wearing a different suit, made an announcement.

'It appears, as you will have seen, that Mrs Salmon, who,

incidentally, is not one of my relatives, no longer wants to work here. We must respect her decision. We shall all miss what she has done to us, I mean for us, but, in the meantime, please tell your parents that for the foreseeable period of time, you must bring your own lunch, in the shape of sandwiches.'

Tim detected some ambiguity in the phrase 'in the shape of sandwiches' but wisely refrained from seeking more precise information.

Later that day, one boy who was passing the headmaster's study, overheard shouting.

'I don't care what you felt about the food but you could have handled the situation much better. Your shouting and swearing at the Salmon woman could have been heard miles away. Now I've lost a cook, who didn't cost me much, and the chance for making some money from charging parents for the lunches. Our finances are not good, so we've got to make some changes. You must go. You're dismissed with immediate effect.'

Tim, whose brainwave had triggered this incident, was amazed at the outcome and basked in his friends' praise. He had managed to ensure that Salmon and Jones were no longer on the staff.

Tim's social life was limited. He enjoyed visiting a Sandgate friend at East Finchley every Saturday afternoon after school and playing Snakes and Ladders, Cluedo, Totopoly, Monopoly, Canasta or billiards before a supper that always consisted of a bag of crisps and some cold meat, followed by an orange. Another treat was watching their large but small-screen television when viewers were treated on Saturday evenings to Café Continental and other variety shows. Later, he was driven home in the parents' Morris Oxford.

Tim's friends never visited the Adams home as visitors were not encouraged. Outings were rare and Tim had to rely on his friend and his parents for taking him out to interesting places such as Hampstead Heath, where the boys played cricket, and Northolt Airport, where it was possible to sit on strangely curved and uncomfortable white chairs only a few yards from the aircraft. His friends also took him to an air show at Ford in Sussex and even treated him to the occasional meal in the West End of London and to speedway at Harringay stadium. Why did few friends visit Tim's home? Admittedly, unlike his friend's home, the garden was small, which prevented any serious attempts to play cricket, and there was no car until the late Fifties. Possibly, as Peter was nearly always away from home, Susan had too much to do.

Despite Susan's entreaties, when Peter was on leave, he was still not entirely happy with his son's behaviour and Tim remained a frightened, shy and unhappy young boy. Once again, Susan challenged her husband in the privacy of their own room and demanded to know why Peter was always so displeased with their oldest son. As usual, the response was 'it's his attitude. He always seems so damned superior as if he's too good for us!'

'As I've told you before, I know he seems so superior but that's just part of growing up. He's trying to build up his self-esteem. I believe that he's made an effort and I think you should do as well. I'm pleading with you to give him a chance. He's shy and doesn't make friends easily and if we go on like this, it'll get worse. Please try, if only for me. I'm just not prepared to tolerate it any more. Tim's not a bad boy but, if we carry on like this we could drive him away from us as soon as he's older and we'll lose our son.' Generously, she had said if 'we carry on' and she knew that she had made the same speech before. Peter grunted and, inwardly, he knew that he was partly responsible for the unsatisfactory relationship. He was the adult and he promised to do what he could. The relationship with his son did improve but war had only given way to a truce.

One day, when Tim returned from school, he wondered where Ann was. She always greeted him and their relationship was good. As soon as she had let Tim in, Susan had rushed upstairs. Tim also wanted to know why the doctor's car was parked outside. As he stood at the foot of the stairs, he heard him say 'it's not good, I can only give her a week at best. I'm sorry but there's nothing more I can do'. Tim was dumbfounded. He knew that, but for his grandmother's efforts over the years, his own life would have been even more difficult. Now, suddenly, and without any warning, it seemed as if she would be dead in less than a fortnight. His face became ashen and, without any shame, he began to cry. He scampered into the kitchen when he heard his mother and the doctor come downstairs.

'Thank you, doctor, for coming so promptly and being candid about my mother's condition. I hope that your family's in good health.' Tim was dumbfounded. Her mother was dying but Susan seemed so cheerful. She then saw Tim, pale-faced and crying. 'What on earth is wrong? Has there been trouble at school?' Was his mother made of wood?

'I just heard the doctor say that he could only give nana a week at best, that he could do no more and you thanked him for being so candid. I don't want nana to die. She's been my friend.'

Unusually, Susan attempted to put her arm around her son but he wriggled free. 'Why don't you care about nana? She's always cared about me.'

'Listen, nana's not going to die. She felt unwell and the doctor says that it's just flu. When he said he'd give her a week that was when he thought she'd be better. I'd asked him that as nana was due to go on holiday.' Much relieved, Tim allowed his mother to cuddle him and tell him that there was nothing to worry about. She, for her part, realised how much his grandmother meant to him and vowed to be a more loving mother to her own son.

Tim's contemporaries, not exercised by family disputes, were discussing such important matters such as why Sam Costa had suddenly disappeared from the very popular *Much Binding in the Marsh*, with Kenneth Horne and Richard Murdoch. Other wireless programmes were popular and millions enjoyed listening to popular and tuneful songs such as *Buttons and Bows* from the film *Paleface* and *Slow Boat to China*.

One afternoon, in 1949, when Tim was only 12, he saw an advertisement in the newspaper which immediately ignited his imagination. He read it slowly and then consulted his mother who immediately suggested that he should follow it up. 'After all, dear, you can but try and if you are unsuccessful, at least you know you tried.' The BBC was looking for a young person to introduce the new programmes on television that were specifically for children. In those days, some air time was to be devoted to what appealed to children. The position now is reversed with little air time allocated to adult adults who dislike crime, cooking, game shows, deformed humans, reality programmes and football. Favourites with the children who had access to a television set included Muffin the mule, the irascible Peregrine the penguin and, from 1950, Richard Hearne, who amused children with his antics as Mr Pastry. Now they were looking for a young person to help present programmes.

Auditions were to be held in Broadcasting House and, having filled in all the necessary forms, Tim was invited to the west end of London, to see if he could have a career in television. He was not alone. Broadcasting House was over-run by young people, of both sexes, keen to achieve everlasting fame and wealth. The hopefuls were herded into the basement and told by an overwrought and overweight executive to form themselves 'over here' into two massive groups.

'All of you to my left will be the interviewers and you will have just three minutes to show us how good an interviewer you are.' He then added with commendable logic, as otherwise the remaining children would have nothing to do, 'those to my right' and here he waved an arm lest there were any who failed to understand, 'will be the interviewees. Just tell your interviewer what you want to talk about and then one of my colleagues will give you the signal to start.' A small army of BBC personnel emerged to listen to the interviews. Tim did not like the look of his examiner. He noted that his eyes were close together and he resembled the sort of man that Dick Barton would confront. Tim was to interview a young female who, prompted by the BBC man with the facial design defect, muttered that she wished to be interviewed on horses by which was meant the topic was 'horses' not that the girl wished to be interrogated whilst astride several equine animals. Having heard her chosen subject, there was no chance to ask her on what aspect of her interest in horses she wished to be questioned. The interview had to begin immediately.

Tim, perplexed, had to start. Should he question her on a possible interest in horse riding, the role of these animals as 'pets' or should he ask her about the role of the horse in war, on farms, on racecourses or any other activity undertaken by her four-legged friend, such as assisting in deliveries of milk? After failing with the obvious and general first question, he plied her with an admirable variety of posers but the little brute could not be coaxed into any responses that were longer than the most modest monosyllable. It may have been some consolation, that she, like Tim, did not progress to the next round but some years later, Tim saw her on television. She had become a well-known and successful skater.

The Hudson Hall School Years

1950 was the year in which North Korea invaded the south, China occupied Tibet and then crossed the 38th parallel. There were racial riots in South Africa, the UK recognised China and West Germany was admitted to the Council of Europe. George Bernard Shaw and George Orwell, died, aged 84 and 47, respectively. On the radio, Woman's Hour celebrated its 1,000 edition. In London, more than 20,000 stray dogs were rounded up by wardens. It was easy to imagine their excitement when, as the end of the year approached and only 19,950 canines had been found. 'News is just coming in that Fred in Barnet has just found another six. We're still in the hunt. Keep looking, men!'

Tim left Sandgate School in the same year and, having passed the Common Entrance Examination, by dint of slogging, made the transition into long trousers. Now, of course, all children are born wearing long trousers and only don shorter bags in middle age, when they look ridiculous, or if they are postmen working in rural areas. Clement Atlee won the General Election, but, because he was already prime minister and thus did not have to move his place of work, did not have to change his trouser type.

Tim, who hated change, joined Hudson Hall in the Christmas term in 1950 and, tentatively took the next and seemingly inevitable step towards becoming an adult. The Public School, which, of course, means that it was private, was founded in 1765 by Sir John Bar-Stad. He was illegitimate and this, and his surname, led to an unfortunate name for the old boys association. At the end of the Second World War, merely registering a male infant at Hudson Hall, for later consideration as a pupil, cost £1.1.0 which was then known as a guinea. The fee per term was £21 plus another £4.15.0 which was levied for consumption of what was delicately described as 'mid-day dinner', thus neatly alienating those who believed that dinner was an evening meal and those who maintained that mid-day tucker was called lunch.

Hudson Hall had started life as a small school but had grown steadily over the centuries and now, having acquired nearby buildings and constructing more on what had been green fields, dominated the village of Hudson Priory which, despite its name, was now essentially an urban site. Because it was spread over such a wide area, the pupils had to be fit as they flitted speedily from one class room to another or to the nearby playing fields, which had retained their original status. If Tim thought about it at all, and this is doubtful, as virtually every hour was fully occupied, he may have hoped that the teaching staff, after nearly 200 years, might have mastered the art of teaching and stimulating young boys. He knew that, even five years after the end of the war, quality teachers were still in short supply but wondered if he and many thousands of others were not just victims of the consequences of war but of the culture and fear of the masters which had changed little for many decades. In all three schools Tim attended, the masters were pre-occupied with the best students and others were merely exhorted to read, concentrate, read again, memorise and pass tests.

Tim was unhappy and, denied the opportunity of discussing it with fellow students, as he had no very close friends, confided, in a mature way, to his diary. 'Is there anything mentally wrong with me? I've no real friends and I've no prospect, despite being in my teens, of ever having a girl friend. Everyone at school seems brighter and happier than me and all I do is to work hard. I never have any fun and father, whenever he's home, often shouts at me for no reason. Is being young and not very bright a sin? Is this what childhood is all about? Who can I talk to?'

He was totally unprepared for his new life in such a large and rule-dominated community. If schooldays were the happiest days of your life, was it really worthwhile hanging around for adulthood? Was becoming an adult compulsory? Did Tim wish to continue with this odd process of growing up? Briefly, he even considered suicide but decided against it as he knew he was a coward. Why was he unhappy? Was it because he resented the unthinking authority, cruelty and injustice that were imposed? Was it because he was a cowardly rebel scared to flick a finger even at a moribund fly and that he disliked himself for this weakness? Was it because he knew that his education was costing his parents a substantial sum of money and he felt guilty? Peter, who occasionally seemingly even resented his living in the same house, often said 'that boy's so ungrateful for all we do for him'. Did this require daily grovelling? Tim retreated within himself but could not discuss his worries with Susan, when his father was back at sea, because she seemed to support him and continued to favour Harry with whom she spent much more time. Of course, she had been influential in killing any relationships with girls, which was one of Tim's problems, and had implied that there was something wrong with him. As he told his diary, 'if schooldays are the happiest days of your life and nothing better's in prospect, I don't want to become an adult. What on earth will happen to me?'

He became increasingly quiet and introvert.

Tim's time at Grafton House, especially during the war, had not been very happy, relieved only by the friendship of other members of the gang and informal cricket on the green at Preston. The stint at Sandgate was better, partly because of his success at cricket and football which reflected the absence of competition. Tim was a school prefect, vice captain of his house and vice captain of the school cricket team. In line with his mother's earlier fears, he seemed to be well into vice. Just briefly, he had became a large fish in a small pond and now, having reached Hudson Hall, he was a timid tadpole, in a huge, uncharted and dangerous lake that was home to many inhospitable rather large and unpleasant animals. Day-to-day life at school was dominated by swaggering and arrogant senior boys whose only qualification was their age. All this was doubtless an early preparation for a career in, for example, a multinational company where age and age alone was the requirement for promotion. The behaviour of these elderly boys, who aped the behaviour of the teaching staff, indicated that they could become successful teachers themselves, or, more likely, totalitarian dictators or military personnel.

Susan, worried about her eldest son, was keen to hear his views on his new school. Tim realised the sacrifice that his parents were making so his comments were carefully phrased and did little to convey his real and significant worries. He had no wish to antagonise her as he had decided to work hard for peace.

'Frankly, it's all bewildering. Some of the boys are so old, they drive their own cars to school and everywhere you look there are boys, boys running to classrooms and trying to be in two places at once. Nobody's very friendly and that includes the masters I've seen so far. There are so many rules that it's difficult to know what to do and what not to do.'

Aware that any more might worry his mother, he added thoughtfully but unconvincingly, 'but I'm sure that I'll soon be happy and will make lots of new friends'.

Susan nodded but, being less confident, merely grunted tactful agreement. She remained worried about Tim. If he had difficulties making new friends, was Peter's relationship with him partly to blame? The two had tried hard to be friends and some progress had been made, but was it all too late?

In the first week, an ugly elderly, bald, hostile and fat Italian, who was allegedly the school doctor, checked all the new boys and decided that Tim and about ten others were round-shouldered. The reality was that Tim was tired and had slumped during the nasty alien's sadistic inspection. Tim was immediately identified as being in need of 'remedial classes'. The names of those boys who had to attend these sessions had their names plastered on a main notice board so that many other 'normal' but intellectually-stunted boys, and there were hundreds of them, were able to define the group, wrongly, of course, as deformed.

One acquaintance from Sandgate, Adam Field, who had preceded Tim into the school, assured him that he would adjust. 'I know what it was like when I got here. I was bewildered by seeing so many boys in the same school. Everyone seemed to run everywhere, nobody walked. Nobody was friendly and you're told what to do all the time. Some of the masters, I admit, are ghastly twerps but some are OK when they get to know you. At first, I tried to fight it but gave up and now I just do what I'm told and that's easier than trying to fight a battle that you know you'll lose. You have so much work to do, in school and with homework and the dreaded cadet corps, that time does go fast.'

Adam was right: Tim's homework often took until 11.00 in the evening, draining him of energy for the following day's lessons, which created more difficulties, and sports devoured Saturdays until about 5.00 o'clock. Much of Sunday was devoted to cleaning and polishing Combined Cadet Force boots and uniform and finishing homework. There was no remission for good behaviour and total conformity was essential. How, then could any boy become a valuable member of society? Perhaps society, or, to be more accurate, business, the professions and the military only wanted those who conformed to social, economic and political criteria of their choosing? Apparently, a nation that had just emerged from a long and bitter war was not interested in those who challenged dogma even although the need for imaginative thinking was greater than for decades and the media spoke about the nation's thirst for innovation and a rejection of the old thinking. The message did not reach Hudson Hall.

There was little time to develop any interests or hobbies, unless they were organised by the school, and any form of social life was virtually impossible. Tim decided against participating in some school activities as he had no wish to involve his parents in additional expenditure and he lacked the time as he had to study so hard. Nothing much happened in the holidays apart from outings organised by the parents of his friend in East Finchley, and, whilst Peter was usually away, Susan always seemed too busy to take the boys out although they visited some of the London museums occasionally.

After the first term had been completed, Tim told his mother of his deep unhappiness. He had made a few friends but had been subjected to regular verbal bullying by some of the older boys. He had tried hard in the class room but found that many of the masters were, at best, sarcastic, and, at worst, sadistic. They seemed interested only in the brainier boys and Tim admitted that he was not in that group. Although he did not regale his mother with all his fears, as he was aware of their financial sacrifice, he said enough to worry Susan.

She hardly knew what to say but was saddened by what she heard.

'Would you like me to come to the school for a chat with any of your masters?'

'Thanks, but no, I think that would make things worse. It's the whole thing. It's as if we're being trained to boss people around and the first part of this process is to be bossed around ourselves. Then, when we get older, we can boss younger boys around and, then, presumably, we can boss adults around as we've been to Public school. ' He was not too happy at the way he had expressed himself and thought that there was rather too much bossing in his comments but Susan knew exactly what he meant. Despite his naiveté and youth, he had probably discerned the role of the Public school in the Fifties. Tim had tried to do his best and almost counted the days to his escape into adult life, whatever that was. Surely, it could not be worse than school?

The school was a few hundred yards from its three main playing fields. Morning lessons ended at 12.30 and the boys were often required to be changed, ready for some sporting exercise, on the closest field, half a mile away at 12.30. Discerning readers might have noted that this required them to perform the miracle of being in two places, often in different clothes, at the same time. They failed which provoked some adult oaf or elderly schoolboy to shout at them for failing to manage what mankind has never achieved. Similarly, swimming might end at, say, 2.30 and at precisely the same time the boys were required to be present, dried and changed, in another part of the complex. Despite having wet heads, which, surely, suggested even to the red-braced buffoon taking the next lesson, that their pleas that they had just come from a swimming lesson, gave some credence, they were harangued. If most of the masters who chided the pupils for failing to be in two places simultaneously, were that stupid, how could the boys rely on them to prepare them for life? In some cases, they had not experienced life, having gone to school then university before returning to the same school to teach. How would they have reacted to being in an adult community and workplace?

The 15 minute breaks in mid morning were periods of sustained lunacy. The boys had to leave the previous classroom, collect what was needed for the next lesson, consume some truly distasteful and bitterly cold milk that, in winter, like the classroom, was close to freezing, check on numerous notice boards to see what was happening, who was required to see who and when and other globally-important information, and report to their next class room, which could well be some distance away. A failure to check on a notice board and to take immediate action was a serious crime. Even more absurd was that dozens of boys would be jostling to see the same notice boards.

Membership of the Combined Cadet Force was compulsory. Older boys could opt to join the RAF group, but, like virtually everyone else, Tim was forced into the army section and became a junior member of the Middlesex Regiment. The Ministry of Defence seemed strangely unmoved by his new links with the army although, doubtless, away from the public gaze, there was much rejoicing that the British military had been strengthened. These military chaps are taught not to show their emotions.

The CCF was probably only just behind music and sport in the school's list of priorities. Academic activity lagged in fourth position. Tim hated the CCF, did not understand music and had not shown any real promise at cricket. Academic work was important, especially for the more gifted pupils, but the remainder, if they worked very hard and memorised chunks of this and that, should be all right, especially if they had the right accent. Memory, not understanding or analysis, remained the key to success.

Every Tuesday afternoon was devoted to what was euphemistically called CCF training, which meant that the unfortunates had to plod through the streets in the morning, and on their way home, in their baggy uniforms. Predictably, some of the lesser intellectuals enjoyed this and could be seen practising a swagger that marked them down for a senior position in the forces in later life. Tim's self-esteem was so low that a dachshund with a chequered background and an unhappy puppy life, would have towered over him. The opening ceremony on the parade ground involved some boys marching up and down, sideways and any other way the former self-important regimental sergeant major invented. In addition, armed with rifles that, miraculously had survived the First World War, the cadets sloped and did other things with these relics to satisfy their instructors. Some boys enjoyed this charade and it proved crucial for what they might have optimistically called their future. Cleaning the rifles was on a par with attendance at chapel each day. A dirty rifle was a sin about which decent people never spoke.

Tim dreaded the Tuesday opening drill and prayed for rain which prompted the introduction of a totally different programme. The weather was seldom bad which implied that his prayers were unanswered which probably accounted for his life-long agnosticism. He knew his left from right but always had difficulty in keeping in step and had the utmost difficulty in performing arms drill. However, these fundamental defects in his character, about which he never spoke, were not the prime cause of his first major military humiliation. The Tuesday parade began with several relatively senior boys from each platoon performing something that reflected both the circus and the Royal Tournament. These boys swaggered around the parade ground, to the apparent satisfaction of the sergeant major. Tim had not learned the elaborate procedure, partly because he had some kind of mental blockage on military matters, and partly because he was one of the most junior members of his platoon so was confident that he would not be required to perform.

A few months after his 'conscription', an outbreak of flu attacked his platoon. This is not to suggest that his group was singled out for attack and, indeed, many thousands of people, none of whom were in his platoon, succumbed to the winter illness. Tim was not indifferent to their plight but they were not involved in the CCF so they were not uppermost in his thoughts. Consequently, during one infamous Tuesday morning, as his young colleagues toppled over in ever greater numbers, Tim found to his unmitigated horror, that he had to participate in a drill, of which he had no knowledge, with which the parade commenced. It seemed that the options were limited. He could either to turn to the left or to the right or perform an about turn. He remembered that stopping and starting were also involved and decided to imitate these boy soldiers as closely as possible. Hopefully, he would be facing in the same and correct direction. Wrong. Early in the drill, he found that he was alone and swiftly increasing the distance between himself and the others. Clearly, he was in a minority of one as his colleagues strode purposefully into the distance and the sound of their boots on the tarmac faded away.

Some fellow rebels enjoyed his performance although it was plain from his caustic remarks that that the crew-cutted and battle-hardened RSM did not share their sense of fun. He was a dour unimaginative man who did not appreciate initiative and individualism. Tim recalled the old joke when one soldier, at dinner, asked another to pass the rice pudding. The request was refused and when challenged by the intending rice-eater for the reason for this blatant lack of co-operation, the other soldier said that it was wrong to encourage a member of the military to desert. The RSM would not have appreciated this minute joke.

Once a year, on Field Day, the entire CCF paraded on the main sports field and undertook some modest manoeuvres, as well as marching around, looking absurdly important, and showing admiring parents and guests how clever members were at dismantling a very elderly Bren gun and re-assembling it, very quickly, without having any parts left over. Presumably, judging by the parents' applause for this activity, they felt reassured that, when the family Bren gun failed to work, their sons' expensive education would prove invaluable. Re-building guns had never been one of Tim's ambitions and, thus far, his life had not caused him to revise his interests. Indeed, the Adams family never owned a Bren gun and

Tim had never requested one for his birthday or Christmas. Then, despite being but a boy, one day he discovered that he could take one to pieces and put it back together again correctly. Joy was unconfined at this rare success.

For many who participated in this Field Day show, it was a major nuisance, especially when they were preparing for the General Certificate of Education examinations. In those days it was necessary to study to pass an exam, or, to be more accurate, memorise huge chunks of knowledge, even if the boys were not told why it was all relevant. This was in those challenging times when examiners did not discuss likely examination questions with teachers to ensure a high pass rate. No, the young men had to be prepared for the day when the country would need them for National Service. Military service was more important than academic progress. Confronted by one of the country's enemies, and the UK always managed, artfully, to find some to challenge each succeeding generation, it would be useful to draw on the experience of taking a Bren gun to pieces and restoring it to a working condition in but seconds. A pass in seven subjects at the General Certificate of Education, ordinary level, a system introduced in 1948, would not deter an aggressive enemy. Would even a placid one have opted not to shoot Tim on hearing that he had passed in seven subjects?

Why was this weapon, apparently, prone to refusing to function adequately when required? Did Tim want to depend on such a gun when confronted by the enemy? He imagined what might happen.

'Hello, I've seven passes in O level and my beastly gun has jammed. I say, do you mind frightfully whilst I repair it?'

'Seven O levels, that's mighty impressive. No, of course not, you repair your gun and let me know when you're ready.'

'Thanks, old man.'

Some minutes later, the conversation might have resumed. 'It's all right now, can we carry on, now? Thanks awfully for waiting. Jolly decent of you.'

One intended highlight of Field Day was when the boy soldiers lumbered past some pompous military big wig who took the salute.

Tim's legendary inability to keep in step meant that he had to look at the boots of the chap in front and try to make any necessary adjustments to his own marching as surreptitiously as possible. Consequently, looking right at the MBW and keeping in step for a few paces was an annual and worrying challenge. Before that, the boys lined up in rows and it was Tim's misfortune that he was always facing the MBW as he ambled past in what was euphemistically called an inspection. As the boys had spent a high proportion of their limited leisure time polishing boots, shining all that could shine, with the aid of brasso for belts and badges, blancoing for webbing and pressing for trousers, before the big day, he might at least have looked in their direction and grunted something that could have been taken as military approval of their appearance.

The Field Day activities were always held in the hay fever season: Tim was not wont to brag but he was one of London's leading sneezers. One early sneeze from him and those chatting within a 200 yard radius knew their words would no longer be heard. Western leaders would seek the instruction booklets that told them how to push the button that could plunge the world into world war three and then be irritated that the only copies available were translated from Japanese. It was clear that there was a great possibility that, as the khaki-clad fellow wandered past, Tim might sneeze, causing his rifle to shake vigorously before he could regain control of the firearm. Imagine the headline and first lines of a relevant story if his gun did have a bayonet attached and nature decided, not for the first time, to embarrass Tim.

Sneezing schoolboy charged with knifing leading general blames hay fever

General Sir Bloggs Norton-Jones, a much-decorated hero and veteran of two world wars, widely regarded as one of Britain's leading military figures, was reported to be recovering in a North London hospital last night after a bizarre stabbing incident at a London Public School. His condition was described as serious but not life-threatening. He was inspecting Hudson Hall School's Combined Cadet Force when a junior boy in the front row, seemingly a victim of a major convulsion, according to those who heard a rushing and bellicose sound, lunged forward, stabbing the national treasure with the bayonet attached to his rifle. Apparently, the general, whose new television series was due to begin next week, was saved from more serious injury as the bayonet had been partly deflected by one of his many medals.

A spokesman for the school, denying that the boy was a known terrorist, confirmed that, going forward, and it wished to make this clear, it would be co-operating fully in the enquiry launched by the Ministry of Defence. 'This has been a bad day for our Combined Cadet Force, and, of course, the General, but we shall regroup, learn the lessons, draw a line in the sand and go forward.'

The name of the pupil, now helping the police with their enquiries, has not been revealed. However, according to a fellow student, he 'seems British' and had claimed to be suffering from hay fever. Allegedly, he had told the school authorities that an accident of this kind was always possible but they had ignored him, telling him 'not to be so silly'. However, the school spokesman said that they had no knowledge of his condition but that, on entering the school, he had been put on a remedial course because he was seriously round-shouldered but was not deformed in any other way.

Tim had several choices. He could be ill on every Field Day but that would have been suspicious as he was already unwell whenever the contingent was taken somewhere very military and made to shoot at things. Thick as those involved with the CCF were, they might have detected the whiff of a correlation. Secondly, he could explain and seek permission to avoid this part of the ceremony. That would not have been well received and he had no doubt that his sensible suggestion would have been rejected as many fellow juvenile soldiers would have suddenly developed HF.

That left but one option. He had discovered that it was possible to delay a burst of sneezing, and there were always at least 12 in every batch, even before inflation took hold, by distorting his facial features, sniffing loudly and, as a last resort, changing his breathing patterns. He did not wish to adopt this last approach on Field Day as it often led to violent hiccups that resembled distant gun fire. Making such a noise as the MBW wandered past might have persuaded him to take immediate cover and could have brought the school into disrepute and exposed the failure of the old rifles and the Bren guns, newly checked, as they tried to fire against an unseen enemy. Again, he pondered the likely headlines and decided that altering his breathing and reorganising his facial features had to be his last resort.

If Tim was to avoid potential disgrace for the Combined Cadet Force, it would be necessary to pull faces as if his life depended on it. Inevitably, one year, when the high pollen count had even been mentioned on the radio, when the multi-medalled military man was about to reach him, Tim sensed that a sneezing fit was imminent. He could not allow himself to sneeze even once as that would, not just metaphorically, open the flood gates. He had practised his defence at home and the system worked on about one in three occasions. The situation called for some world-ranking grimaces. It was not his fault that he was at the peak of his facial contortions when the multi-medalled military big wig reached him in the line. He looked straight ahead and managed an excellent imitation of a pig about to snort, silently, for his life. Presumably, the MBW must have thought that he was mentally deficient or suffered from some strange disease and that, in the interest of good manners, it was best to say nothing. Tim had succeeded in repressing an attack of sneezing.

Later in the day, in a thrilling climax, thrilling for him as the day was nearly over, the military man addressed the cadets but made no reference to Tim's facial outburst and, as he stared at him, Tim kept his facial expressions to an absolute minimum. The military man looked perplexed, not least in Tim's inconsistency in pulling faces, but, being a man of some considerable experience, he did not show it. Tim's fellow pupils, dressed, as ever, in baggy ill-fitting army uniforms and boots that shone, or would have done if the weather had been more friendly, moved uneasily whilst sitting on the grass, as their puttees decided that they no longer wished to be associated so closely with their trousers. In an army accent that was based in part on Churchill and partly on Montgomery, the Big Wig assured the cadets that 'you fellows are destined to become leaders of men'. Tim looked around his young temporarily military colleagues and did well to suppress a laugh without even pulling a face. The trouble was, some believed him and did become leaders of men. Possibly some also led a few women and, doubtless, some may have misled a few women.

Life in the CCF was not always misery: the imitation soldiers were marching near the school and some jumped-up little boy whose unthinking obeisance had propelled him to Lord High General Supreme Commander, (Small Boys) or some such title, was marching backwards, on the pavement, so that he could watch the platoon which was odd as, frankly, they were not particularly interesting. Personally, Tim found the red single-decker RF type London Transport buses more interesting. LHGSC (Small Boys) enjoyed shouting in public but his vocabulary was limited to just 'left' and 'right'. That said, he was word perfect. Frequently, this seems to be all that is usually required in a military man but he bumped into something, abandoned his boring recitation of left and right, drew imaginatively on his vocabulary and immediately apologised saying that he was 'most frightfully sorry' before he realised that he was addressing a lamp post.

Participation in these Tuesday frolics was to lead to an attempt to pass Certificate A in parts one and two. Additionally, each member of the corps was supposed to become a first class shot. All this created problems for Tim but, amazingly, eventually he secured passes in all the tests. His claims to be a first class shot seemed unjustified by the evidence but, after several attempts, which, mercifully caused no deaths or harm to humans or animals, he passed. All this was supposed to be of help when, in due course, the young boys were sucked, compulsorily, of course, into two years of boring and totally pointless hell in National Service.

A minority of Hudson Hall teachers were amiable and keen to teach and understood the need to stimulate young minds. They did not merely command their charges to read and memorise their text books after which the boys were subjected to a test. That, surely, was the way to train any parrots who could read but few had detected that young boys were not birds. The man who taught history was a good teacher and enjoyed deserved success in promoting a genuine interest in his subject. He and a few masters did stimulate enthusiasm for their subjects and this, combined with some very hard work, enabled Tim to secure passes in six subjects at O level. He failed in Mathematics but re-sat and passed the exam again in the Christmas term of 1953, which was to be his final term at Hudson Hall. Oddly, some of those teachers who attracted greatest contempt from Tim were the very same masters who commanded much affection from other boys. The latter were the brighter ones which suggests that some teachers never tried to stimulate those whom they perceived to be less intelligent.

In the early Fifties, schools were still suffering from the losses of thousands of young potential teachers from the war. Consequently, many of those in the profession, now advanced in years, carried on as if they were still in the pre-war period and ruled by fear. That was the context in which their own schooldays had been experienced and they did not have the intelligence or imagination to challenge the outdated custom. Others, who had been in the forces, seemed unable to distinguish between former adult colleagues, always told to obey without questioning, and young impressionable boys. Many 'teachers' lacked formal training and the ability to improvise to hide their defects. Some masters were there only because there was no competition from those who were genuinely keen to teach.

One master, a decent gentleman, was, regrettably, the butt of collective class humour. Silver-haired and still sporting a modest quiff when most of his generation were obliged to accept baldness, Anthony Gordon understood the need to stimulate young minds but his problem was that his periods were seen as opportunities to relax after the rigors of trying to memorise vast tracts of other subjects. His subject, biology, was neither interesting nor relevant to most of the boys. They had very little interest in frogs, either fully assembled or in parts. Dissecting a frog, for Tim, was even less important than being able to re-assemble a Bren gun. At least you could rebuild a Bren gun. Although he feared that the latter 'skill' might be useful in subsequent national service, he never imagined himself pulling a dead frog to pieces, either to save his own life or to advance his country's interests.

Gordon had little understanding of how to impose discipline. Cruelly, a contest was organised to see who could irritate him most in each term and the winner was presented with a wooden shield. Jack, shrewdly aware of the master's likely reaction, brought an alarm clock to school and set it to ring during the class. Precisely as he had anticipated, the master said 'I want the owner of that clock to stop it and bring it to me'. Nobody stirred and then, with impeccable timing, Jack said 'I think that I can help there, sir' went to the back of the room and fetched the offending timepiece and caused it to cease its noise. 'When I asked for the boy who owned the clock to collect it and to stop its noise, why didn't you come forward?'

'You said you wanted the owner of the clock to collect it, sir, and it belongs to my sister.' Then, looking around the room, he added, unnecessarily, 'and she's not here'.

On another occasion, a boy was playing with a clock rather than learning some French. The master, for whom the word impetuous had been invented, grabbed the clock and immediately hurled it out of the window. A few moments later, a dustman, sorry, that should now be a community domestic refuse removal officer, known popularly as a CDRRO, entered the room, without knocking, clutching his head in one hand and the clock in the other. 'One of your boys threw this out of the window, mate.' The master apologised, promising that he would investigate.

The man allegedly responsible for teaching both chemistry and physics, merely carried out experiments himself and required the boys to write up, with drawings, what had been done. All this was totally foreign to Tim and the master, whose head bore an uncanny resemblance to a well-worn scrubbing brush, told Susan that Tim ought to drop these two subjects. He did not point out that he, like so many of his colleagues, was only interested in talented boys. He had a Lancashire accent and would have been ideal for the role of the Mad March Hatter, in more ways than one, at Sandgate. Tim upset him on one occasion by answering a question correctly, long before his star pupils reacted. Worse still, when had overcome his shock that Tim was right, whilst his favourites continued to strain every mental muscle, he listened to Tim's explanation with increasing incredulity and irritation. The problem, inevitably, involved baths and hot and cold water. Baths and taps and flow rates were the very staple diet of maths and physics in those days and it was surprising that they did not feature in English Literature or History. For example, what do we know about William Shakespeare's ablutions and did Francis Drake say that he would only engage with the Spanish after he had had a bath? It was difficult to imagine a lesson in which these topics were not featured and doubtless many young boys were indirectly encouraged to become plumbers.

The class was given the flow from each tap and relevant temperatures of the H_2O entering the bath, the capacity of which was given, and asked to determine the overall temperature of the water. Tim realised that the flow from each tap resembled a batsman scoring runs whilst playing cricket. Some scores would be good or hot and others would be poor or cold. It was only a matter of working out the average. The poor little physics master looked crestfallen as his methods were undermined and his favourites overtaken by such an ignoramus.

There were two vicars on the staff. One was inadequate and merely gave out instructions on what to read and to tell the class when the test would be and the other was a sadistic brute who was a disgrace to the church, education and humanity. Like so many others in this profession at this time, he would doubtless now be in jail but, presumably he is in heaven as a fully paid-up former vicar rather than in hell, as merited by his cruelty.

The highlight of these years was Tim's ownership of a very fine bicycle which he used, on fine days, to go to school. It was also used for the return journey which seemed sensible as he had no wish to leave it at school and walk home. Unfortunately, to buy this BSA Golden Wings, he had had to sell many of his possessions, accumulated over the years, which, if he had been able to retain them, would now be very valuable. This drop-handlebar bike had white plastic mudguards, a three speed Sturmey-Archer gearbox, a dynamo lighting system, a pump and a fine saddlebag. Gradually, other items were added including a speedometer, bought for 25 shillings, an odometer, which measured distance travelled, not smell, and two drinking bottles. Tim's first foray using these bottles proved a failure. He had filled them with a fizzy drink and when he stopped to partake of the contents, the bouncing motion of the bike had stirred them so much that the drink flooded out all over the bike and caused the handlebars to become very sticky. He also added an additional rear light, which was used as a brake light. He could flick it on from a switch which he put on the handlebar. Whether any other road users realised its function is debateable. To prevent his feet from slipping off the pedals, which had never happened, Tim bought and attached some specially designed clips. They were successful in that his feet continued to remain where they should have done but the toe caps of his shoes sustained considerable damage.

The family was to visit the Isle of Wight for a holiday in 1952. Tim volunteered to cycle there and, in any spare time, trained by riding up some of the steepest hills in north London. On the big day, he set out early and reached the hotel, 98 miles away, without incident and in good time. Peter, grateful that he had been saved a return train fare, bought his son a black, green and white check sleeveless pullover which was his first non-school piece of clothing, apart from the greatly-prized blue lumber jacket sent just after the war by an 'aunt' in Canada. Matters between father and son were improving.

When Tim first participated in sport at Hudson Hall, in September 1950, he was 14 and was bewildered by the variety of different football teams that each house fielded in various intra-school competitions and by the different positions in which he had to play. Apart from keeping goal, he played in all positions and, in an early match, scored four goals for the house third eleven which was almost the lowest of the low. He added eight more before the end of the season and, in the following year scored another 21 but never was even close to a trial for a school team. Before leaving Hudson Hall at the end of the Christmas term in 1953, his 47 goals in 45 games and being captain of various house sides counted for nothing when school teams were selected.

In the early days, Tim hoped, that when he was older, he might challenge for a place in the school's first eleven at cricket and he was encouraged by what he thought was a low standard. His hopes of even achieving house colours at cricket were not to be fulfilled. He had a trial for the Under 15 team but his four overs, from which just 11 runs were scored, ensured that he would never play for the school. In three seasons at Hudson, Tim took 90 wickets at a cost of just six runs apiece, in only 218 overs, of which 64 were maidens. In his last season, in 1953, at the age of 16, younger than most of his fellow students so chosen, he was selected for the Senior House side. Tim's very poor team was confronted by two very talented young spin bowlers but, despite some success with the bat, Tim was never awarded his house colours and he despised his house master for this. All his friends seemed to be awarded house colours. This distinction allowed them to wear fancy blazers and walk around, or even run if they so desired, providing it was not at school, or crawl, as they often did in the direction of teachers, capless during the summer term. Tim remained incarcerated in either his plain blazer or grey suit with his head dominated by the school cap, indicating that he was no good at sport. Life was so unfair.

Despite not even securing house colours, Tim enjoyed playing cricket, albeit at a lower level than he felt was justified, and, encouraged by his modest success joined the highly-regarded North Middlesex cricket club where, in the 1953 school holidays, he played for each of the first four sides, including the first eleven, where he prayed that the ball would not come to him, as well as for the colts. This was useful experience but, of course, his inclusion in the senior sides reflected not his ability but the reduced availability of the adults. His first-ever club game was for the first team against

Ealing Town. In 14 matches for the club in total, he only bowled in three games and took three wickets for 30, including 2-10 in his bowling debut, against North West Polytechnic.

Tim's social life was confined to visiting his friend's home in Finchley, after sport on Saturday afternoon. As in the earlier days, the two boys played billiards on his father's large table, cricket in the long drive to his house, watched television and ran some model trains on an extensive layout. Peter and Susan could never compete with this array of enticements and Charlie never came to Tim's house.

Another friend invited Tim to spend a weekend with his rich parents on their fine cruiser which was parked near Kingston in Surrey. Tim went direct from school on the Saturday afternoon, still clad in his grey flannel uniform suit. He had no other daytime clothes, except his special pullover.

'How do I get on to the cruiser as it's a few feet away?'

His friend Robin replied.

'It's easy, we have this canoe, attached by this long rope to the cruiser, you step on to it and then press down hard with your feet and force it to come alongside the cruiser.'

Tim was far from convinced, even after his friend demonstrated how easy it was.

'Your turn now and I'll help you as soon as you're close.'

Tim knew that disaster was imminent, even before he stepped on to the canoe.

Predictably, the canoe refused to obey and opted instead to move sideways. Indeed, if this had been continued, and Tim had remained standing, which was most unlikely, he would have collided with a nearby bridge. Inspired by fear, as he passed the part of the cruiser where his friend was positioned, Tim managed to grip a fleeting part of the cruiser but his grip became progressively more tenuous and potentially difficult. Desperately, he tried to persuade the canoe to behave but it was all to no avail. It was clear that the Thames and Tim were about to meet face on. He had anticipated this for some seconds as had Robin, who had raced to where his friend was parked, albeit for but a nanosecond before he embraced the Thames. Anticipating a damp end to this incident and, thanks in part to his friend's action, Tim's back was hardly wet. The same could not be said for the front of his jacket and trousers to which traces of river life had adhered.

Tim had been a regular visitor to Torquay United football club when the family lived in Devon and when the family moved back to London, he discovered that home was about the same distance to Arsenal's Highbury ground and Tottenham's White Hart Lane. Tim favoured Arsenal as it was possible to walk half way home, thus saving 1.5 old pence, but patronised both clubs in the school holidays, taking care to ensure that they were playing as otherwise it would have been such a waste of time and money. Attendance in those days was around 50,000 but the crowds were well behaved and it was safe for young boys who were even carried over the heads of the crowds to a suitable vantage point.

Tim's first visit to Highbury, on 25th September 1948, was with Jeremy, an uncle who knew someone important at the club, so the two had fine seats in the grandstand. Tim spent much of the second half of the match, checking the half time scores on the static signboards around the pitch. Arsenal beat Wolverhampton Wanderers 3-1. Such was the uncle's influence that Tim was given a slender booklet detailing the club's 1947-48 season in which they won the first division championship. Indeed, Arsenal had been unbeaten for their first 17 matches. The booklet not only contained a few words about each player and a photograph but their genuine autographs which had been collected just for Tim. Some of the stars included Denis Compton, Laurie Scott, who, bizarrely, revealed that he never ate green vegetables, except peas, Wally Barnes, Alex Forbes, Don Roper, Jimmy Logie, George Swindon, the goalkeeper who played in all 42 league matches and who conceded only 32 goals, and Ronnie Rooke who scored 33 of the club's 81 goals. Collecting autographs was a popular hobby in those days and at one stage, Tim had a substantial collection which consisted mainly of printed autographs which were sent out, on request, by the country's leading football clubs. His proudest possession was his cricket bat which had been signed by the redoubtable Denis

Compton.

In the early Fifties the family was visiting Peter when his vessel came into South Shields. That needs clarification. Firstly, Peter was on his tanker at the time, which was right as he was in charge. Secondly, the vessel stopped well short of the urban complex and the family was not on board when the tanker arrived. Thirdly, it was no fluke that it had docked in South Shields as this had been the intention from the very outset of the voyage. Peter took his son to Roker Park, then the home of Sunderland, who, coincidentally, were playing the mighty Arsenal. Peter was short which meant that, although the ground could accommodate about 60,000, father and son should be in the queue early and were about number 12 in the line and even Tim, a pessimist's pessimist, knew that the two would have a good choice of standing positions. However, when the ticket turnstiles were opened, one man, number six in the queue, realised that he was being overtaken by number nine and a squabble ensued. Arsenal won the more serious encounter.

Outings with either parent were rare but on 19th August 1953, Peter, who was now much more friendly towards his eldest son, and Tim were amongst an enthusiastic crowd at the Oval in London, hoping to see an England victory which would have secured the Ashes for the first time for 19 years. England were set 131 to win on the last day and, despite losing Hutton and May and confronted by the bowling of Lindwall, Miller and Johnston, the home side were victors by eight wickets. Denis Compton, who hit the winning run off Arthur Morris, was not out 22 and Bill Edrich, who had opened the batting with Len Hutton, was undefeated on 55. The crowd, almost delirious with joy that the spell of remorseless defeats had been broken, ran on to the field to celebrate. It was an emotional moment and, in modern jargon, helped to bond father and son.

When in Devon, Tim had been a regular follower of Paignton Rugby Club, which played at Queens Park in the middle of the town. Later, in London, he went to a few rugby internationals at Twickenham, by himself, and also attended an athletics meeting at White City. He watched ice hockey and speedway at Harringay stadium and recalled the happy occasion when the local ice hockey team, strengthened by some aliens, beat the United States.

Tim's brief and unsuccessful relationship with girls, curtailed when the family left Preston and non-existent whilst at Sandgate, had not flourished. Now, in 1953, aged 16 and greatly daring, as introductions had not been made, he offered a polite good morning to a red-haired schoolgirl whom he saw each day as they passed en route to their institutions. This relationship never really started, despite several dates, and Tim was soon justly dismissed, largely because he had no idea of how to converse with or behave towards a young person of the opposite gender. One potential ploy might have changed his social life. Some school friends and he had enjoyed going to the nearby Harringay stadium to watch the Racers play ice hockey. Terry, an astute lad, whose early life in New Zealand seemed to be have been spent entirely on skates, judging by his skill, suggested that they might meet some girls if they took up ice skating. Tim had never tried to skate and, predictably, was so incompetent that his skating made his marching out of step look slick. Despite all his efforts, he failed to improve and the only new friend he made was the side barrier. The keen skater soon had girls interested, if not the rink officials who were not keen on his speed skating over a crowded rink. Other friends, almost as incompetent as Tim but who were more adventurous, would skate to the middle and then fall over, sometimes deliberately. Their efforts to stand upright again soon attracted girls' attention but Tim never had any luck and never mastered skating or how to acquire female friends via his efforts. Frustrated by the attempts to find a girl friend and by the lack of opportunities, Tim gave up any further attempts for some years. It was marginally less painful not to try than to try and fail.

The End Of The Beginning

Tim had studied hard. Peter, now back at sea, was very pleased with his progress and had congratulated him on his exam success. Both parents were now much more friendly to their son, who was beginning to understand the magnitude of their sacrifice to send him to a good school.

Susan now felt that she had to take the initiative in helping him to move into the adult world, and more specifically, finding a job. He, for his part, was also concerned with what he might do with adulthood, as its arrival seemed inevitable. For many years, he had yearned for adulthood, if only because it was different to school life, or so he imagined. Now that it was almost there he was not at all sure that he wanted it. He was keen to lose some of the restrictions of being young but unsure that he wanted some of the apparent responsibilities of being grown up, whatever that was.

All his friends who were leaving school had secured places at university or jobs and were looking forward to their new lives. The problem for Tim was that neither he nor his mother had any idea of what he might do. He had no outstanding ambition as his desire to be in medicine, because his doctor had a new car immediately after the war, had vanished. Similarly, the idea that he could become a cricketer had faded as his lack of skill became apparent. His form as a very young player for North Middlesex, suggested that, at best, he might become a reasonable club cricketer. When he was but ten, he had thought that he might want to become a writer but that idea had long since disappeared. The realisation that he was on the threshold of becoming an adult but had no idea of what he wanted to do depressed him. What was he going to do with the rest of his life?

Susan tried to cheer him up.

'You've got seven GCE O level passes and that's pretty good. I've an idea. Why don't I make an appointment for us to visit the so-called Elite Schools Appointments Bureau in London? I really don't like their name but they might have some ideas.' Tim seemed apathetic but warmed to the idea when Susan said that he could take an afternoon off before school broke up for Christmas.

The appointment was made and the 134 bus route took the anxious mother and her son to an old-fashioned building, seemingly staffed by old-fashioned people, in Victoria. ESAB was on the third floor and, with some trepidation, mother and son entered the lift and slammed the door behind them. After some wheezing and not a little effort, mainly from the lift, they were delivered and knocked on the door of the office which was occupied by the man they had come to see.

'Come in, come in.'

They did as bidden and glanced around the office. It was littered with files and could easily have been mistaken for a storage area visited by burglars, who denied their prey, had peevishly turned filing cabinets upside down and created the maximum amount of mess. Papers were perched on the edge of an elderly desk, on the thin carpet and on top of the dusty office furniture. There was only one window and, as it was so dirty, the room was very dark and a single 40 watt light bulb did more to emphasise the gloom than to alleviate it. The walls were covered in dark brown paper but were adorned by several yellowing certificates which suggested that the occupant, when much younger, had achieved some academic success or, possibly, they were certificates of attendance relating to a local dancing academy. Mountains of brochures and leaflets looked as if they were intent on reaching the ceiling. The adviser seemed in character with his surroundings. His round face was lined and distinguished by what seemed a failed attempt to grow a military-type moustache and his remaining hair was grey. His suit was ill-fitting, suggesting that he had lost weight since its purchase many years before. It was, overall, not a scene to inspire hope.

'Sit down, sit down.'

Tim, unsure of whether this duplication was one for his mother and one for him, or whether it was standard office duplication, opted for the latter and said 'thank you, thank you'.

The adviser, Arthur Stevens, made a few general comments about examination results and the fine career opportunities available in the diplomatic service before admitting that he should have mentioned that as a degree was essential and, he added, unnecessarily, 'of course, you haven't one, have you?'

'My son is just about to leave school. He has seven GCE O level passes and we're very proud of him.'

Stevens ignored this and suggested that jobs in the church, accounting, banking and the military could be recommended.

Tim tried not to groan.

'Any experience in the forces, young man, I mean the CCF?'

'CCF?'

'Yes, the combined cadet force. All good schools have one.'

'I was in mine.'

'Good, good, did you reach any rank worth mentioning?'

'I was a lance corporal but this was only because I was the oldest boy. I hated everything to do with the CCF. I didn't like being bossed around by older boys and men who were very stupid. We spent so much time marching around and I didn't know why. Then we had to keep our rifles clean which was pointless as they were so old that I doubt if they would have worked anyway. I didn't see why we should know how to dismantle and rebuild bren guns and..'

At this point, Susan, sensing Stevens' increasing irritation, as etched on his lined features, intervened and motioned nearly invisibly, as only mothers and wives can, that Tim should be more polite in his answers.

'I think, dear, that you have made your point. I'm sure that Mr Stevens realises that you and the military will not be getting together.'

'Are you interested in the church?'

Tim was now in form. His words were sharp as he had just developed toothache and Stevens irritated him.

'If I judge the church on the two sadistic and incompetent monsters who pretended that they were teachers, I would be an enthusiastic atheist. In fact, I think that I am and those twisted men should have been locked up in a lunatic asylum. They were evil.'

Stevens blinked. This was most unusual and he was concerned as he only had one more profession to offer, apart from teaching. Bravely, and expecting a critical torrent, Stevens mentioned another profession.

'What about accounting?'

'No, I didn't even understand book-keeping. I prefer words to figures.'

Stevens, pleased not to have provoked any more criticism of one of his favoured professions, tried another approach.

'What interests, hobbies or sports interest you?'

It was an indication of his nervousness in front of this rather blunt boy that a retrospective analysis of this sentence displeased him.

Tim pondered this for a moment and realised, to his horror, that he had no hobbies worth mentioning but, at the last moment, before another negative sentence was allowed to escape, he thought of his interest in cricket.

'Well, I suppose cricket is my main hobby and interest.'

Stevens was silent as if his brain had just been switched on and was warming up after years of neglect. This boy liked words and cricket. Could it be that, for the first time for years, he managed to fit a round peg into a round hole?

'I think that I may have just the job for you, then.'

Tim allowed his scowl to fade and Susan's smile suggested a 'told you so'.

The advisor disappeared from behind his desk, scurried around on the floor and emerged triumphantly, much in the manner of Chamberlain after his abortive yet, to him, successful mission to Munich. The beaming Stevens sat down again and announced the outcome of his brief foray.

'I knew I had it somewhere. There's an opportunity on one of the leading national newspapers for a young person to help their senior cricket correspondent.'

Tim nearly fainted as he named one of the most famous of cricket writers and broadcasters, James Duckton. Surely, finding a career was not as easy as this? The adviser resumed.

'The main requirements are that you must hold a driving licence and do shorthand. I presume that's no problem?'

Tim's hopes were destroyed immediately. Did the fool really think that a 16 year old boy, just about to leave school, could have met either of these two requirements? Was he so ignorant of school life that he thought that shorthand was on the syllabus? It was apparent that this man was only marginally more useful than the Hudson Hall careers master who, divorced from the real world, knew nothing apart from jobs in banking, teaching, accountancy, the church and, of course, the forces.

Tim's toothache was becoming more painful and this added pungency to his final pugnacious but uncharacteristic comment when asked by Stevens if he had any questions.

'Yes, I have, as a matter of fact. I would like to become a careers adviser. I think that I know as much about job prospects as you and it's clear that no real knowledge is needed and you can...'

At this point, Susan intervened. She had seen Tim holding his mouth and guessed that he was suffering from toothache again which had flared up earlier in the day.

'Please forgive my son's rudeness, but he's got toothache and I think that I must take him home immediately. Thank you for your time and for your help.'

Tim muttered 'what help?' and the two legged it into the real world.

'Why were you so rude to that man? He was only trying to help.'

'It was a waste of our bus fares. He didn't know of anything that was suitable and the idiot seemed to think that 16 year-old schoolboys can do shorthand and drive. What a twerp. Anyway, I had toothache but it's gone now so I feel better.'

Where would Tim find a job?

It was December 1953 and Peter was on leave. To Susan's great relief, he had become much more friendly with Tim in recent weeks. Peter had realised that he had been jealous of his son's relatively calm and almost affluent childhood, free of the problems that he himself had experienced. He now admitted that he could not expect Tim to understand any of this, not least as he still could not bring himself to convey the hardship and squalor of his early years in any detail. Tim, for his part, was tired of rows and was trying to be more appreciative of all that had been done for him. He also knew that, in his relationship with his father, he had been supercilious and superior. Peter had promised Susan that he was going to apologise to their son for his attitude over many years and would tell him again that he was proud of what he had achieved at school and that his greatest wish now was that the two of them would become firm friends. Indeed, he had asked Tim when he would be out of school for the last time as the three of them would then go to have lunch in what he described as a 'swanky restaurant'. It seemed that a new and much better relationship was in prospect.

Tim, not knowing what he was to do with the rest of his life, set out for school for the last time. There was one difference: he was wearing recently-acquired brown shoes in a final but weak act of defiance. He had not reached the giddy heights of school monitor or prefect whose apparel, as well as their pomposity and ludicrous sense of self-importance, distinguished them from ordinary boys. Tim was but a house monitor so was required to wear black shoes. Wearing brown shoes 'illegally', was a serious offence, on a par with being heard advocating the annihilation of all the staff. A jumped-up little twit, wearing a black jacket which signified that he was a school monitor, immediately recognised that Tim was not in his select group and challenged him on the colour of his footwear. Tim had anticipated this and took pleasure in lying to the mentally-challenged buffoon that his black shoes were being repaired. The school monitor was the sort of boy who would have believed the army man who, when addressing the young boys, told them that they would become leaders of men.

Tim later regretted not having taken greater advantage of his last day when he could have caused some degree of mayhem without fear of retribution but his innate cowardice had suppressed any such thoughts. The last morning passed in the company of several of his form mates who were staying on to sit exams at advanced level of the General Certificate of Education.

The hated headmaster, Sebastian Edwards, was grey in character and appearance. His hair had left him prematurely, following his wife's example some years before, and his brown eyes peered out from beneath shaggy eyebrows as if fearful that their function might easily be undermined by the hairy bushes. All this and his slight stoop suggested that he was much older than he was. His sense of justice, and humour, had long since departed and his self-importance was boosted by the knowledge that he held power over hundreds of boys. He was an impenitent snob who appealed to the majority of parents who felt that the country was going to the dogs and wanted their offspring, when, inevitably, they came to power, to change the country's direction. They, the parents, not the dogs, knew little about education and, indeed, the modern world, but realised that their sons were destined to become leaders of men and paid the school to prepare them for this role.

The final punishment, for all boys leaving school, irrespective of their behaviour during their internment, was to sit through what was supposed to be an inspirational farewell speech from this unpleasant and unthinking man. So Tim and some acquaintances were in the group of 35 leavers who had assembled in the Great Hall, built several centuries ago, for the man's supposedly motivating peroration. It was, of course, nothing more than the misguided, ill-informed, snobbish and tactless ramblings of a conceited man who had never worked in the adult world but, who, thanks to his own background, had no need to change his outdated and objectionable views. His address, scheduled for 30 minutes, from 12.00, never ended on time. The term ended officially at 12.30.

The brown-shoed Tim had wended his way into Great Hall for the last time as a pupil. Apparently, Edwards' presentations were always consistent. The delivery and content were uniformly dull, incoherent, uninspiring and insulting to anyone with even a modest-sized brain. He could have earned good money, sending insomniacs to sleep. The ritual and the speech were always the same. When the audience had gathered, he would seize the microphone and laboriously count up to eight, ending with the daft message, 'testing, testing, this is your headmaster speaking'. Satisfied that all was well and that he had reminded his youthful audience that he was still in charge, he would then clear his throat and grab the microphone afresh much as he would have done an unruly boy.

He began as if he were in church.

'We are gathered here together to celebrate your life here as pupils. Some of you started in the junior school and now, here you are, some years later, sitting in Great Hall for the last time as pupils, on the very threshold of life.'

There was a murmur from some of the boys who had foolishly imagined that they were already alive even if they did not think much of it. They were silenced immediately by a twitch of the headmaster's eyebrows.

'As you know, it has been my practice, over many years, to speak to boys as they begin the great trek through life. Now I am speaking to each and everyone of you, as I say, for the last time as pupils.'

At this point, Mr and Mrs Adams arrived at the school's reception office and were told that their son was in Great Hall but would be out shortly. Helpfully, the parents were directed accordingly and stood outside, listening to the headmaster whose aristocratic tones echoed around the large and near empty hall.

Edwards' speech then took an aggressive tone.

'Some of you have failed to take full advantage of what was on offer here. I regret this and so will you, whatever you may think now. Some of you, for example, spurned the chance to play fives and only a few of you participated in the Dramatic Society. Some of you decided against participating more fully in the excellent work of the Combined Cadet Force and you may well regret that if this country is involved in any wars in the future as it undoubtedly will be as some of the upstart colonies feel they should rule themselves.

'I know, too that some of you, happily a minority, failed to take full advantage of the inspirational lessons provided by my excellent colleagues. I just hope that that will not prove to be too heavy a handicap over the years. You may now feel guilty but that said, I'm confident that, with hard work, you'll become successful students in the University of Life. You can succeed and you must always remember that.'

Tim groaned at the ideas, the language, the condescension and lack of understanding. He had not played fives because he did not want to incur extra costs for his parents and he had not joined the Dramatic Society as he had been forced to spend most of his spare time on homework and trying to keep up with the rest of the class. He had not participated 'fully' in the work of the CCF as the whole concept was alien to him but he had tried to do his best at academic work.

'You boys are about to step into the real world. It will not be easy for you but I believe that each and everyone of you, except possibly a few currently skulking at the back of the hall, have the capacity, if you work hard, to become leaders of men.'

Where had Tim heard this before? Oh yes, it was that military twit on a field day. What did Edwards know about the real world? He had gone from school to university and then back to school. Tim had no wish to lead men.

'You will find the real world is often unfair, unjust and that many people will anger you as they parade their smug, ignorant and ill-informed opinions as if they have been handed down by a superior being.'

One brave boy in the second row bellowed out 'hear hear'. Edwards, unaware that it was a criticism of himself, beamed gratefully, pleased that he had provoked such a positive and understanding reaction to one of his key points.

'Sometimes, it will be difficult to make your voice heard but you must persist.' Again, he was rewarded by two boys who had often tried to make a point in the headmaster's lessons and were ignored. A grand total of four hear hears were added to the total. Edwards looked pleased: his presentations in the past had rarely provoked such a positive reaction. Some eagle-eyed pupils maintained that he almost smiled.

'People will disagree with you at work, if you have to have a job, and in the family. They may not share your views but you must remain unyielding and determined to adhere to your principles, which have been current for centuries which speaks volumes for their values and which we have passed on to you via my colleagues and me, I mean I. But, with all this you must be tolerant, especially towards those who have not had such a fine start in life as you.'

Tim thought that school had prepared him well for injustice, intolerance and ignorance.

'But you will also find that hard work, dedication and a concern for one's fellow human beings will bring its own reward. We who have had the good fortune to benefit from a valuable education, must accept our duty to assist fellow men.'

At this point, Tim wondered aloud if he also had a duty to assisting females, prompting Peter and Susan, just outside the main door, to smile in unison. Tim's quip provoked a laugh from those sitting near him and Edwards looked up, puzzled that a serious point had provoked sniggers. He thought that it was probably that failure, Adams, who had made a silly joke. He was doomed but it served him right for not fully entering into the cultural life of the school.

Edwards resumed his unstructured ramblings. 'I like to think, that, in your years here, each and every one of you will have benefited from wise guidance, a sense of fair play and the rewards that come from hard and dedicated work. Whilst you have been here, you have lived in a small world and some of you have become big people in this small world. Now your world will become much bigger and, in many ways, potentially more frightening as you become smaller, at least for a few years until you make your mark, when, assuredly, you will become bigger again.' For some reason, Tim recalled Alice in Wonderland and smiled at the recollection of his role as a gardener.

'You must not be afraid of becoming smaller. We all start small, at our nanny's knee but by the time that you're going to the opera, you'll have grown. I want you to know that. It's a challenge that we all face at one stage or another in our lives and it is my earnest hope that I and my colleagues have prepared you for this new world. I think, nay, I know, that we have.

'Many of you, the more-gifted ones, will be going on to university and you will find that life there, especially at Oxbridge, is much like school here albeit a little more free, although I think that my colleagues and me, I mean I, have given you a taste of freedom but with freedom comes responsibility and that brings duty. Ignore those jealous people who claim that you are privileged. Society always needs leaders and that is your role. Remember, you have a duty.'

One boy wanted to know where Oxbridge was as he had never found it in his atlas and another asked the headmaster to please tell him where Camford was. Both were ignored.

'For those of you going to other places of learning, I wish you well and hope that you succeed in adapting to a very different culture. Oxbridge offers the best education but I'm told that other institutions, although lacking Oxbridge's history and reputation, are quite good.

'I understand that most of the rest of you have secured posts in banking, accountancy, the church or the military and I'm sure you will all wish me to thank Mr Regan, our esteemed careers specialist, for his invaluable inexpert, sorry, expert, advice and help in assisting you to put your feet on the first rung of a difficult but not impossible ladder. It's a pity that you have to go straight into business but I know that family circumstances permit nothing else. At least I know that it is not the fault of the teaching staff that you have failed to undertake further education.'

Tim glared afresh and allowed two distinctly contemptuous and noisy snorts to escape and embellished them with a powerful pah. As pahs go, it was one of the best. One snort was for the absurd view that Regan was a fine careers master and the other was dedicated to the grade one rubbish dropping from the lips of this odious and dangerously deluded man. Tim had hardly seen him in the three years whilst he was a student, sorry, pupil, and, as this snobbish and demeaning tripe was directed at him and his colleagues, he wondered how society could allow such a man to be in such a place of influence.

Edwards interpreted the snorts not as a criticism but the forerunner of a cold.

The tactless oaf continued.

'I'm told that two of you do not have any further education or jobs lined up. I think, Adams, that you are one of them?'

Peter and Susan stared at one another and, inside the hall, everyone turned to look at Tim as if they had never seen him before and had to examine a manifest failure whilst they had the chance. Tim, hard put to maintain silence but determined not to lower himself into the same gutter, glared at the idiot headmaster who resumed.

'You mustn't despair. Apparently, most people can find work if they look hard enough and I'm sure that it won't be long before you become an office worker or, of course, you might find employment in a shop. I understand that many people who work in shops are totally happy and fulfilled, although how, God alone knows.'

The offensive man was out of touch with the modern world. Tim, greatly insulted, vowed that he would do all he could, over the years, to damage or eliminate men like this from public life. In the meantime, before he could affect such significant change, and he knew that it was unlikely that he would ever succeed, he vowed to take more immediate action. He had two plans and, given the personal hostility towards him, Tim decided that both would be implemented. There would be a gap of one week between the end of plan one and the beginning of plan two. The first required Tim, posing as the headmaster, to book a taxi for 7.00 in the morning to take him to Heathrow airport. Five companies would be asked to call, on five successive mornings. Plan B called for a substantial amount of manure to be deposited, cash on delivery, on the fool's drive.

The moron continued and confirmed Tim's justification for implementing plan B.

'On occasions such as this, it's sad for me and for my colleagues to see you go and to say goodbye. We shall always have memories of you, good and bad, and will follow your careers with great interest, yes, even if it's working in a shop, as you step into the outside world, not least as we like to think that we have played, and forgive our collective immodesty, a significant part in the development of each and everyone of you.'

Tim looked at his watch. The fool had been rambling on and this boy decided to take an immediate step into the outside world. It was 12.32 and he was no longer a pupil. He pushed his chair back as noisily as he could, causing Edwards to look up. Tim rose and began to walk calmly but purposely, towards the exit. Freedom beckoned beyond the medieval door.

Edwards had no precedent for this and shouted out in obvious anger, 'that boy, that boy, come back, this instant'.

Tim noted the phrase. His grandmother and father had often referred to him as 'that boy'. Now his headmaster, no, he corrected himself, his former headmaster, had followed them. All the frustration and injustices of his life, at home and school, where had been ordered what to do, frequently without justification or explanation, rose to the surface. Now, confronted with a unique opportunity, he would be a man, not a mouse.

Edwards, similarly confronted with a unique situation, bawled out 'come back'.

To the great pleasure of his former pupils, who had moved around, as if one man, to watch the failure and wonder what would happen next, Tim stopped walking, turned and responded.

'I'm not going to listen to any more rubbish from you. I think you're an incompetent fool and you shouldn't be a headmaster. You haven't enough intelligence to work in a shop and you're not even fit to be a car park attendant. You are totally contemptible and an ignorant and unpleasant snob.'

As he said this, he wondered if it were possible for any fools to be competent but did not allow this to divert him from what he wanted to do. His former school mates, also destined to leave shortly, who, like Tim, hoped that their schooldays would not prove to be the happiest of their lives, burst into unrestrained applause, stood up and cheered. Edwards had suddenly shrunk. The pompous ogre was now but a nervous dwarf.

Desperate to regain the initiative, he shouted at Tim as he resumed the long walk to the door.

'Adams, come back this instant. There's more that I want to say. I haven't finished.'

The retort from one boy who was not likely to be welcomed into membership of the old boys' society, was admirably brief.

'No, Edwards, but I have and I never want to see you or hear from you again.'

The cheering from his former fellow pupils was now accompanied by vigorous stamping and scraping of the chairs as the headmaster stood, gaping, gormless and powerless. So saying, Tim resumed his march out of the first part of his life into what passed as adulthood. He had no idea what the future held for him and speaking to his former headmaster, as he had, was the most satisfying moment of his teenage years. Oddly, as he contemplated what lay ahead, he was seized with the bizarre thought that it must be like old age. He was waiting for the future but ignorant of what was to come but he did know that he had taken his first steps as an adult. It felt good. Had 'that boy' become a man?

As he pushed at the partially open door, he was greeted by a tearful Peter who put one arm around his son's shoulders whilst using his other to shake him by the hand. 'My God, that was great, I'm so proud of you. That was magnificent. That took real guts. I'm so sorry that I've been so unfair to you over the years. I was wrong and I wish I could take it all back. You're a big man. Saying what you said was courageous. Please can you forgive me and can we now be friends?'

'I've been wrong too. I'm not proud of my behaviour when you came back from the camp and although I was young, Nana explained it all to me and I should have shown more understanding. I felt left out and that I had to defend myself and I'm sure I seemed superior even 'though that wasn't my intention. I know that I must have come across as ungrateful and condescending and I decided to ignore you but I can promise you, I'm very grateful for the sacrifice you both have made for my education and...' His confession was halted by a paternal finger wagging in his face which indicated that he was to say no more but Tim added 'most definitely, it was not all your fault. I'm ashamed to say that I deliberately provoked you but I can't just be friends with you now. You must be my best friend.'

Susan smiled and the three caught a taxi to the swanky restaurant.